Road Trip to Nowhere

By
Barbara De Smedt

www.DarkInkBooks.com

www.AMInkPublishing.com

Prologue

Sometimes your body knows something terrible has happened before the information reaches your brain. The persistent buzzing in her head, the cramping muscles, the pounding heart. She registers it even before her consciousness returns. Cautiously, she opens her eyes. Sharp pangs of pain shoot through her head. Flashes of light dance through her vision like fireflies on speed.

Where am I?

She lies on her stomach, feeling the cool floor beneath her. Unfamiliar smells enter her nostrils, and again, her body reacts first: a sob escapes her throat involuntarily. Only then does she realize, *my daughter!*

She raises her head from the floor, trying to find support with her hands. She opens her eyes wide, and her pupils dilate, attempting to dispel the darkness. The pain becomes more intense, and she feels nauseous, but she must find out where her daughter is. Whether she's safe. Her heart thumps against the floor at lightning speed. Panic spreads through her body and takes her breath away.

Why isn't she here? She's always with me, I never let her out of sight.

She can't use her hands to push herself up, something is wedged in her fist. Something that feels heavy and sticky. She tries to focus on it, but the image remains blurry. Confused, she looks around, scrambles to her feet, and leans against... what? A wall? Her eyes are getting used to the dark. She sits on the floor of a cramped space. A container? She can hardly fit into the space, although she isn't tall.

Why am I here?

She closes her eyes. Tries to conjure up images, to remember something.

Dragonfly is the first word that comes to mind, followed by the image of a plastic cutlery drawer. A cutlery drawer? She opens her eyes again, and vaguely sees the outline of that same cutlery drawer right before her. And then, as if someone has called out "action," the film of what has happened starts playing on her retina. One by one, the images come back: how she walked to the camper in the dark and saw the door was slightly open. How she first knocked on the door, but when nobody answered, she decided to go inside. How she then, on impulse, pulled open all the cupboards and drawers, looking for what she needed. How, to her dismay, she found something else, carelessly discarded between the knives and forks, rubber bands, and old crown caps.

She reaches for her pants pocket with her free hand and immediately feels it there. Tears of relief roll down her cheeks. She has found it again. She found *him* again.

"Now, I'll never let you go," she whispers.

Her attention shifts to the object in her other hand. She raises her arm slightly, trying to catch the light on it, but to no avail. Then she remembers she has her handbag with her. She puts the heavy thing down and lets both her hands search the floor until she feels the familiar shape of her leather bag. The light on her cell phone springs on, and she aims the beam at the strange object. She screams.

Chapter 1

One Week Earlier

Two young women are standing on the beach, their faces turned toward each other. Pink morning light glides over their naked skin. One is tall and blonde, the other small and dark, with hair almost reaching her buttocks. I flinch, seeking shelter behind a rock, unable to stop watching. They have no idea I can see them. The beach is theirs. They belong here, I don't. A few feet behind them, the waves thunder down with a roar. White foam splashes up meters high, like fireworks, showcasing the power of the waves in this area. The girls seem to be at one with nature, and the rising sun. Their movements (are they doing tai chi?) are synchronous and fluent, their nakedness is as natural as the moon that is still vaguely visible in the sky. Everything fits. With parched lips, I gaze at their slender figures, the curvature of their buttocks, the radiance of their skin.

It wasn't my intention to spy on them, I just wanted to see the ocean at sunrise, so I got up early, packed my tent, and drove to a beach where, according to the manager of the camping site, hardly anyone came because the current was too dangerous. I went down the steep hill until I arrived at a village of about ten houses. The road ended at a small parking lot where you could clamber down along a rocky path to the beach. A few cars were parked there, including a camper van with a German license plate. I thought the occupants were still deep asleep, little did I know. I was rushing because the first warm glow of the sun was already starting to spread over the beige sand. Quickly I parked my Volvo, got out my ukulele, and climbed carefully over the slippery rocks. It was still cool. Summer nights on the Portuguese coast are a lot cooler than those inland. Especially if you sleep in a tent like I do. I pulled my jacket closer around me and descended. Only then did I see them.

Now I feel like an intruder, a voyeur. Suddenly, the girl with the long dark hair turns her head. She can't see me, can she? She stands with her legs apart and holds her hands over her eyes facing my direction, where the sun rises above the dunes.

No, she can't see me. Impossible. The sun blinds her and I am hidden behind the dark rocks that smell of the sea. The blonde girl says something, glances at me too, and then looks away. She's much taller, with long legs, like me. She shrugs her shoulders and starts running, heading for the ocean. After a brief hesitation, the dark-haired girl pulls her gaze away from my hiding place and follows her friend. Together, they dive into the mighty waves, and I take the opportunity to sneak back to my car, unnoticed.

My heart keeps beating hard for minutes. My hands shake when I start my car. I can't place the feeling I have in my lower abdomen. Is it craving? Jealousy? Fear? I experience it all. Part of me wants to be with them, another part would like to hide, my cheeks red with shame, and forget I ever saw them. That last part wins. It always does. According to my therapist, I'm subconsciously sending out signals that make it hard for people to connect with me. He means I repel people, just like a citronella candle repels mosquitoes.

I inhale the eucalyptus scent of the woods whizzing past me and enjoy the wind blowing through the open window. For the first time, I'm doing something all by myself. This road trip is precisely what I needed. I feel liberated from a prison I wasn't aware of before.

But I can't get the two girls out of my head. They looked so serene, so completely at peace with the world.

So different from me.

Instead of repelling people, they attract them. If I'm a citronella candle, they're flytraps. They weren't looking for who they are, or why they exist. They already know, and they have each other. While me... I don't have anyone anymore.

Chapter 2

I left my mother's home on the first sunny day in July 2009 and drove until I couldn't keep my eyes open anymore. Without realizing it, I had driven straight to the seaside, the Belgian coast. It had taken me hours to get there because many day-trippers had the same brilliant idea. The first sight of that mass of water did so good after the gray tones of the city. I had to adjust to the fact that I could suddenly see for long distances, instead of just across the street. My eyes were using muscles they hadn't trained in years. All this time, my vision had been so limited, always focused on the ground.

I got out of the car and let my untrained eyes wander. I let them take in everything: the colors, the shapes, the vastness. This was what I needed, I realized. So, it seemed logical to keep following the coast, for lack of another plan.

The first night I slept in a cheap little hotel just across the French border. I knew I couldn't afford it, not every day, but I was too afraid to camp on my own at the time. The second day was difficult too. When you've spent your whole life doing what others expect of you, making your own decisions is challenging. Go left or right? Fill up now on the expensive highway, or drive off and search for a cheaper option in a village? Stop to eat and pee in a lurid parking lot, or not at all? I had to pay close attention not to lose sight of any details that could alter my fate and darn it, that responsibility weighed heavily.

Only after about three days, did I start to relax a bit and I slept in my tent for the first time, although I watched every hour on the clock that night. I had nothing to distract me, except my ukulele. Not a single book had I packed in my wild escape. On the road, I could only listen to the radio, while driving. I had a lot of time to think. Too much time.

France was a blur. I remember almost nothing of the places where I stopped. I saw Honfleur, where I walked into a beautiful museum; the Mont Saint-Michel in Normandy; and a terrible rainstorm in Brest drove me to despair and out of my tent. Bordeaux; I know I was there, but not much more. My first vivid memory is of Biarritz, where I saw surfers for the first time.

I was sitting on a rock staring at the water when I suddenly saw these little black figures floating in the distance. They reminded me of seagulls. It fascinated me. I remember watching them, seeing how the swell of the waves increased, lifting them up and gently setting them down again. The ocean was cherishing them, it seemed. They danced together, and I was the wallflower standing by. Then I clambered off my rock and got back into my car.

But these and all other memories were flooded with tears that wouldn't stop flowing. Whatever I did, wherever I went, my pain followed me everywhere. I couldn't be further away from the ideal image I had in my head; I wasn't a strong, independent woman traveling alone, I was a wreck.

Once past the border with Spain, things started to get better. The weather improved; the sun became my traveling companion. Finally, I could wash my clothes and let them dry. I wandered around the Guggenheim in Bilbao and was stunned by a painting of Gerhard Richter. A seaview. I had to look twice to ensure it was a painting, not a blurry photograph. The sharp line forming the horizon, the fictitious cord separating, so it seemed, the sea from the sky, made me gasp. Suddenly, I understood why I had been staring at that same horizon every morning and every evening for the past few days, and why it had stirred so much in me. I was a tightrope walker. And if the horizon was the fictitious cord, then the ocean was my inner world, which nobody saw, and the sky was what I showed to the outside world. That they touched, where the cord was, was only an optical illusion. The ocean and the sky were, in reality, miles apart, just like my head and my heart. And that, I realized there in the Guggenheim, was the reason for my despair. Now the only question that remained was what I would do about it.

My journey was progressing. As the sun's intensity increased, my tears dried. I bought a dusty paperback at a flea market, *Eat, Pray, Love* by Elizabeth Gilbert. I had never heard of it but read on the flap that it was about a woman who, after her divorce, set off on a journey around the world all alone. That seemed appropriate.

I drove along the Spanish north coast in admiration, stopped in San Sebastián to look at the surfers again, and visited Guernica, a small village that was once wiped out. Galicia, still unspoiled, stole my heart, with its jagged coastline of cliffs and rivers. I recognized myself in the melancholy of the Costa da Morte, where once hundreds of ships broke to splinters on the sharp rocks. I imagined the sailors' spirits still haunted where I stood.

Still, I had no idea where I wanted to go. For a few days now I had seen pilgrims walking and cycling everywhere, carrying heavy rucksacks, and on impulse, I decided to follow the signs with the yellow shell to the Galician capital, Santiago de Compostela. Who knew, maybe a place of pilgrimage would bring me what I was looking for. If so many people sought their salvation there, surely there had to be something for me too? At the sight of the cathedral, however, I almost turned back, it reminded me too much of my mother, with her crucifixes and rosaries, but something in me made me walk on. On automatic pilot, I followed some backpackers to a huge square called Praza do Obradoiro. Like a magnet, I was drawn to the center. Under my feet, I noticed that several straight paths led to it, and realized they formed a star with its center in the exact spot where I was standing. Full of awe, I looked at the monumental buildings: the university, the imposing city hall, the cathedral itself. Around me, groups of people came to a halt. Two men fell into each other's arms, their faces sunburned, their shoes dirty and their soles worn. A woman stopped just before me, plopped her backpack on the ground, and stretched out her arms to me.

"*We made it!*" she called out, laughing.

Before I realized what was happening, she had taken me into her arms, and I was intoxicated by her scent, a spicy mixture of sweat and curry. I cringed, mumbled an apology, and walked away from her with my heart pounding. It was the first physical contact in a long time, since I took off, and it became immediately clear to me: I was not ready for this.

That same evening, I stopped at a beautiful spot in Sanxenxo. The Galician coastline is of a raw beauty that can't be described. I had parked the Volvo where there were many other cars. It was quite noisy, and I wondered if I should drive on, looking for a proper campsite, but the setting sun lured me to the beach, my ukulele in hand. I hadn't missed a single sunset until then. It was pretty much my only foothold. When I woke up, I never knew where to sleep that night, but I knew I would see the sunset. *No matter what.*

I followed a footpath through the dunes until I came to a white stone bench. There was no one in sight. The sky was turning orange, and I sat down. This was my moment. I pulled up one leg to support the ukulele and started strumming — just a little tune. My gaze was fixed on the orange fireball in the sky, only minutes away from the horizon, when I suddenly saw something jump out of the water. Stunned, I stopped playing and let my eyes slide over the darkening water.

Had I imagined it?

No, there it was again: a black thing jumped out of the water, immediately followed by another one.

And another one.

And another one!

They were dolphins. I couldn't believe my eyes. Quickly, I looked around me. Was there anyone here I could share this with? I wanted to shout, jump. Look! Dolphins! In the ocean! But there was no one there. No one but me and the setting sun. For minutes, the school danced before my eyes, tumbling one after the other under the golden glare of the sun. When the last bit of sun disappeared into the sea, I saw them no more. The spectacle had lasted no more than three minutes. I was all alone again, on my bench. I looked at the ukulele in my hands, at the dune grass that waved gently back and forth in the twilight, and felt my cheeks wet with tears.

When I walked back to my car and turned around one more time, I saw a text on the back of the bench that said: "*Grazas pola vida*" or: "Thank you for life".

My trip could have been beautiful, I now realize. But that was my last stop before entering Portugal. Before everything went to shit.

Chapter 3

After a few quick stops, I decide to pull over for lunch. By now I know I must follow the signs that say "Praia," and I make a few turns around the parking lot until I find a spot for the Volvo. No shade, unfortunately.

I walk across the warm dune sand, alone with my thoughts. A group of surfers approaches from the opposite direction, shouting. They don't notice me, and I almost lose my balance when they pass me. Irritated, I turn around to scold them, but none of the muscular bodies bothers to stop. It's like I'm air to them.

I plod on, toward the beach, a drop of sweat escaping from the pond that has formed in my cleavage and tickling its way toward my navel. I peer through my sunglasses, check to see how much longer this path is, and then stand still with a jolt.

There they are again. The same girls. I recognize them immediately as they walk in front of me. One tall and blonde, the other small and dark.

I see how the muscles in their tanned arms tighten to hold their surfboards upright against the ocean breeze. They are wearing nothing more than a bikini, no wetsuit. The smell of coconut oil floats past my nostrils. I have trouble taking my eyes off them as they descend the dune together. As if she has noticed, the dark girl turns around and looks me straight in the eye. This time she sees me.

Really sees me.

A curious, amused look. Mocking, even. Immediately, my cheeks start burning. I duck my head, seeking protection from my enormous sun hat, but the glow spreads to my ears and neck, coloring my skin as red as my hair. There's no way she knows I saw her naked on the beach just this morning, is there? That's impossible. Then why do I get that feeling? She turns around again and walks with her friend towards the surf. I make my way to the beach bar, where a reggae song blares through the speakers. I plop down at an empty table and pretend to be busy looking for something in my handbag, while my eyes peek at the girls from behind my sunglasses. But they are already on the beach doing yoga exercises, their surfboards next to them.

I crave a glass of wine but order a Coke instead to accompany the fish of the day. My meager salary won't be deposited for another week, and I've already used up much more money than I had expected. Road tripping is a lot pricier than I thought, but not drinking alcohol makes it cheaper. I haven't had a drop to drink since I left my mother's house with little more than a hangover, a tent, and a duffel bag full of terrible memories. It seems like an eternity ago.

My therapist says I drink because I haven't learned to love myself. At the time, I laughed smugly at that. So, what should I do? Get a haircut and do my nails? Look in the mirror every morning and wink, saying "Hello, tiger!" to myself? Come on. But now I am slowly beginning to understand what he meant. Yesterday, on my daily walk along the beach, I saw something special. If you go early enough, there are still plenty of treasures on the sand, left there by the tide. Usually, items like broken anchors, pieces of rope, or colored buoys come loose from the fishing boats, but this time I found something different. It was a small car tire, rim and all, completely covered in shells. It looked like a Christmas wreath made by the ocean itself. The shells sparkled pearly in the early sunlight, turning that ugly old tire into something beautiful. But the shells also reminded me of something else. Like me, they clung desperately to the first thing they came across. Like me, they couldn't live on their own, without something to hold on to.

I grab my cell phone and connect to the bar's Wi-Fi. Maybe I'll find them online, my soulmate shells. It gives me something to do while I wait for my food. After a few misses, I get a bite. My beautiful shells turn out not to be shells at all but mini lobsters, *percebes*, they call them here. The English name is goose barnacle, which sounds a lot less beautiful. Fascinated, I read on: "They begin their life as free-swimming larvae until they encounter a solid object to which they attach themselves. Adult goose barnacles attach to floating objects, such as driftwood, ships, and even sea turtles."

So, they attach to whatever they come across, basically.

Wow, I realize, I am a goose barnacle.

But there's more: "Goose barnacles cause a lot of economic damage because they attach themselves to the underside of ocean-going vessels, slowing the speed of the ship." I wash away a lump in my throat with my ice-cold Coke. I can't deny that's true, too. If William was the ship, I was the goose barnacle clinging to him and slowing him down. Now I almost regret not ordering that glass of wine.

Arguing voices in the distance make me look up. The two girls are floating in the ocean, their upper bodies on their surfboards, apparently engaged in a discussion with a third figure. A man, it seems, in a wetsuit. I sit up and try to figure out what's going on, but the scene is too far away. Based on their body language, I can tell they're not having a friendly conversation. I observe the two girls emerging from the water with animated gestures. Why are they leaving already? They just got in. It seems odd. The man throws up his arms and lingers alone in the ocean. Strange.

No one on the terrace seems to be paying any attention to what's happening, so I suspect it must have been a "you stole my wave" thing, as I've seen happen between surfers before. They seem very territorial.

My eyes search for the two girls again. They are on their way back. The man is still standing in the surf, calling after them. The dark girl is leading the way; she looks fierce, and the blonde girl can barely keep up with her despite her much longer legs. She looks worried and calls out something in English, but I don't understand it, they are still too far away. I watch the two figures as they walk towards the parking lot. Something seems amiss, but I know better than to interfere. Avoiding all contact at the slightest hint of danger and disappearing like a turtle into its shell, is my tactic. That's the advantage of traveling by car: you can always leave, as long as you have gas in your tank.

The waiter appears with my grilled fish — a *dourada* — and I continue my lunch. It's a beautiful day and I'm determined to enjoy it, but the memory of the dark-haired girl's gaze keeps haunting me. I still can't place the feeling I had. There was something about her, something dangerous, like a sudden thunderstorm. I almost laugh out loud at the comparison, as if I, Michelle Deckers, the goose barnacle, have any people skills at all. I shake my head chuckling as I sop up a piece of bread in the sauce and enjoy wriggling my toes in the warm sand. No, I don't have any understanding of people.

My mother may have her flaws, but in this, she was right: you can't trust anyone. Although *she* meant you can't trust any *man*. But can you blame her? My father left when I was four. I can't remember him and there are no pictures of him, my mother burned them all. I know he must have had red hair like me, and pale skin with freckles. That's it.

I lick my fingers, put a few euros on the table, and grab my cell phone to see which way I'll be driving next. Everything is new to me. Before I left on this trip, I only knew foreign countries from TV, from shows like "A Place under the Sun," in which families leave their familiar surroundings with all their possessions to start a B&B somewhere among the French cows. It's one of my mother's favorite shows; the worse it got for those families, the better she liked it. And now I am doing exactly the same.

Being totally unprepared and still hoping for a happy ending.

After I pick up the bill, I get up and throw my bag over my shoulder but then I notice the man who was arguing with the girls before. He's in the restaurant, talking to an older gentleman who is sitting in the shade of an umbrella with a cup of coffee; a newspaper is folded in front of him on the table. It looks like they are negotiating something. Wetsuit man hands a dripping bag to the gentleman, who in turn hands him some money. Again, I decide not to wonder what is in the bag. Avoid all contact.

With my sun hat pulled low over my ears, I start walking toward my car, but the sound of quick steps makes me glance back: the wetsuit-clad man is striding purposefully behind me, and he has a dogged expression on his face. Now that I can see him up close, I notice his skin is almost as white as mine, he is clearly not Portuguese. And he's not a surfer either, unless he lost his board somewhere and the argument with the girls was about that.

"Desculpe," he says, as he marches past me and almost mows me down with his broad shoulders. He's tall, his towel cape can't disguise how broad his shoulders are, and under his wet wetsuit, I can see his muscles bulging. His gaze remains fixed on the ground the whole time. I stop to regain my balance. This is the second time I have been ignored on this path. It must be me, right? Michelle, the citronella candle, burns with passion. I throw an irritated look at his back and then decide to give my attention to the ocean. The waves are going in all directions now. So wild, so turbulent, so many whitecaps. There are no more surfers in the water, the ocean has chased everyone out. Good for her. Let them go fight somewhere else.

With my flip-flops in hand, I walk on. Once past the dune, the sandy path turns into a wooden walkway. Wetsuit man is no longer in sight. With the dunes protecting me from the sea breeze, I immediately feel the temperature rise again. As I approach the parking lot, my back is wet with sweat and I have to cool myself with my sun hat. As soon as I catch sight of my car, I feel that something is not right. The hairs on my arms stand up, my body tells me something is wrong before my eyes can see it. Only when I am standing nearby do I know why.

Chapter 4

My love,

Being without you is so hard, much harder than I could ever imagine. Do you miss me too, I wonder? Are you happy? It is so unfair that you are gone, so unjust. Why am I being punished so severely?

Sometimes I wish I had never met you, but I quickly dismiss that thought because a life without you is like music without sound: meaningless. All days are alike, bland, and insipid, lacking in salt.

At first, I would rather not live anymore. I imagined how I would die and when, but that was a senseless thought, I realize now. I was desperate.

Today I saw the sign you gave me, my dear. I could hardly believe it. Is it true? Will I get a second chance? Will we soon be together again, you and me?

Show me the way, and I will follow you.

Chapter 5

"Goddamn it!" I yell out loud, pushing open the forced door. Inside the car, it's a mess. My clothes are scattered here and there. Clean and dirty, all mixed up together. Knowing someone has had their hands on my dirty panties gives me a woeful feeling. Agitated, I try to survey what is gone. My car radio is still in place, oddly enough. Too old, probably.

I stuff my clothes back into the overnight bag lying on the back seat, my eyes shooting from left to right. My GPS is gone, along with the charger for my cell phone. Why hadn't I put my valuable items in the glove compartment so you couldn't see them from the outside?

The glove compartment!

I pull it open and feel my knees buckle. The envelope of cash I put there is gone. I clench my teeth. I don't know who I'm angrier at: myself or the thief who grazed me. I couldn't use my debit card at most of the small campgrounds where I have stayed so far, nor in many cafés and restaurants. So, a few days ago, when I came across an ATM, it seemed like a good idea to withdraw a larger sum of money and put it in the glove compartment.

It feels like a hand being clamped around my throat. I grab my wallet from my handbag. If only I hadn't had lunch at such an expensive beach bar just now. If I had known this was my last money… Thirty-six euros is all I have left to live on for the next six days. There is still a little credit on my debit card, with which I can hopefully fill up the car. I'll have to camp in the wild, I realize. No more B&Bs, no campsites. And live on bread and canned food.

"I told you," says a voice in my head. "It's dangerous out there. You should never have left. And definitely not by yourself. That group of young surfers you passed earlier struck gold. You're lucky nothing worse happened."

I shake my head. I know who that voice belongs to. Time after time, my mother read me the story of Little Red Riding Hood. She had only one task: to bring a basket of food to her grandmother without deviating from the path. Because those who stray from the path get into trouble.

"It was Little Red Riding Hood's fault that the wolf swallowed whole her grandmother," my mother told me as she closed the book. "After all, that's what happens when you don't listen."

I shudder. I've been afraid of dogs for years because of that story. Frantically, I try to pull myself together. It's only money. And I have a map on my phone, so I don't need the GPS, right? After all, it is 2009. I refuse to be swayed by this. But, wait, how can I use my mobile phone with my charger gone? For the second time that day, I feel my cheeks burning, not from embarrassment this time, but from anger. With a bang, I slam the passenger door shut, but it remains slightly open because of the twisted metal. This is bad. I can't drive safely like this. I throw my full five-foot-ten against the door and try to close it as well as I can. The result is not very satisfying, but at least the door is shut now. Then, apprehensively, I make my way to the trunk. To my relief, the thieves haven't bothered to pry it open, or perhaps they were interrupted. In any case, it is still locked. Thank goodness, because my camping gear and precious ukulele are in there, as are some cans of food, which will also come in handy.

I get in the Volvo, put the key in the ignition without turning it, and start biting my nails. What should I do? I need to get that door fixed, but then I won't have money left to eat. I could call my mother to ask her to wire some, but the tension in my chest tells me that's the last thing I want.

Here I am. Michelle the goose barnacle, thirty-one years old and completely alone in the parking lot of a Portuguese fishing village, with no money, no GPS, and — in a few hours — no working cell phone.

"One setback is all it took to bring you to your knees, Michelle," I shout to myself in the increasingly hot car. "One stupid robbery, and you're already giving up." When I feel my eyes getting hot with tears, I slam both hands on my steering wheel. "No! No!" I can't give up now. I don't need that stupid GPS, as long as I keep following the coast toward the south, I'll be fine. And I can always buy a map along the way and ask for help finding a camping spot. That I will actually have to talk to someone to do that, so be it. The whole point of this trip was that I would come back stronger.

But that car door…

I decide to try it. Best case, it stays shut. Worst case, it doesn't, and then I'll have to think of another plan. I turn the key in the ignition and slowly drive out of the parking lot. I know I must turn right and ignore the arrow to the highway because to drive on it; I have to pay the toll and I can't afford that.

The back roads then.

The car door rattles a little, just like my heart.

Chapter 6

The entire time William and I had lived together, I had never realized what it meant to have no money. Even though I didn't earn that much as a kindergarten teacher, he more than compensated my salary. We had a bank account for our joint expenses, but I can't access it anymore.

The first two weeks of my trip, I spent far too much money on food, especially in France. And that was without drinking any alcohol. *Fortunately, Portugal is so cheap*, I think, as I continue along a road that could use an extra layer of asphalt. If I just keep thinking positive thoughts, maybe it will all work out.

A dragging sound breaks through my inner monologue and I feel I can't control the car properly.

Now what?

I want to scream in frustration, but instead, I grind my teeth and carefully pull the Volvo over. I'm on a country road, with bumps and holes everywhere, with no footpath or parking space, where two cars can just drive side by side. *Please don't let me have a flat tire*, I pray as I get out of the car to inspect the tires. Alas, my prayers are not answered. I sink to the ground next to my car. Less than an hour ago, I was in a beach bar feeling so proud of myself, now I sit here, all alone in the heat of the afternoon sun, with a flat tire and a door that no longer closes.

I throw my arms in the air and slump down onto the grass.

"Fine, I got it!" I yell.

The small stock of self-confidence I had accumulated over the past three weeks doesn't give me enough strength to take a second setback. I feel my energy waning like a candle whose wick is barely glowing. I have lasted this long at least, longer than anyone ever thought possible, including me. Maybe I should just be happy about that and end my road trip here and now.

In the distance, a van approaches. Instinctively, I hide behind my car. It would make much more sense to jump up and call for help, but that's not my first thought, being here all alone. My heart is hammering in my chest.

Keep driving, keep driving. I'll call a tow truck. Please keep driving.

The van passes me, then slows down and, to my horror, comes to a halt a little further down the road. I realize that the driver will soon spot me, and I quickly get up, brushing the sand and grass from my pants. I know that my panic is silly. My head knows this, but my body is in a state of high alert.

The van door opens. A man gets out and comes walking toward me, his stride hesitant. He, too, seems not quite sure of this.

"Hello, do you need help?" he calls from afar.

Only when I open my mouth to answer do I realize he's speaking Dutch, despite his Portuguese license plate. Another two seconds later, I realize who he is: Mr. Wetsuit.

"No!" I shout. "Everything okay! Thanks!" With my hand, I make a flapping gesture.

The man still has his wetsuit on. That is, the top part is hanging loosely along his body, and he's wearing a long-sleeved T-shirt that says #RESET in big letters. On his head, he has a green fishing hat. He keeps walking towards me and nerves are coursing through my body. He is abnormally tall. I am not the smallest person in the world, but he towers over me. If he means any harm, I'll be in that van of his in a minute. With clammy hands, I spy around me, pricking up my ears in the hope that someone will drive by to save me from this situation, but apart from some chirping, nothing can be heard. Meanwhile, the man has come to a halt a few meters in front of me and is looking at me inquisitively. His gaze is watchful, like that of someone who is used to running away at the slightest threat.

"I saw your Belgian license plate and thought you could use some help. What's wrong with your door?"

I can't place his accent.

"My door?" I had completely forgotten about the problem of the forced door now that the broken tire was taking up all the space in my head. He hadn't spotted that yet. "Oh, it's nothing, just a little bent."

He frowns. On his nose and cheeks is a thick layer of sunblock. What is a man with such pale skin doing in a sunny country like Portugal? I know how painful that can be, being a redhead myself.

"Did they break into your car, too?" he asks, moving closer and inspecting the door.

Too? I think. It hadn't occurred to me at all that I might not be the only victim of the thieving surfers.

"They grazed me too," he continues grimly. "I think I know who did it, but I have no proof and the police can't do anything. Did they take much?"

I don't know what to say. On the one hand, I want nothing more than to share my problems with someone who might be able to help me, if only to not feel like I'm alone. On the other hand, my head is screaming that I shouldn't trust strangers. Especially not strange men of around six foot five driving a van on a deserted country road. Again, I peer down the road hoping to be relieved by a passerby, but there is no one else.

I decide to tell him the truth.

"No, they didn't. I don't have anything of value with me and I guess they didn't have much time. I'm only missing my GPS, some money, and my charger. My biggest problem now is a flat tire." I point next to me to the right rear wheel. "I need to get that fixed, and then I'm going home."

Without saying a word, he comes and stands close to me. I step back. He crouches down and studies the rubber. "You've driven through glass," he nods. "Do you have a spare? If so, I'll put it on."

I have no idea but open my trunk for form's sake, making sure I don't have my back to the man. After lifting out my camping gear and placing my ukulele on the back seat, I let him pry the bottom off himself. To my relief, there is indeed a spare tire where it should be. With skillful hands, he takes it out of the trunk, along with a jack. Without another word, he crouches down and gets to work.

As he slides the jack under my car, I realize that I must have driven through glass in the parking lot. I hadn't been paying attention to whether any other cars had damage but they must have had. The thieves were obviously not just targeting my car.

I can't help it. I feel sorry for myself. Why is this happening to me? All I wanted was to make this trip, and now it seems that's no longer possible, I just want to go home, that's not asking much, is it?

According to my therapist, there is no point in wondering why things happen. Why my mother is like she is. Why William did what he did. Why the surfers robbed me. Why Marie died.

I understand his perspective, except when it comes to Marie's death. If I can't think of a reason for her death, then there must not have been one. In that case, she might as well still be alive, and William and I would still be together.

Maybe I am being punished for something I did in a past life. I must have been a witch. A wicked red-haired witch.

I swallow and focus on the wetsuit man again. "I'm Michelle, by the way," I say, as he cranks up my car. Because politeness is the other trait I inherited from my mother, besides distrust.

"Daniel," he replies, without looking up from his work. He's not very talkative. I would almost venture to say that he is as reticent as I am. But why did he stop then? An uncomfortable silence falls.

"Are you here on vacation?" he asks. He has removed the broken tire and is rolling it out of the way. I decide to tell him I left for a road trip two weeks ago and just now returned home. Wherever that may be — I can't go back to William, and I don't want to go to my mother. But I don't tell him that.

He lets me tell my story and skillfully secures the spare tire into place. Then he inspects the broken door, pulls it open, and slams it shut with such force that I'm sure it will never be opened again.

"There, now you can lock it again," he grumbles. Sweat runs down his temples. He's still wearing half his wetsuit and a long-sleeved T-shirt and has no intention of taking them off. Which is odd, but I would rather not dwell on that too much because all I feel is relief. I am saved! Now I can begin the journey home. I want to thank him, but the words get stuck somewhere halfway down my throat. Should I offer him something to drink? Give him money?

"I... Thank you... I don't know how I could have continued..." I stammer.

He shrugs. "No problem. I respect that you're doing this alone. Are you sure you want to go back to Belgium? Surely, you can keep traveling now?"

"I don't have a GPS anymore, nor a phone charger. I don't know, it just doesn't feel right. That robbery already rocked me and this flat tire tipped me over the edge." However, I must admit that the feeling of desperation, panic, and loneliness that made me collapse earlier has almost completely disappeared.

He seems to notice my doubt. "Okay, you know what," he replies, "I still have an old GPS that I never use. If you'd like, you can have it. And you can buy a phone charger on the road, right?"

"That's very sweet, but I can't accept that, sorry."

"Why not? That old thing is lying in my van gathering dust, I never use it. And I can't sell it, so…"

"Why are you doing this?" I ask in surprise, "You don't even know me."

He looks back in equal wonder. "Why do I have to know you to help you?"

"It's just, most people wouldn't, I guess, not in my world at least." I know how cynical it sounds, but I can't help it. Images of the last confrontation I had with my school management flash by. Harsh words, reproaches. No one stuck their neck out for me when I needed help.

His gaze becomes more serious. "I'm sorry for that." He hesitates for a moment, seeming to want to tell me something personal, but realizing just in time that this is neither the place nor the time for personal outpourings. "When I see someone in trouble, I help that person. And I hope the opposite is also true," he says.

I let his words sink in for a moment. I would never stop if I saw someone in need. Never.

Daniel has turned around again and is marching with big strides to his van. I load my camping gear back into the trunk while I think about what to do. Back to Belgium or continue?

Forward towards the unknown or backward towards certainty? To trust or distrust? Daniel is right, I could drive on. My wrecked door is shut tight now and if I'm frugal, I'll make it until my next salary. Then I won't have to go back home with my tail between my legs, but with my back straight and my head held high. A more than appealing thought.

"Here. This is the GPS and this is my number. Who knows, it might come in handy."

I hadn't noticed that he had come back. Gratefully, I take the GPS from him. For a moment, I keep staring at the note with the phone number quickly scribbled down, then I put it away in my bag. Michelle the goose barnacle would now cling to this strange man and never let him go. Grateful for every ounce of attention she gets. But I left that Michelle behind in Belgium, so I politely keep my distance.

"I don't know how to thank you, I'd like to offer you a drink, but I'm afraid I'm rather short on cash," I say, shrugging my shoulders apologetically.

"No problem, you're welcome. And it's nice to speak my language again."

"So, do you live here? In Portugal?" I ask.

"More or less," he replies. "Have you decided what you're going to do yet?"

He's evading my question.

"No, I need to think about it, get my thoughts aligned. I wanted to do this trip on my own because I needed a new perspective. And what you said just now, about helping people, that's something I want to learn. I think it's great to go through life with such confidence, even if you've been robbed."

"Oh, that. Believe me, I had to learn that too. And I'm not that confident, I'm just good at faking it."

Again, I have the impression he wants to say more but doesn't. We say our goodbyes and I get in my Volvo.

It is only when I see him drive away, his hand raised out the window, that I realize I still would like to ask him so many questions. Like why a kind man like him was fighting with those two surf girls earlier. And what was in the dripping wet bag he gave the restaurant owner? But I'll never find out now.

Chapter 7

I am not a bad person. No one is born bad, so neither am I. I did bad things, but that's something else entirely. What I did, I did because I had to. Not because I wanted to. You know that, my dear. You know how it was. Of course, I realize that this time I have crossed a line. That I can't go back. That it will never be like it was before.

Maybe things would have been different if I had been born into a different family. Maybe. But I'll never know because we only get one chance, right? And we have to make that one chance work. Some succeed a little better than others. Some fail miserably. Of course, if I had gotten a better start, perhaps I wouldn't have done the things I did. Then I wouldn't have disappointed you. I wouldn't be in this situation now. All of that is true.

But, my dear, then I would never have met you either. Then I would never have known the love that existed between us. Never felt your warm breath on my neck. Never knew what it was like to be happy. Truly happy. I know that for a fact.

I can't bear the thought of it. Although I would have been spared the pain. Yes. The all-consuming pain of losing you. The tearing sound my heart made when you abandoned me. The void you left behind is greater than I can comprehend. It's an emptiness that I try to fill every day. But I'd rather try to fill that bottomless pit every day than give back one second of the time we had together.

I would give everything to have you back. Everything.

Chapter 8

I need to think about what I'm going to do next, so I pull over on a packed parking lot at the beach. I know only one way to unwind, to gather my thoughts: playing my ukulele. The beach stretches endlessly before me, but unfortunately so does the crowd, so I begin a brisk walk.

I am exhausted when I finally reach a spot that is too far for the beachgoers, with their umbrellas and beer-filled coolers. Just to be on the safe side, I walk on for a few more minutes until I am sufficiently out of sight. Then a white silhouette on the sand catches my attention. I sigh. I'm tired, but I need to be alone, so I'll have to walk further. I approach the figure but keep a reasonable distance, just in case it is a nudist enjoying his privacy. The shape becomes clearer. It doesn't look human.

I come closer. It's quiet and deserted here. Except for the sound of the waves, but that's a tune I've almost stopped hearing, it's been playing in the background of my trip for so long now. Strange things often wash up on the beach, so I am prepared for anything. As long as it's not a corpse, I chuckle.

But it is.

Luckily, not that of a human, but it's still a corpse. Of a shark. And not a small one at that. Carefully, I approach the colossus. The animal lies on its side, a few meters in front of the surf. Its belly is pearly white and shines in the bright sunlight, its eyes are still clear and look like glass with a blue-green color. Breathlessly I walk around it, trying to estimate how big it is. Huge. For a fish, that is. Cautiously, I lie down next to the dead animal, stretched out. We're almost the same size, five foot five or six even. Jesus!

I know nothing about sharks, is this a species that is dangerous to humans? Are there others here? Is this a baby and is its double-sized mother looking for it? Are the kids who are playing in the monitored area of the ocean in danger? Should I call someone?

I decide not to. I don't want to be afraid. Not now, not here on the sand next to the dead shark. I refuse to give in to the fear and try to control my breathing. Nothing can happen to me. I am safe. After a few minutes, I feel peaceful again. Together, we lie on the warm sand, the shark and I. In the sunlight, that occasionally disappears behind a cloud to produce a silver lining. At least now he's not alone. Or she. How would she have died? I prop myself up a little, using my elbows to support myself, and study the giant fish a little more intensely. Was she sick? Maybe she got plastic in her stomach? I imagine how she swam for many miles through the plastic soup, gasping at the bags used to package my groceries at the supermarket, thinking it was a tasty fish. I shake my head; I watched too many National Geographic documentaries.

After a little while, I decide to do what I came here for. I grab my ukulele and start playing while watching the breaking of the waves. I start strumming the strings and moments later I am humming a tune.

The thunder of the ocean drowns out my voice, which gives me the courage to sing louder, something I rarely do. I close my eyes. The high waves are now no longer just arising in the blue-green water before me, but also within me. Deep inside, I feel how they raise, crystal clear and stately, until they can go no higher, only to let their white heads crash down with thunderous noise.

This is how I want to live. Surrendering. Fearless. Without reins. Like the woman in my book, I want to set aside my fear by telling myself a different story than the one I grew up with. The one of the fears of being alone in the dark, of being scared in an elevator, of distrusting strangers, especially men. I decide I am safe, strong, brave. Who I was and what I did no longer matters. I can choose what story to tell myself, right? After all, why should I be afraid anymore? The worst thing that could happen to me has already happened. So why shouldn't I continue my journey? I realize that this is the only logical decision: I'm not going back to Belgium yet, but I'm going to keep driving south.

"Thank you, Daniel," I say aloud as I pluck on. "Thanks for showing me I'm not alone."

"Wow, that's a blue shark!" someone shouts right next to me, in French.

My eyes fly open and I stop playing. An older man dressed in beige shorts and accompanied by a walking stick stands right next to the shark, his female companion following a few feet behind him. She's wearing the same beige shorts.

I scramble to my feet and pat the sand from my clothes, shaking the grains out of my hair with one hand and holding the neck of my ukulele with the other.

The man gives me a broad smile. "Do you speak French?" he asks in French. Which I wouldn't have understood if I didn't.

"I do," I answer.

"Nice find you have there. Blue sharks can easily reach three meters. This one is young. It must have gotten separated from its family and couldn't survive on its own." The man crouches down by the dead animal. "They live up to twenty years in good conditions, did you know that?"

I don't know if the question is directed at me, or at the woman who is standing next to him by now and is giving me an apologetic smile, so I just hum back.

"Yes, yes," he continues enthusiastically, getting back up. "They don't normally get this close to the shore, you know."

I clear my throat, determined not to show my anxiety. "Are they dangerous? To humans?" I ask.

He shakes his head. "Not really. They mainly eat squid, but on bad days, they can confuse a human with a seal." He laughs heartily at his own joke. "By the way, did you know…" He now bends down so close to me I can smell his wine breath. "…that male blue sharks bite the females so hard during the mating ritual that the females develop a skin that is three times as thick? Ha!"

"Luc!" his wife hisses through her teeth. She's clearly tired of his ramblings.

I try to produce something resembling a smile. I seem incapable of being impolite to people, another trait of mine for which I must thank my mother. But I wonder: why do some men feel the need to display their knowledge when they are in the company of women? Or does it only happen to me?

The man, meanwhile, ignores his wife, puts down his backpack, and takes out a professional-looking camera. While he adjusts the complicated equipment to take the perfect picture, I see my chance to escape.

"I'll be off now," I say, and I cast one last glance at my shark. In a few hours, the ocean will claim it again, unless someone finds it sooner and puts it on the barbecue as they do with every fish here. Or are sharks not edible? I could ask Luc but decide not to.

As I walk back to my car, the warm sand beneath my feet, I keep thinking about Daniel. Having his phone number makes me feel safe. At least now there is one person I can ask for help, should the need arise. You never know, after all. Even if I put my fear aside and tell myself as often as I can I'm not in danger, there will always be sharks in the sea.

Chapter 9

Music is about the only thing I live for other than the children I teach, who I carry in my heart. Grateful to still have my car radio, I softly sing along to "Sweet Child O' Mine" by Guns N' Roses. Seen from behind, you could easily take me for Axl Rose. I chuckle. Same red, wiry hair.

My spirits are high again. I've always enjoyed driving. It was one of the few "dangerous" things my mother allowed me to do, although perhaps it was mainly out of self-interest, since Vera Deckers herself can't drive. The feeling of being on the road with a gas tank that's almost full, a door that closes properly, and a GPS that works, makes the events of this afternoon dissolve like sugar in my daily cup of coffee. I suddenly see everything clearly again. Of course, I'm not going back home. Not yet. When I think back to the night before my sudden departure, my stomach churns.

***

My mother had made dinner, but she had never been very good at that. We had chops with canned peas and boiled potatoes. I couldn't get a bite down my throat. The conversation I had with William a few days earlier was still going around in my head. He had humiliated me so deeply, hurt me so badly.

"Don't you think?" my mother said. She had been talking for quite a while, but I had tuned my inner radio to another station.

"Sorry?" I replied.

"That it's all better this way," my mother clarified.

"Better?"

"That in retrospect it's a good thing you and William couldn't have children."

The piece of dry chop I had been chewing on for minutes stuck in my cheek. "What exactly do you mean?" I asked, though I didn't want to hear the answer.

"Surely, you could never have handled kids, they are a heavy burden, you know. You have no idea what you would have had to give up. It was God's will." The tormented look on her face made it clear how much Vera Deckers had put her life at the service of her daughter. At least that was what she believed she did. How could she say something like that? Didn't she know me at all? I was a bloody kindergarten teacher, so where exactly did my knowledge on the subject fall short?

I swallowed the piece of chop and in one gulp downed a glass of wine — which earned me a disapproving look — whereupon I left the table without a word and disappeared to my room with the rest of the bottle.

***

Even now, with my hands clasped around the steering wheel, I grit my teeth in anger. If there is one thing for which I am grateful to William, it's that he offered me a way out. Thanks to him, I was able to break free from my mother's grip, even though she continued to cling to me like a mussel to its rock for a long time. It was William who made me realize that my mother was sick. Not physically, as she had led me to believe all my life, but in her head.

With all my might, I try to regain my good mood of a moment ago, but I fail to. Daniel had given me the address of a cheap campground, a *Quinta* where I could pitch my tent in a field for five euros. I have never camped in the wild. I also never pitch my tent anywhere where I'm alone. The more campers I see, the better. It is the end of July and therefore high season, so the latter is not a problem. Most people travel as a family, but only a few, like me, travel alone. Occasionally, one of the campers tries to strike up a conversation, but so far, I have discouraged these attempts whenever possible. Except for a friendly good morning, there is not much to pick up in the way of conversation with me. That just seemed like the best strategy.

According to the GPS, I have arrived at my destination, but I am in the middle of a dirt road. I continue at a walking pace. Although it's not quite dusk, the sun hangs so low in the sky that it blinds me. It's time to pitch my tent. A little ahead of me a sign looms with the familiar AL logo: *Alojamento Local.* And indeed: an open gate forms the entrance to the Quinta. Relieved, I enter the domain. A second arrow shows me the way to the campsite. Here and there, small tents glow in the golden hour. I pick a spot, far enough from the others but not so far that I am isolated from them, and put up my tent. It's up in a few minutes and I throw in my mat and sleeping bag. There is something comforting about being in a different place every day and yet always coming home.

Sitting on my little low folding chair, I light the gas ring and warm up a can of soup that I found in the trunk. It may seem sparse, but when I spoon up the soup, my soup, from my bowl, I feel rich. I close my eyes with pure pleasure. All around me are various comforting sounds: someone laughing, the clink of cutlery and crockery, and a small child coughing loudly. Other than that, only the crickets provide background music to the event.

When my meal is finished, I take out my ukulele and begin to strum softly. I taught myself to play during college, and it is still the most fun moment of the school week for me when I rehearse a new song with my class. Is it only a month ago that I led a normal life? That I went to school every day, took care of my class, wiped snot bubbles and gave hugs, then did some quick shopping and after that made dinner? Was my life that mundane?

I stop strumming and run my fingers over the strings of my ukulele. I left my guitar at my mother's; I didn't dare to take it along on my trip. The ukulele is smaller and therefore more convenient. It's almost dark now, and I softly start to play a tune, not too loud. I don't want to disturb anyone. The lyrics of "Somewhere over the Rainbow" come to mind and with my eyes closed I start humming the song, and my fingers automatically find the right chords. When I play music, fear loses its grip on me. Then it's as if a protective layer hangs around me, a musical armor that shields me, through which nothing bad can pass. At those moments, my thoughts just stop, my mind goes blank and I just am. I don't think about how I look, with my sleek red hair, and my pale face turned toward the moon, which has appeared from behind the trees. With my long white legs, crossed over, one bare foot skipping along to the beat of the music. So, when suddenly a voice sounds next to me, I almost flip over backwards with folding chair and all. That's how convinced I was that I was alone.

Chapter 10

"That guitar is really tiny!!"

A girl of about five, dressed in yellow pajamas, with a stuffed elephant in her arms, looks at me curiously, her eyes bright and big.

"Oh, hello," I reply with a broad smile. "This is a ukulele! And who are you?" With children, I have always felt most at ease. I may not have a little one myself, but the boys and girls in my class give me so much love that I would almost call it compensation. They never have a hidden agenda; they just say what they need without all the extra layers that adults create.

"I'm Frey. I'm here with my mommy," the child says, pointing with her free hand to somewhere behind her in the dark. "My mommy plays music too, but she didn't bring her piano because it was too big."

I laugh. "Yes, I can imagine. What a pretty name Frey is!"

She smiles and takes a step closer. Her hair is white-blond and there is still a little toothpaste on her chin. I hesitate for a moment, but then ask, "Would you like to sing a song with me?"

"Yes!" Frey replies radiantly.

"Do you know 'Elephant in the Woods'?" I ask, my eyes fixed on the plush animal in her arms.

She shakes her head in denial.

"Okay, it's not hard at all. I'll teach you," I say as I begin to play the simple chords. But when I open my mouth to sing the first words, a figure comes running towards us in the dark. My heart skips a few beats and in a reflex, I pull the girl towards me.

"Frey!" the figure shouts. "Frey!" The voice skips with panic.

The child jumps up, startled, and pulls away from me. "*Maman*! I'm here!"

"Frey! *Merde*!" The woman comes to a halt panting and grabs the girl roughly by the arm, away from me. Her lip quivers.

Relief and anger fight in my chest to have their say. Anger takes over for a moment. "Easy," I say rather harshly. "She just came to say hello. I think the sound of my ukulele lured her here. Nothing to worry about." The woman has Frey rather firmly by the arm, I notice.

When the woman stares straight back at me, she looks like a lunatic: her pupils are wide open, her chest heaving up and down. But she is the kind of person who, even with a face full of rage, still looks beautiful, like a movie star from an old film noir. With dark curly hair and eyes that seem jet black. *Gypsy eyes* shoots through my mind. She looks at me, at my ukulele, and then at my tent. Without a word, she then turns around and pulls Frey with her.

"I just wanted to sing a song, *maman*," I hear the little girl's voice before they disappear into the darkness together.

Perplexed, I am left behind. Geez. No one in their right mind would react like that, would they? I slump down on my chair again and look ahead sullenly. I hate being falsely accused of something. Because that's what that woman did, right? Reacting as if I wanted to do something to her child. Is it her child, by the way? The little girl spoke perfect Dutch and looked nothing like her dark-skinned mother, who had an obvious French accent. But then again, I don't look like mine either. And she called her "maman" after all.

It has cooled considerably by now, and I shiver. Unconsciously, I put my hands on my belly. How different would my life have been if I had had children with William? I wouldn't be sitting here now, that's for sure. I would be a stay-at-home mom; we had discussed it during my first pregnancy. Because of William's practice, that was the wisest choice, he had said.

With a deep sigh, I get up, fold my chair, and unzip the tent. The sound of the zipper gives me an instant feeling of happiness. It reminds me of my goal: to find myself again. I look forward to the security of the night to process today's events and plop down on my inflatable mattress. With my hands behind my head, I stare at the canvas ceiling. I wonder how the baby shark would be doing. Would it still be alone on the beach? In the dark? Or has the ocean reclaimed it?

I hear something outside. Someone is there.

I lie frozen still, my feet hanging outside the tent and my throat spontaneously drying up at the realization of how vulnerable I am, with nothing but a piece of tent canvas between me and the outside world.

I hear it again; someone is approaching softly, with careful steps. I am not alone. My heart is pounding and I hold my breath. Very slowly, I pull my feet in and reach for my cell phone. If I scream really loud, someone will hopefully come and help me. The other campers are only about seventy feet away from me. In a burst of courage, or desperation, who knows, I shine the beam of my mobile toward the sound.

"Hello? Is anyone there?" I call out with more conviction than I feel. A dark shape approaches and fear squeezes my throat. If I'm going to scream, I have to do it now.

"Hello? I'm calling for help, mind you," I screech.

"Hey, I didn't mean to scare you," the phantom replies in a French accent. Relief washes over me. It's that delusional mother again. I shine my lamp straight into her face, she holds her hands protectively in front of her eyes.

"You scared me," I say.

"Sorry, this was a mistake. I've frightened you. Of course, stupid of me to come back in the pitch dark. I just wanted to apologize for my behavior just now, with Frey. I'm going again. Sorry. Really. My mistake."

"Wait," I reply bewildered. Whatever the reason for her tantrum was before, it's clear that there's nothing left of it now. "Apology accepted," I say bravely, lowering the glow of the lamp a bit, so the woman doesn't go blind forever. "I'm Michelle."

Her shoulders relax and she smiles shyly. My lamp reflects brightly on a pendant around her neck, a cylinder of some sort. I don't know why, but my attention is drawn toward the silvery thing.

"I'm Isabelle. Frey asked me to come and apologize, she said I behaved horribly," she says, her fingers clenched around the pendant.

"Yes, you were very fierce, indeed," I reply.

"I know. Sorry. As far as Frey is concerned, I can react rather violently. I wasn't thinking. I'd gone to the washroom and had told her to stay in the van, but she'd slipped away when she heard you playing your ukulele. When I couldn't find her anywhere, I panicked." Her gypsy eyes are soft, shining in the glow of my lamp. Despite her French accent, her Dutch is perfect, which makes me suspect that she comes from the French-speaking part of Belgium, perhaps from the area around Brussels. I can easily imagine what must have been going through her mind when she couldn't find her daughter anywhere, though of course, the girl could never be far away. I thawed some more.

"Well, children are like that when something has aroused their interest. They immediately start to investigate. Don't worry, I understand your reaction." I get ready to crawl back into my tent, now I really want to go to sleep.

Thankfully, she's taken the hint. "Okay then, good night," she says as she turns around.

"Goodnight, Isabelle," I reply.

"Call me Isa," she says, turning back again. "By the way, Frey asked if you might like to go to the beach with us tomorrow."

"To the beach?"

"Yeah, you know: where the ocean hits the sand," she smiles. "No problem if you don't want to, mind you. I had to promise to ask, but of course, Frey doesn't always have to get her way."

The way she talks about her daughter is so loving that even in the dark I can see how her eyes are shining. I suck in my cheeks. This day just keeps getting crazier. As if the universe has opened up a can of "challenges for Michelle" to quite literally lure me out of hiding. I had planned to go to the beach tomorrow, like every day. It would be strange if I rejected Isa's invitation now, and then she would see me there tomorrow. To avoid that, I would have to drive further first thing tomorrow morning, to the next beach, which is ridiculous. And besides, Frey seems like a nice kid and I miss the kids in my class. It would take my mind off the eternal brooding over William and Marie.

"Well yes, why not," I hear myself answer.

Chapter 11

The sun rises early and my tent barely blocks the light. The canvas looks like it's on fire. I turn over onto my stomach to catch a few more minutes of sleep but soon have to give up. By now I am used to living to the rhythm of the sun: going to bed when it sets, and getting up when it rises. I stretch my body so that my toes almost poke through the tarpaulin. "Matchstick," the bullies called me in elementary school, because of my lanky body and red hair. I breathe in deeply. The smell of a tent is something I will always associate with summer.

It was a good night. For the first time in weeks, I didn't dream about William. I wonder if my chance encounter with both Isa and Daniel had anything to do with that. The conversation with Daniel in particular has made me think, his words continue to resonate: "When I see someone in trouble, I help that person. And I hope that the reverse is also the case."

I hope it too, of course. I know I have to learn to trust, but it's bloody hard. William's betrayal has added to it, even though it was he, of all people, who made me realize that my mother was poisoning me with her mistrust. It was he who helped me get away from her. Though today I don't know which of them I feel more betrayed by.

"She's a narcissist and a hypochondriac," he had said. "She will do anything to make you stay here with her. Anything."

I knew it was true. Just as I realize now, I clung to William as much as my mother clung to me. Apparently, the goose barnacle gene is dominant in our family. Of course, in hindsight, it is easy to see through behavioral patterns because they have already been woven by now. As a child, I had neither the knowledge nor the insight to realize that something was wrong. After all, children don't see their parents' mistakes. They grow up with the norms and values they are given and accept them as truth. Only at puberty do the first cracks appear because teenagers can see those too loosely woven stitches and ugly patterns. They even have a trained eye for it.

I remember that time when, as a sixteen-year-old, I had finally had enough of my mother's meddling. My school was going on a week-long ski trip, but she wouldn't let me go. I had tried everything: I had begged, prayed, and caused trouble, but to no avail. In the end, I came up with the idea to engage the school management, so the principal summoned my mother. And I had to come with her. Oh, how nervous I was when I was staring at the yellow tiles in the chilly school corridor while she was inside the principal's office. The look she gave me when she stepped outside said it all, as did the amiable smile she gave the principal. She had given her consent; the pressure was too great. Only I knew with how much reluctance she had signed. Despite my nerves, it was a euphoric moment for me, for I had found my mother's weak spot: what other people thought about her. Unfortunately, my euphoria was short-lived.

The day we were leaving, I walked into the kitchen for breakfast, but my mother was not downstairs. I set up my suitcase in the hall, made some toast, and poured myself a cup of coffee. It was not unusual for me to have breakfast alone, rather the other way around, and I suspected this was my mother's way of punishing me for my "betrayal." It was half past seven. In fifteen minutes, my best friend, Heleen, and her mother, Magda, would pick me up by car. Like me, Heleen didn't belong to the A club of pretty teenagers with trendy clothes. She was more into reading and math. We differed in the latter because I was terrible at mathematics. I'm more of a language girl. Heleen was a bit chubby and wore glasses with thick lenses, which didn't help her popularity at school. But what particularly annoyed our classmates about her was that Heleen never exchanged a word with them. She never responded to their jokes, insults, or even their rare attempts to make conversation. I knew why. Heleen had a firm opinion about each of them, and she was not subtle about it. Her black humor often made me roar with laughter, something I am still grateful for. One look was enough for us to make it clear what we thought about someone. Childish, but after all, we were teenagers, just like the rest. Every insecure teenager should have a Heleen.

When I finished my cup of coffee, I washed my mug and plate and put them in the drying rack. Still, my mother had not come downstairs; according to my watch, it was twenty to eight. I only had five minutes left. With leaden legs, I walked up the stairs. I couldn't leave without saying goodbye to her. No matter how angry she was. My knuckles rumbled briefly on the bedroom door.

"Mom?"

I listened intently, but there was no answer. Gently, I opened the door to the room I rarely entered. It felt like I was committing a traffic violation, like running a red light.

"Mommy?" I said again, but it remained strangely silent. The room smelled a little sour, of sleep and something else, something I couldn't immediately pinpoint. My mother was still in bed, I could see her body outlined in the darkness as my eyes adjusted. "Mom, Heleen will be here soon. I'm leaving, I just wanted to say goodbye."

Chewing the inside of my cheek, I waited for a response. When it didn't come, I touched my mother's arm. In retrospect, I think I already knew then, with the way her body reacted to my touch. Or rather: didn't react at all. But as I stood there, in the dark bedroom, I only realized what was going on when my foot bumped into an empty bottle of pills.

"Mom! Mommy!" I cried, shaking her limp body. "Mom! Wake up!" But my mother did not wake up. When the bell rang, I ran downstairs crying. Hysterically, I explained to Heleen and Magda that my mother had taken an overdose of sleeping pills.

It was Magda who called the ambulance, who felt if Vera Deckers still had a pulse, who checked if she was breathing. It was Magda who then drove me to the hospital and stayed in the waiting room with me, nail-biting, hoping for good news. It was Magda who dried my tears until I had none left. Who soothed me and told me it would be okay, though she couldn't be certain. Magda and Heleen took me in, Heleen didn't go on the ski holiday either, although I told her she should.

"Are you crazy, with those losers? I'd rather stay with you," she said. I slept on an inflatable mattress in her room and heard her snoring softly while I lay awake for hours. I remember exactly how the guilt tore me apart, lying next to her on the floor. How could I have done this to my mother? Time after time she had asked me not to go.

"It's too dangerous," she had said. "You don't know what people are like, Michelle. People are evil. It's in our nature. We are born sinners."

But I hadn't listened, and now she had committed a terrible act just because I wouldn't listen. It was my fault. The thought that I could lose my mother took my breath away. That it was me who killed her. My mother and I were a team, we only had each other. What was I supposed to do? If my mother didn't survive, I would have no parents. Then I would be a sixteen-year-old orphan. Would I still be allowed to stay in our house? Would I go to a foster home?

"Heleen!" I shook her awake, sniffling.

"Mmmm?"

"When Mom dies, can I come and live with you?"

"Mmmm… Of course, silly. But she will not die, though," she mumbled back. "Mommy says she'll be all right. Now go to sleep."

And she was right, a week later my mother returned home. She said I was lucky the doctors got there in time, that they had managed to pump her stomach, and that there would be no permanent damage. At least no visible damage.

Yes, I was extremely lucky.

***

A groan escapes my mouth, why am I thinking of this now? I rub the sleep from my eyes with both hands and open the tent to let in the fresh morning breeze. I stick my head out and sniff the scent of soil and grass, letting the freshness penetrate every corner of my mind to chase away the memories.

After a breakfast of warm oatmeal accompanied by a strong cup of coffee, I can take on the world again. It is still early, so presumably Isa and Frey are not yet ready. I walk across the camping grounds to the small building where you can take a shower for fifty euro cents, and decide to save my money by sticking to a sink bath today. In the slot provided for that purpose, I dutifully throw five euros for my overnight stay.

What would my mother think of this, I wonder. A lot of the smaller rural campsites operate in good faith. You pay because you want to, not because anyone tells you to. Not the larger campsites, of course. They have barriers and security and stuff. But the smaller ones do. I love it. In my first week on the road, in France, I ended up on a free campground owned by a wine farmer. In a wooden shed, I found a refrigerator filled with bottles of red and white wine and Crémant, a French sparkling wine. Next to it was a price list and a mailbox to deposit the money into. I loved it so much that it had cost me a lot of willpower not to buy a bottle myself.

I walk back to my tent. Most of the cars on the site have a Portuguese license plate, there are also some Germans, a few Dutch, and a few French cars. No other Belgians. Which car would Isa and Frey be traveling in? I get an instant answer to my question when I see Frey coming out of a yellow camper van with a French license plate.

"Hello!" she calls out cheerfully. She's wearing a summer dress with blue and white stripes and her mouth is smeared with chocolate.

"Good morning," I reply. "Do you feel like going to the beach?"

"Yes!" exclaims the girl. "I'm going to make a snowman out of sand!"

I laugh. "Okay, that sounds good. Shall I help you with that?"

"Yes!"

"Frey, you haven't brushed your teeth!" shouts Isa, who is standing by the van. She looks at me with an apologetic smile and raises her mug in the air as the girl runs back. "Coffee?"

"No, thanks, I've already finished mine," I reply. I'm still having a hard time erasing her performance from my memory; she did leave an impression.

"We'll be done in a minute, shall we pick you up in half an hour?"

I raise my thumb and walk back to my tent. There is no harm in going to the beach with a little girl and her mother, I tell myself. No harm at all. Back at my tent, I start packing my things, so I can drive on later, after the beach visit. The south of Portugal beckons.

Chapter 12

"Are you here on vacation?" Isa asks, without taking her eyes off Frey, who is clambering up the dune in front of us. The chocolate now washed off her mouth, her toddler legs moving surprisingly fast.

"Well, sort of," I reply. "And you guys?"

"Also sort of," she smiles.

The question of where Frey's father is burns on my lips, but I manage to hold back. From experience, I know how annoying it is to have to answer it when there is no father to speak of. Maybe later, when Frey is out of earshot. Or maybe not. After all, it's none of my business.

Frey looks like she has lived at the beach all her life, with her golden skin and white-blond hair. She doesn't look a bit like her dark-haired mother. In the daylight, by the way, I estimate Isa to be a little older than I first thought. Last night I could have sworn she was younger than me, today I'm not so sure anymore. Especially because of her eyes. Old eyes they are, with a deep wrinkle between them. At times, when she thinks no one is looking at her, she looks so sad. As if those eyes have seen too much to be happy anymore. Her dark curls are bleached here and there by the sun, her skin is so tanned it's almost black. My milky white arms stand out brightly against hers.

"Is it hard, traveling like this by yourself?" she asks.

I shrug and pretend to be a little tougher than I feel. "It's okay," I say. She doesn't need to know how desperate I was only yesterday.

"Don't you ever get scared, as a woman on your own?"

"Do you?" I shoot back. "I mean, technically you're alone too, right?"

"Yes, you're right. I always pick spots where there are families. That's where I feel safest," she replies, but her eyes wander away. For a moment, it seems as if she wants to add something, but she fixes her gaze back on Frey.

"The first nights, I couldn't sleep," I admit. "Every sound, every rustle, made me lie in my tent with my eyes wide open. But I can't afford to sleep in a B&B, so I had to get used to it."

"I know what you mean. For a while, I even slept during the day and traveled at night; otherwise, I couldn't manage," she says, nodding.

"Seriously?" I exclaim in surprise. "But why? There's no fun in that, is there? Then you had better not go on vacation."

"Fun?" she responds, caught off guard. "Oh, no, don't worry. It only happened twice, you know. No drama. I exaggerated a little," she says, but the words roll out of her mouth too quickly. She clearly regrets her outpouring, which she now tries to minimize. What is this? Why is she backtracking? If she drives at night and sleeps during the day, what is she doing with Frey? I want to call her on it, but a group of surfers coming out of the dunes towards us catches my attention. One of them, a boy with a long, wet ponytail, takes the floor and says something in Portuguese. I don't understand him. Questioningly, I look at Isa, but she clearly doesn't understand either.

"Français? English?" she asks, whereupon the surfers confer with each other for a moment. The coconut smell of the wax on their surfboards floats into my nostrils. They radiate something young and adventurous, as they stand there in their shiny wetsuits. All boys, no girls. Is this the group that broke into my car? They all look so similar in their black wetsuits. After a short deliberation, a surfer with a blond beard takes the lead. "Go back," he says.

Frey has come to stand next to her mother and takes her hand. "What are they saying, maman?"

"I don't know, honey, wait a minute. Go back? Why?" Isa turns to the blond boy; her body is tense like a coil spring.

The young surfer shrugs his shoulders. "Police," he replies, before shouting something to his comrades and walking further towards some parked vans. They must think they've gone to enough trouble already and that we should sort it out ourselves. I keep an eye on Isa. She stands as still as a meerkat. If she could pierce the dunes with her eyes to see what lies beyond, she would.

"What could it mean? Why aren't we allowed on the beach?" I ask, but she doesn't respond and remains standing.

"Isa?"

She blinks and jolts awake from her trance. "I don't know. I think the police don't allow us to go onto the beach because something has washed up or something. Shall we turn back?" Her voice sounds strained, and her eyes shoot back and forth as if she expects to see someone. It makes me uncomfortable. Especially since I don't understand what provoked her reaction.

"How about we just walk up to the top of the dune?" I suggest. "Maybe we'll see what's going on. Who knows, it might just be a shark that washed up." Possibly the mama-shark, I think.

"A shark!" shouts Frey. "We've already seen a dead dolphin, haven't we, maman?"

But Isa's mind is still somewhere else. I touch her arm for a moment. "Isa?"

"Hm?"

"Shall we just walk up to the top of the dune?" I try again, while Frey looks at her mother expectantly.

"Hm, yes. Okay, I guess that wouldn't hurt," she replies, but all of her body posture has changed from a few minutes ago. She doesn't let go of Frey's hand as we continue our journey, and although my legs are much longer than hers, she still is the first one up. I stumble behind her, panting. At the top, I need to catch my breath. I support my hands on my knees and look out over the beach.

There is absolutely nothing to see. The stretch we can see from here is deserted, which is not so strange at this early hour.

"Probably those surfers just wanted to keep their paradise to themselves," I say. "Or scare us. Maybe that's what they think is funny, scaring the crap out of two women."

Isa's shoulders are still tense. "Yes, it must have been something like that," she says, but it's clear she doesn't believe any of it.

Why is she so scared?

"Shall we return anyway, just to be sure?"

"Maman! No! I still have to make my snowman out of sand!" cries Frey. She lets go of her mother's hand and runs down the high dune.

"Frey!"

"I'll go after her," I say, jumping down as well. The wind makes my hair flutter and I feel like I'm flying. I had forgotten how liberating it is to be in the company of toddlers. Delightful!

Isa comes chasing after us with her beach bag full of Frey's stuff. "Frey! Merde! How many times do I have to tell you to stay with me!" she shouts, and even from a distance I see another glimpse of the dark fury from last night. My uneasiness grows, but I feel caught between two fires. I promised myself to put aside my fear and not surrender to that irrational distrust of everything and everyone. Then I might as well have stayed in Belgium. Besides, I'm here at her invitation, she may as well take that into account.

"Come on, Isa! Don't be silly!" I call back, my hands in my sides. "Everything is fine."

My body posture must speak volumes because she tempers herself and a moment later, she's down on the beach with us. "Little bugger," she says to her daughter.

Frey looks a little guilty, but can't hide the lights in her eyes. My heart melts for that child. Then the look in Isa's eyes changes again. "Oh, no!" she whispers, staring at something behind me.

"What?" Quickly I turn around. In the distance, police ribbons flutter like colored pennants in the morning sun. I turn to Isa whose skin has become a few shades lighter. "Why are you so worried, Isa? It happens more often than not that something washes up here, doesn't it? Frey said you've seen a dead dolphin, and I've found a shark myself. There's nothing to be afraid of, is there? And we're far enough away, Frey won't see a thing."

She swallows. "I… I… You're probably right, but would you mind going there and looking around?" she asks softly, but forcefully. "Then I'll stay here with Frey for a while?" She fixes me with her eyes, which have darkened another shade in contrast to her skin. "Just to be certain?" Her whole body is tense. And I thought I had issues.

I shrug. "No problem," I say, being far too curious myself. But I am tired of her attitude and I'm secretly glad that soon I will be traveling on my own again. It was a mistake to go to the beach together. With large strides, I walk toward the commotion in the distance. Police ribbons. What could that mean? A whale, perhaps? But of course, it could also be something else. Maybe someone drowned. As I walk over the lukewarm sand, I try to push away the thought of Isa's reaction, but I can't. Something is wrong. Up there on the dune, when she heard the word "police", she stiffened completely. Could she be on the run from the police? But then why is she making me run up there? And if she's fleeing from something or someone, or is in danger, why does she have her daughter with her? I chuckle for a moment, my imagination running away with me. As if my life is that exciting. The most logical explanation is that she just doesn't like me anymore either, and this is a ruse to get rid of me. When I return, they will probably be gone.

I approach the police tape and notice I am not alone. A small crowd has gathered on the beach. The cordoned-off area is not far from the main entrance, where there are a few parked cars. The police have done their job thoroughly and cordoned off the place well, but they can't hide where everyone's gaze is drawn. Where my gaze is also sucked towards.

Chapter 13

A white tent is set up in the middle of the cordoned-off strip. Serious-looking men and women walk in and out, their bodies wrapped in plastic. I stand next to some tourists who are busily taking pictures and try to catch a glimpse of what is going on inside the tent, but that is an impossible task. One of the tourists, a woman with a long sarong tied around her body, notices my presence.

"Exciting, isn't it!" she squeals. "Finally, something interesting is happening!"

"Do you know what's going on?" I ask.

"They've found a body, of a man. A fisherman found him this morning."

"A dead body," I say, startled. "What happened? Did he drown?"

"I don't think so," she responds grinning, one eyebrow raised a little higher than the other. She clearly enjoys having more information than I do, but I'm too curious to be bothered by that.

"Why, why not? What happened?"

The woman bends toward me conspiratorially. "The police," she says, nodding in their direction, "won't say anything, but I've heard from good sources that the corpse has no head or limbs left."

"What!" I exclaim.

"Yes, gruesome, isn't it!" she gloats.

"But... how..." The image of the shark haunts my mind. That Frenchman in his shorts had said they could easily reach three meters. But they didn't attack people, did they? With my mouth hanging open I stare at the tent.

The woman interprets my silence as shock and is visibly pleased with the effect of her words.

"No idea how, but we'll hear all about it on the news, I'm sure." She points to the news vans approaching and promptly loses all interest in me. A reporter, microphone in hand and followed by a cameraman, makes his way through the crowd to the police tape. The woman almost trips over her skirt in an attempt to get to him.

***

With my head full of horrific images of severed limbs, I walk across the sand back to the place where I left Frey and Isa. To my relief, they are still there. They are taking pictures of the sand castle they made, and Isa is standing with her back to me, so she doesn't see me right away.

"Frey! Will you stand next to the sand castle for a moment? Yes, good. Smile!" I hear her say.

"Look, Michelle! Mommy and I made it together!" Frey proudly shouts at me, and Isa turns around with a jerk.

"Everything okay?" she asks.

I don't answer immediately and focus on her daughter. "Nice!" I say. My voice sounds shrill. Between my teeth, I hiss to Isa, "Can I talk to you for a minute?" as I take her by the elbow and pull her further away from Frey.

"What is it?" she asks when we're out of earshot. "What is happening there?"

"There's a dead body over there, Isa," I say breathlessly.

The change in her expression is so subtle that I wouldn't have seen it if I hadn't been watching her face so closely. I understand what she's doing, she doesn't want to alarm her daughter, but I still think it's remarkable that she can have so much self-control. Based on her earlier behavior, I didn't expect that. She nods at me briefly and walks back to Frey.

"Put your things back in the bag, dear. We have to leave," she says.

"What, already! We just got here!"

"I know, doll, but according to Michelle, a storm is coming, and we'd better leave as soon as possible."

Frey looks up at the clear blue sky in amazement and wants to open her mouth again, but then meets her mother's compelling gaze.

I come to Isa's aid. "Yes, Frey, a storm! Come on, whoever puts the most stuff in the bag wins!"

Fortunately, my little trick works. Frey even starts singing a tidying-up song that I know only too well. In no time at all we are on the way back.

"Details, please, what happened?" asks Isa between her teeth once Frey has run ahead of us and is out of earshot.

"There was a body on the beach, under one of those white tents. I haven't spoken to the police, but according to one bystander, a man's body washed up there. Or was put there, I don't know."

"What do you think happened? Did he drown?"

"I don't think so," I reply grimly. As we continue walking, I give her the account of the missing limbs and the shark I saw.

"O, mon Dieu," Isa exclaims, her self-control completely gone.

"Shhh," I hiss at her. "If Frey hears what happened, she'll never go near the ocean again."

"Yes, yes, of course," Isa stammers. She muffles her voice. "But surely a shark couldn't have done it, right? There are no dangerous species living in this area," she whispers back. Under her dark complexion, the skin around her nose has turned white. She thinks for a moment. "I think Frey and I had better leave as soon as possible. It's not safe here."

I highly agree, I don't want to stay here a second longer myself. My relief is great when we arrive at our campsite. I am eager to get into my car and drive away, far away. A beach where shark-eaten limbless corpses wash up or fall off cliffs or are dumped from boats or whatever else my head can think of that happened is not the place I can unwind at. Let alone where I can restore my faith in the world. It's time for a change.

I say goodbye to Isa and Frey. I give the little girl another hug and walk to my Volvo, ready to leave. Everything is packed already, my freedom beckons. I'm not ready to mingle with other people yet. I realize that now. It's just too complicated.

Then I hear a horrible sound. A scream that sounds like that of an animal. Primal. My first thought is: "Frey!" and with a pounding heart I run back, just in time to see the child running toward the van.

"Maman!" she cries out in a panic. It must have been Isa's scream that I heard, coming from the van.

I instinctively run after her. "Frey, wait!" But she's already inside.

I come to a stop in front of the open door and behold the scene: Isa is inside, on her knees, her head on the floor, as if praying. Frey runs to her, but I pull her away and keep her protectively behind me. Meanwhile, I try to process and, above all, understand what I see. I look for blood, shards, or other signs of something horrible having happened here, but Isa doesn't seem to be hurt, though she lies there groaning. The van is a mess. Cupboards and drawers are open, clothes are scattered here and there.

"Isa? Isa? What's going on? Isa!" I try.

She doesn't answer and stays on the floor, crying. I can feel Frey trembling behind me.

"Isa, you're scaring Frey, what happened? Say something."

The woman moans some kind of mantra that I don't understand. It bears a resemblance to a prayer, although I'm sure it's not. At least it seems to calm her down. Minutes pass, and the moaning lessens. Then she seems to pull herself together. She scrambles to her feet, holding a wooden box in her hands. Her face is swollen and wet with tears. Frey, too, has started crying. I take her in my arms.

I feel torn. I don't know what to do. Isa needs help, but I don't know why. My concern for Frey takes over, and I touch Isa briefly with my hand. "Frey is upset," I whisper. "Shall I take her to my car for while so you can calm down a bit?"

"No!" Isa roars. Before I realize what is happening, she pushes me out of the van and pulls Frey out of my arms. "My daughter stays with me!"

I fall out of the van, on my backside, at which point Frey cries even louder. Trembling, I get up. What on earth is going on here?

"Isa! Please! You're scaring her," I shout. A few people have come to see what the fuss is about. What should I do? My instincts tell me to help a child who is caught in a critical situation, but the look in Isa's eyes makes me question whether it's a good idea to separate the two. Whatever the reason, Isa is terrified of losing sight of Frey. But that doesn't mean she can traumatize her daughter. To my surprise, I walk over to the van again, where Isa is sitting on the floor with Frey pressed against her, the wooden box next to her. The girl is still sobbing. Her mother stares into nothingness with a frozen face. I decide to step inside. I raise my hand briefly to the few people who are standing outside watching and close the door. Silently, I sit down on the floor next to Isa and Frey, my arms wrapped around my knees. I can't just walk away from a child who has just seen her mother in an emotional breakdown. No way.

Chapter 14

Let me tell you about my first corpse.

When I was sixteen, I saw my very first dead body. Matthew was my mother's latest husband. His time to go had come, according to her. She had no choice, she told me. He didn't want to leave, even though she had asked him to. So, she had smashed his brains in with a cast-iron wok.

I didn't know then that she had done the same to my father, ten years earlier. Who knows, maybe she even did it with that same wok. The wok in which I made teriyaki noodles at least once a week.

He had abandoned us, she had always told us, me and my siblings. Only a year after she killed Matthew did she tell me the truth. Why she confided in me like that, I don't know. Perhaps she needed to share her secret with someone. Someone who would never betray her.

She told me a lot — I was the oldest—but not everything.

"You are my rock," she said. "The only person in this evil world who I can count on. The only one who understands me."

That felt good. It's nice to know your existence matters, even if it matters only for being someone's rock. And I never betrayed her, that's true. You're still the only one who knows what I did, my dear.

That night, after putting the others to sleep (something I did every night because Mom often worked late), I helped her put Matthew's heavy body in the trunk of the car. He was still warm and his head with the bald patch on top of it fell back strangely. We drove to a secluded spot in the woods behind the farm and made a fire. All night we stayed vigil next to the flames that greedily consumed his body until nothing was left but some charred bones. Mom made me gather the ashes, and I burned myself as the remaining bones disintegrated between my fingers. We drove back home and I emptied the bag of ashes through the window of the moving car.

"Never leave a trace," my mother said. "And if you do, let it point clearly at someone else."

The burn marks on my hands remained for days. Now they are scars that remind me of what I did. Of course, it was wrong. But I had to do it. What would have become of me and my brothers and sisters if we'd had to go into foster care? The twins might have been split up. It's hard enough to find a foster home for one child, let alone for six. I couldn't let that happen, Belle. I did what I had to do, just as I am doing what I have to do right now.

Chapter 15

The mundane sounds of the camping intrude into the van from outside, but beyond that, I can only hear my breathing and Frey's diminishing sobs. I take my time taking in my surroundings. From the outside, the yellow van looked very ordinary, old, and unremarkable, but as I sit here, I can hardly believe that this is the same van. The walls are lined with fine dark wood slats and the ceiling is painted in a fresh white. A double mattress takes up almost all the back of the space, and the soft pillows scattered on it suggest that this is where Isa and Frey usually cozy up together. A lot of thought has gone into the interior of the bus. Isa has made it a real home. In my mind, I compare this place with my home and I must admit that the bus wins. A bit over the top for a holiday vehicle, maybe. The windows have wooden shutters that can be pushed aside. They are painted with magnetic paint and covered by black and white pictures. Almost all of them are of Isa and Frey, but some are of an elderly couple. No picture of Frey's father, as far as I can tell. As cozy as the van feels, it is abundantly clear that it has been broken into. All the closet doors are open, and their contents are scattered across the white comforter.

"Tea," I decide when I spot a small stove. I'm here now, so I might as well make myself useful. I get up and put a small pan of water on the stove. Then I find teabags in a pot under the stove. Two mugs are still dripping in a washing-up bowl and I dry them while glancing at Isa. Frey seems to have fallen asleep in her arms. I pour the boiling water into the mugs and wait. Meanwhile, my eyes wander back to the pictures on the wall. The older woman is no doubt Isa's mother; the resemblance is striking. The same gypsy eyes, the same curls, but silver.

"Those are my parents," she confirms my stare. Her voice is husky and raw, whispering.

I nod and study the photos one by one. Isa gets up carefully and lays Frey on the bed, cautiously, so as not to wake her. With one arm, she supports her child, while with the other she sweeps the havoc out of the way and makes room for me to sit down. She places the wooden box on her lap. I hand her a mug of tea and take a seat next to her. Frey rolls over in her sleep and heaves a contented sigh.

"Sorry you had to see that," Isa says.

I remain silent.

"You must be wondering what kind of crazy woman you've ended up with."

"The van was broken into and you freaked out," I say. "I get that. But something tells me that's not the only reason for your outburst."

She shakes her head. "No, it's not." She plays absently with the box, then looks at me, her eyes tracing over my face. As if she can read from them how much she can tell me.

"Family is everything to me," she says.

I feel a heartbreaking story coming on and seek support in the reassuring warmth of my mug.

"I come from a small village near Nantes, in France. Two years ago, I got divorced. It was a difficult time, very hard." She swallows audibly, takes a sip of her tea, and looks at the pictures on the wall. "I had a lot of help from my parents during that period. They supported me through thick and thin. Never once did my father reproach me for marrying Remco, although he had warned me several times that he was not the right man for me. But then again," she shrugs, "that's what every father thinks, right?"

I hum affirmatively but say nothing. In turn, I take a sip of my tea — chamomile—which prompts Isa to continue.

"Now, of course, I know he was right, but at the time I thought my parents were just overprotective. They were already getting on in age when they had me. I was their little miracle. After the birth of my older brother Jacco, my mother never dreamed that she would be able to get pregnant again because according to the doctors it was no longer possible. She was forty-three at the time, it was a real miracle."

I feel a tugging pain in my stomach. I hate stories about miracle babies. My jaws clamp together.

"So, when I fell in love with a Belgian guy from Antwerp, they were afraid of losing me. But they didn't stop me. They never did. They spoiled me rotten. Come to think of it, I always got everything I wanted. Maybe that's the reason I fell into my ex's romantic trap." A tear rolls out of the corner of her eye. She sighs deeply and waves her hand as if to repel the memory. "Anyway, after my divorce, I went to live alone. My parents wanted me to come and live with them in France, with Frey, but I couldn't. I had to stay in Belgium because Remco and I were co-parenting. If only I had known what would happen…" she sobs.

I put a comforting hand on her arm. "You don't have to tell me," I say.

"Yes, I do. It feels good. There aren't many opportunities for me to talk about my parents," she replies. Her gaze slides to the pictures again. "My mother has diabetes, and she's been getting worse for a few years now, but my father was always in perfect health. A man like a tree. He took care of her. She was his greatest love. Dragged her everywhere so she wouldn't become isolated. And then, a few months after my divorce, he died unexpectedly. Cardiac arrest. Gone." Isa snaps her fingers, then puts her hand on her bare neck, right where I had noticed a pendant hanging just last night.

"It was like I lost a piece of myself, like I had to continue on one leg. My father was my hero and my only buffer against Remco. When he died, I was as vulnerable as a hatchling. But I could not and should not collapse; I had to be there, not only for Frey but also for my mother. She was deteriorating rapidly and slowly becoming blind. My brother Jacco and I faced an impossible task: he couldn't just leave his farm and I couldn't just take Frey to France, not without Remco's approval. It was impossible to combine the care for my mother, the care for Frey, my work... In the end, Mom suggested going to a nursing home, and Jacco and I had no choice but to agree. Our parents' house was sold to pay the costs..." She gets a lump in her throat and I sympathize with her, but still don't understand why she's telling me all this.

With her hand on her neck, she continues. *"Bon.* So, together with the house, all my memories were sold. But since his death, I always carry some of my father's ashes with me. I had a silver pendant made, a cylinder, on which I had his name and date of death engraved. Other than these photos, it's all I have left of him." Her lip trembles and red marks appear on her neck. "The feeling that my father's death is somehow my fault never leaves me. If only I had listened to him, to his gut feeling, then he might still be here. This whole situation with Remco... it killed him. Again, she grabs at her neck, her tearful eyes focusing on me. "I only take off my pendant to go to the beach. Why didn't I take it with me, Michelle? Why did I leave it here?"

Finally, I understand why she's so upset. Not because of the break-in itself, but because the only memento of her father has been stolen from her van. "Oh, Isa! I'm so sorry," I whisper. "I don't know what to say. How awful!"

She shrugs her shoulders, sniffles, and shakes her head. I squeeze her hand for a moment, letting her recover a little. Somehow, I'm relieved that there's an explanation for the outburst I witnessed. Isa is not a delusional freak but a woman with a great deal of grief and some serious emotional baggage. No wonder her eyes are often so sad. My own problems suddenly seem so insignificant. I am almost ashamed that my world is turned upside down because of William. In my urge to help, I say, "You have to talk to the police, there's obviously a gang at work. My car was broken into too, I'll go with you. We'll find your pendant."

But that doesn't have the desired effect. Isa snatches her hand from mine, her eyes wide. "No, no police." She almost shouts it, and I look up in surprise at the fierce reaction.

"How come, why not?" I ask.

She clenches her hands in frustration. "I really can't explain, Michelle. But please believe me when I say we'd better leave it."

I stare at her in bewilderment and think of all the reasons someone wouldn't want to get the police involved, when there is a loud banging on the side of the van. Isa stiffens, wide-eyed, as she looks at me. Someone is shouting. I hear running. Has someone called the police, after all? For seconds, we remain still. Frey sleepily gets up. We now hear voices echo from everywhere.

"Isa, something's wrong. I have to see," I say.

She nods, pulling Frey towards her. I open the door. Greater chaos than what I see at that moment is rarely encountered. A man runs up to me.

"*Fogo!*" he shouts.

Behind him tents are being hastily dismantled, and one by one the campers are getting ready to leave.

"Fire!" he calls again.

And then I smell the smoke.

Chapter 16

The fire started in a eucalyptus forest and is raging only a few miles from the campsite. Thick plumes of brown-gray smoke rise in the distance. I hastily help Isa pack. My car is already waiting. What a morning.

"Where should we go now?" she calls out. "Which way?"

"To the south! Away from the fire!" I call back. I am also struggling to get my bearings in the chaos. We leave together and follow the other cars, hoping they have a plan. How far should we go to escape the fire? How quickly does something like this spread? Forest fires are commonplace in Portugal, unfortunately, but this is the first time I've been in the middle of one.

Isa is driving right in front of me. We exchanged numbers before we left, and I call her, my phone clamped between my head and shoulder. "If we lose each other, just keep driving, okay? You don't have to wait for me!" I say.

"Okay, I'll drive to Lisbon, we'll be safe there. Will I see you there?"

"Maybe," I reply because I don't want to be rude. But I honestly have to think about it. I would rather not travel together with Isa, but I feel bad for the little girl. Will I be selfish and think only of myself, or shall I stay close to Frey for a while longer, until I'm sure Isa has calmed down? I let the distance between my Volvo and the van widen a little. A car pulls in. And then another. And another one. Until I can't see the yellow van anymore.

Exactly like I had allowed the distance between William and myself expand.

After we lost Marie, we were still okay. He understood my grief and shared it with me so it didn't get too heavy. He dried my tears. The growing apart came later. It started subtly. When I would reach for the bottle of wine at dinner to refill my glass, he would look at me briefly without saying anything. He didn't have to. I knew what he meant, and I answered him by filling my glass to the brim and looking back defiantly. Even when he wasn't home, I uncorked a bottle. I would never have done that before. But I found no other way out. Who could I talk to? I still didn't have any friends; I didn't want to bore Heleen on the phone with my whining. My mother? Yeah, right.

I sought refuge in the wine and found it there. And when that one glass could no longer provide enough oblivion, it became a bottle. And when the bin of empty bottles suspiciously filled up, I replaced the bottles with cartons. And what did William do? He would come home later and later.

"A lot of work," he said.

I was often already asleep or pretended to be when he entered the bedroom. When he pressed his warm body against mine, I rolled myself away from him with a feigned moan until he gave up. I was so angry. So angry. Not even at him, really, but he was just the only one who was there. I was angry at my mother, at her God, at my defective body. I was angry at pregnant women and baby store owners. I was angry at diaper commercials. I was angry at women with strollers. Oh, how I hated those.

I took it out on William. I was sure he was seeing someone else. After all, why would he stay with me? He only married me because he thought he had to, right? He denied everything. I began searching his pockets, looking for evidence, but I found nothing. I surveillanced his practice, followed him home, and then pretended I just happened to come home, too, with a shopping bag in my hands. I still found nothing. Maybe there was nothing to find. I don't know. In any case, now there is. If you look long enough, you'll eventually find something. Even if it wasn't there before.

***

When I can no longer see the plumes of smoke behind me, I leave the highway again and wind along the coastal road: prettier and cheaper. Now that the adrenaline has worn off, I feel my stomach rumble. My oatmeal was digested hours ago, and I desperately need to pee, so I decide to stop.

One of the things I love about this country is that regardless of where you stop, there's always a country road somewhere that takes you right into nature. I park my Volvo on the shoulder of the road, take out my bag, and walk through the fields. The blue of the ocean shimmers in front of me. It's so beautiful here: the sandy beige of the path I'm walking on, the green of the thorns and bushes on the shoulder. I seem to be walking in a painting. Above me, I hear the shrill cry of a bird of prey. I squint my eyes and see that not one but two falcons are circling above me. I come to a fork in the road, both roads run parallel to the ocean and for a moment, I don't know which way to go. Then I see that the birds are flying on my left and I follow. I don't plan to go much further and am just about to settle in when I see a little house in the distance, built against a hillside. I walk a little more, the birds still hovering over my head. I climb the steep hill and the closer I get, the more obvious it is that the cottage is uninhabited. It is a container that was once converted to a home. Someone worked hard to turn it into something beautiful, but that work has since been undone. Graffiti disfigures the little house, all around is broken glass in the sand. Yet, you can still see that this must have been an idyllic place, flanked by the dunes that block the wind, and with a spectacular view over the ocean. Now, only the skeleton and the roof of the structure are still there.

My bladder begins to protest, so I walk behind the house to a spot where I am definitely out of sight and let my pee go happily. That's one of the few things I miss about home: a bathroom all to myself. The ones I encounter along the way are often not worthy of the name, yet I refuse to do my number two in the bushes. I'm the only one, judging by the many wet wipes found here and there along hiking trails.

I carefully step into the shady cottage and sit down on the wooden floor. My white legs dangle over the edge, where the wall has been removed. Pieces of it lie several feet below in the bushes. From my bag, I pull a pack of dry crackers. It's not much, but about five of them are enough to satisfy my hunger. In the depths ahead of me I can see the dunes, straight ahead is the ocean under a clear blue sky. I try to imagine living here, by myself. In my mind, I redo the walls, place a bed and a small kitchenette in the space, and install an outdoor shower, next to the large palm tree that flanks the cottage. Yes, I could do that, I think. Watching the sun set each evening and saying goodbye to the day accompanied by my ukulele. Eating fish from the ocean, and potatoes from my own little garden. Although, can you grow vegetables in this sandy soil? I shrug my shoulders. Doesn't matter, in my imagination, I can and that's enough.

I take my book out of my bag and continue reading Eat, Pray, Love. The story is not what I expected it to be. For starters, the main character doesn't travel the world, as I thought she would, but in the first part of the book she lives in Italy for months at a time when she does nothing but eat. That's fine by me, but moreover, she is seeking spirituality on her journey. No. Sorry, let me rephrase that: she's looking for God.

Let's just say that I'm not.

Thirdly, to test my empathy to the limit, she doesn't want children. She can have them, but she doesn't want them. I don't know if I'm ready to follow her argument yet.

When I get up to walk back to my car, I spot one of the birds again. It's hovering silently in the air with its wings spread. Since I'm at an altitude myself, I can get a good look at its beautiful brown feathers. Then it dives at lightning speed. The mouse that is probably frolicking happily over there, will be dead soon. A shiver runs down my spine, despite the warmth of the midday sun. Only moments ago, that mouse didn't know that her life would be over in a few seconds. It was perhaps scrabbling around on the ground, thinking it was safe. Maybe it was searching for food, or it was just on its way back to its den. Or who knows, maybe it was just enjoying its freedom while it lasted. Not a hair on its fur would have thought that soon it would be ripped from its familiar life by a calculated killer. A killer it never saw coming.

The bird flies up again, and in a slow spiral, it joins its companion who has been hovering above me all this time. And whom I had not seen.

Back in my car, I drive on with the windows open and let the uncomfortable feeling that the two birds of prey gave me blow away. I think of Isa and how she sat there, broken, the wooden box that had held the pendant with her father's ashes in her hands. Ahead of me, I see a sign with Lisboa – 5 km. I can leave Isa's drama behind me and just drive somewhere else. I already have enough baggage without having to add Isa's. Softly I clack my tongue.

What shall I do, what shall I do?

Before I switch on my turn signal, I shake my head, as if I already realize I'm making the wrong decision. But I can't help myself. Without giving it a second thought, I take the exit and after a short phone call, I park my Volvo at the same campsite as Isa and Frey.

Chapter 17

"I'm glad you're here," says Isa.

It's dusk, and we're sitting on folding chairs in front of her van. Isa had suggested we share a camping spot and given my meager cash supply I accepted her offer. I just finished five games of Memory with Frey and Isa put her to bed.

"You must have doubted whether you wanted to be around me anymore," she adds when I don't answer right away. Her hands are shaking a little.

"For a moment," I admit. "But you went through something intense today, and I thought you could use some company." That's only half the truth.

"Thank you, I'm still shaky," Isa replies; she appears to be very nervous and talks fast.

"Did they steal a lot from you?"

"Not really. My father's ashes are the worst. Other than that, all the jewelry that was in the box with the pendant, a little cash, and my medication, strangely enough."

"Medication?"

"Some painkillers mainly, but also other things I could quite use right now," she says as she gets back up and gets into the van. "Just going to check on Frey."

She apparently can't sit still.

I close my eyes for a moment and breathe deeply. It's a mild evening. At the campground, it smells of pine trees and barbecue smoke. We seem to be surrounded by families with children. I open my eyes again and see how the sky turns pinkish, the shadows grow larger, and I realize that there is another reason I turned up here: it makes me feel good not to be alone anymore. But this time, I decide, I'm respecting my boundaries. My inner goose barnacle is not welcome anymore.

"You're really at ease with children, aren't you?" says Isa, stepping out again.

"I'm a kindergarten teacher, so I'm used to dealing with little ones," I admit.

"Kindergarten teacher? Really? I hadn't seen that in you."

"No?" I reply. I wouldn't know who or what else I could have become. Taking care of toddlers is my second nature, my identity. Who am I if I can't be a teacher?

"No, I hadn't, but now I can see it. And it explains why you can go on vacation for so long. Glass?" She raises a bottle of red wine.

"No, thanks," I say, a fraction too late to sound authentic. I have to fight to push back the "Yes, please," but Isa doesn't notice.

"Sure? Are you going to let me drink on my own?"

"Go ahead, I've got my Coke," I say, pointing to my can.

She uncorks the bottle and pours herself a glass. The bottleneck clatters against it. Then she lowers herself back into her folding chair and looks at me inquiringly. "Are you not drinking now, or do you never drink?"

I hesitate for a moment and watch her take a sip. With a slight flick of her wrist, she makes the red liquid dance in the glass. "Not now and never again," I say. I used to think the wine would help me forget, which is nonsense because I remember all of it. Most of it. If only I *could* forget everything. Do a Ctrl-alt-delete of my memory. That would be nice.

She nods understandingly. "But you don't mind if I have a glass, do you? I really need it. It's been an intense day," she rattles on.

"You can say that again: a dead body, a break-in, a forest fire," I count on my fingers. Man, what I would give to put that glass to my lips for a moment, too. But I won't. "No, really, I don't mind, enjoy. So, what do you see me doing instead of being a kindergarten teacher?" I ask, to move away from the topic of alcohol.

"I don't know, I thought you were a therapist or social worker or something," she replies. "Or something creative, but of course, that's what you are as a kindergarten teacher."

I nod. "That's one thing I love about my job: I get to draw, paint, make music, sculpt. Anything I want, really, and there's no one to have an opinion about it. The children love everything anyway."

It's funny that Isa thought I was a therapist. When we graduated, Heleen suggested I should study Psychology. She said I had the "biggest listening ears" she knew, after which she fell on my bed screaming with laughter. My ears are a little bigger than average, yes. You won't see me with a short haircut or a ponytail. But I know that deep down she meant what she said. I am indeed a good listener, but unfortunately, that is not the only thing you need to become a psychologist.

"I considered Psychology for a while," I confess, "but my mother summed it up nicely: 'With your lack of talent for math, you'll never get through the first year," I imitate her affected voice.

Isa laughs. "You do have to study statistics, but nowadays, it's all done with special software."

I raise both my hands, as a sign of surrender. "Stop, I can feel my stress levels rising. Computers and I don't go well together, sorry. And I love my job, really, I do."

"I admire you. I wouldn't have the patience with a room full of toddlers."

"It's not so bad. The parents get in my hair much more than the children."

She chuckles. "I can only imagine." Her first glass of wine is empty; she seems a lot more relaxed now. Thoughtlessly, she pours another one.

"What do you do for a living?" I ask.

"Guess," she says.

I really have no idea. "IT consultant? Bank teller? Dog groomer? Blogger? Concert pianist?" I try.

She throws her head back laughing. There is no trace left of the paranoid Isa I saw before. "You're not even close!" she chuckles.

"Painter? Astronaut? Grape picker? Burlesque dancer?" I try again, encouraged by her laughter.

"Wait, I'll give you a hint," she chuckles. She opens her mouth in a big grin and then stares at me. I suddenly think she looks a little creepy, her lips stained blue by the wine and her eyes glittering almost unnaturally. I'm reminded of Pennywise from *It*.

"Clown?" I try.

"No!" she giggles. She points to her teeth.

"Dentist?"

"Almost!"

"Orthodontist?"

"No, no, I'll help you. I'm a dental assistant. Or, at least, I was," she says. She shakes a box of matches back and forth, takes one out, and lights the citronella candle that stands between us. The flame of the candle flickers wildly and casts strange shadows across our faces.

"Why did you quit?"

"Long story." Her hand goes to that spot on her neck again, where the pendant with her father's ashes should hang. Suddenly, her smile is gone, as is the sparkle in her eyes. She sinks back into her chair and empties her glass in one gulp. There she is again, dark Isa.

"I'm a good listener," I say.

She sighs, looks at me furtively, refills her glass, and takes a sip. "I quit because of my ex, Remco. I met him during a city trip to Antwerp," she begins. Her s-sounds linger a bit. She has drunk more than she can handle, with her small stature.

"My wallet was stolen, and he was the officer on duty when I went to report it." Even in the dim light of the candle, I can see her cheeks turn red at the memory. "It was love at first sight, no matter how strange I think that sounds now. I mean, you can't tell by looking at someone's face that they're disturbed, can you? I didn't see it, anyway. Remco gave me everything I wanted. Flowers. Romantic nights out. Jewelry. All my girlfriends were so jealous."

I am immediately reminded of William. He, too, had wooed me that way, but I hadn't had any girlfriends to share it with. Only my mother. Fortunately, at nightfall the coolness sets in; otherwise I would be sweating now. The urge to pull the glass out of Isa's hands and drink it myself is almost uncontrollable. I don't want to think about William right now, so I focus on her again as best I can.

"He was a self-made man," she continues. "His childhood had not been as wonderful as mine. Raised by a single mother as the eldest of a large family. He dragged himself out of the gutter, took the police exam, and was promoted to superintendent. Later, he founded his own security company. I admired his resilience, his intelligence, his perseverance."

"That doesn't sound like someone who is disturbed."

"No, he was great. I was head over heels in love. So much so that I moved to Belgium for him, much to my parents' sorrow. We got married and went to live in a beautiful villa in the suburbs, with a long driveway made of cobblestones. Everything I had ever dreamed of became a reality. Until I got pregnant."

Again, she takes a sip, her hands no longer trembling. "I took Dutch lessons, so I could work in Belgium, but he asked me to stop those. At first, I thought that was strange, but he swore to me that it was only for a while until our child would go to school, he said. And I believed him. In retrospect, things went wrong from that moment on, but I didn't realize it at the time. It all happened very gradually, you know?"

I nod affirmatively, having a small inkling of where this is going.

"I didn't have any friends in Belgium, I hadn't lived there long enough for that. No social life. After Frey was born, I stayed home alone more and more. I became increasingly isolated."

"And your parents?"

"They came to visit, of course, but they lived in France so they could never stay very long. The only person I chatted and practiced my Dutch with was Monika, our housekeeper. She came once a week. Can you imagine that was the highlight of my week?" She casts a desperate glance in my direction. "I wasn't doing much other than looking after the baby and running the household. One day, one of my fellow students called me. They were going out for drinks, and she asked if I wanted to come along. I wanted so badly to go out again, and laugh, talk, like I used to." Her hands pick at her hair, and her mouth twitches. "But Remco didn't want me to go. At first, I thought I could persuade him, that maybe he didn't mean it. I was so naïve. That was the first time things got out of hand. He locked me in our house, took away my keys, and left me with no money, and no debit card. Nothing."

"You are kidding!"

"No, I'm not. Before I knew it, I was a prisoner in my own home. Literally. There were cameras everywhere in the house, under the guise of my safety. In the next phase, he even threatened to take Frey away from me if I tried to leave him, so to the outside world, I made it seem that everything was okay. That's how scared I was." A tear rolls down her cheek.

"Oh, Isa, what a hell that must have been... how did you get away from him?"

"My father... I couldn't fool him; he knew me too well for that. As soon as he got wind of what was going on, he helped me get away from Remco, much to his anger." Again, her hand grabs at her empty neck.

I feel my throat squeeze shut. Poor woman.

"Isa... we can still report the burglary to the police. You really shouldn't leave it at that, you know. I mean, that pendant meant so much to you. Why not report the theft? That way, you'll at least have a chance of finding it."

Isa groans. "Oh, Michelle, I know that, but I can't get the police involved. Never."

"But why?"

She empties the last of the bottle in her glass. Then she stares into nothingness for a minute.

"Because Remco is chasing us."

Chapter 18

I don't get it. If her ex is stalking her, shouldn't she call the police? Isa sits defeated in her folding chair; her eyes are not focusing very well when she tries to look at me.

"I think you've had too much to drink," I say. "I don't understand anything you're saying. Why is your ex coming after you? Why can't you call the police?"

She slaps her hands in front of her eyes and groans. "Oh, Michelle, I can't get you involved in this. Forget I said anything."

Is she serious? I feel an urge to grab and shake her, whether or not she's a wreck. "Isa, you'd better tell me what's going on, or I'll go to the police myself," I say. "Should I be worried about that Remco, yes, or no?"

"Of course, you shouldn't," she says in a loud whisper. "And please be quiet, Frey might hear us." She lowers her hands — her gypsy eyes have turned red—and looks at me questioningly. Is she debating what she can tell me? Do I want to know? She seems to look deep into my soul as if she knows who I really am. Or rather: *what* I am.

Isa sighs theatrically. "Oh well, what the hell. I am exhausted. I'm so tired of doing everything on my own. And I have a feeling you will not judge like most people would."

"I'm listening."

She begins to talk: "I was a wreck after the divorce. And then Dad died, and it got worse. I tried to give Frey a normal childhood, so she wouldn't miss her father when she was with me." Her words occasionally slur because of the booze. "She only went to see him every other weekend. But Remco hadn't come to terms with the fact that I had left him, that he could see Frey so little and…" She swallows audibly.

"And then? What did he do?" I ask in a small voice.

"He started stalking me, harassing me. Strange things started happening in my apartment, things that were suddenly in a different place. I was sure Remco was behind it, even though I had no proof. There was nothing the police could do. I changed the locks but to no avail. I was living in total fear. For Frey, for myself." She looks at my face in desperation, searching for understanding. "One day I came home from work, after picking up Frey from school. We walked into the apartment and I knew immediately that he had been there again. The pictures I was in were all lying face down. Only Frey's were still standing up. My underwear had been worked on with scissors. My piano had been scratched. A bracelet he had given me as a gift had disappeared from my jewelry box, along with my wedding ring. His scent still hung in my bedroom; the mattress was even warm. And yet, the police supposedly couldn't prove it was him." She rubs her eyes. "They didn't even believe me! Thought I had staged the whole thing. Their pal Remco would never do such a thing, they were covering for him. He was still one of them."

"But you did report it?"

"Yes, I did. And I hired a private investigator. Luckily. Then the complaints came in about Frey. In kindergarten, they questioned some of the bruises she had."

"Oh no, did he do something to her?" My throat squeezes at the thought.

"I don't know, Frey never said anything, but I had an awful feeling about it, so I reported it again. One day, a woman from Child Services came to the door. Of course, I thought she was coming to discuss Remco, about what I thought he did to Frey. But it wasn't like that, on the contrary. She framed me and claimed that I was responsible for Frey's bruises. She said I was a confused woman. That I hadn't processed the divorce and my father's death properly. That I suffered from delusions. That I unjustly accused my ex. Unjustly! That woman was there with a mission: to take away my custody of Frey at the behest of Remco. He had orchestrated the whole thing. It was his way of showing how big his influence was. I knew I was going to lose her, Michelle." The tears stream down Isa's cheeks again, and I feel her helplessness. "Remco was going to take Frey away from me. Forever. I would barely be able to see her. I couldn't let that happen. I couldn't let that monster do that to her."

"Oh, Isa, how awful! Couldn't that private detective help you, then?"

"Yes. It took months, but eventually, the judge ruled in my favor. Thanks to the detective's evidence we were able to get around Remco's "friends". He lost custody and I got a restraining order against him."

I'm baffled by this plot twist. "I don't get it, then it's all right, isn't it?"

"No, Michelle, nothing's all right. Remco had no reason to abide by that restraining order. In the police force he had friends everywhere, and thanks to his security company he had incriminating material on numerous magistrates. It was only a matter of time before he would come after Frey."

"But that's illegal!"

"It is, but what could I do? I feared for my life and Frey's. It was my mother's idea to run away. I didn't want to at first, I knew I'd probably never see my mom again if I did, but she forced me to do it, for Frey. I left that very night; I didn't have a second to lose…"

She blows her nose, stares into the distance, and shakes her head as if answering an inaudible question. "My mother notified my brother Jacco and told me to go there, in Bordeaux. So, I drove all night, with Frey in the back seat. I haven't seen *Maman* since. I miss her terribly." She wipes away her tears with her sleeve.

"Jacco owns a farm and lives off what he grows there. Frey loved it, but I was too afraid to stay in one place for too long. People in the village might ask questions, so together with Jacco I refurbished this camper van. It is registered in his name. After that, our journey began."

"That must have been a tough decision," I say, but I know what it's like to have no other option than to run away.

Isa nods. "Yes, it was. And the worst part is: my mission failed. I may not have seen or heard from my ex since we left, but every so often I just feel he's there, you know?" She gets up. "I don't know, I must be paranoid, but there have been a few occasions when I was at the beach with Frey that I was sure he was watching us. I felt his eyes following us. And then the break-in, my pendant gone..." She points to her empty neck, "while... he can't know where I am, can he?"

"Do you think *he* broke in here?" Why?" I ask.

"Because my pendant is gone. He's the only one who knows how important it is to me."

I'm confused. "But wouldn't he have taken Frey, if he knew where you were?" I whisper.

Isa shakes her head. "You don't know Remco. He's enjoying this. He knows he can do whatever he wants. But if he takes Frey from me now, the game is over. That's why he's not doing anything yet: he wants to continue playing first."

"That sounds like a true psychopath," I say, a shiver creeping down my spine.

"Indeed. He's terrifying. That's why I stay here on the coast where there are plenty of people. At first, I didn't. I was avoiding major roads, and we slept in Spanish villages that were so deserted they seemed haunted, but when summer came, the temperature rose to the point where it was unbearable. It was also harder to get food and water. I became afraid. Imagine if he found us there, all alone, we were sitting ducks. And Frey wanted to see the sea so badly that I decided to take the risk. But maybe I shouldn't have. Especially not now with that corpse on the beach. It is going to attract the attention of the media. And of the police."

I'm not quite sure what to make of it. One side of me is shocked by the story and wants to get away as quickly as possible. Surely, the police can protect her? This Remco's influence won't reach that far, will it? On the other hand, I realize that Isa must be desperate to do something so drastic. To leave everything behind, her sick mom, so she doesn't lose her daughter. You wouldn't do that when you have other options.

"If you want to leave, I understand," she says. Her bottom lip trembles.

I shake my head. "I don't know, Isa. I really don't know. I'm going to sleep; you should do the same."

Chapter 19

I haven't slept a wink. I tossed and turned all night. The story about Remco gives me the creeps so badly that I almost wish Isa hadn't told me. Although now I do understand her strange behavior. For hours on end I, weighed the pros and cons: should I stay, or should I go? When I leave, I leave this bizarre situation behind me and I can look ahead again. Even if that means being on my own and without a penny in my pocket. If I stay, I save money and at the same time can keep an eye on Frey. That last argument turns out to be the deciding factor.

"As we're in Lisbon now, shall we visit the city?" I suggest over breakfast, which we eat together as if it's always been that way.

Isa's eyebrows shoot up. "I doubt that's a good idea."

"Why not? In a big city, you don't stand out as much as on the coast, don't you think?" We talked about it yesterday: if Remco knew where Isa was at all, he must have lost track of her after the forest fire. But it did not reassure Isa, understandably so.

"Okay, but... you don't have any money, do you?" she tries again.

"Not much," I admit, "but apart from a bus ticket, it doesn't have to cost much, mind you. Looking around is free."

"Yes, but there are so many people there!" she exclaims.

"Indeed, that makes it even easier to just blend in with the crowd," I argue, chuckling. I have already decided that I will go myself anyway, even if she's not up for it.

After washing up, I take a nice hot shower in the sanitary block. I do a mini clothes wash and hang my things to dry. When I hang up the last pair of panties, I look around. That's weird. It looks like I'm missing a pair. Have I lost it on the way back? I retrace my steps for a moment to the washing area, but there is nothing there. Then I turn my tent inside out to see if the panties might have ended up under my sleeping mat, but I only startle a few ants.

It may sound silly, but I travel so lightly that I know exactly what I do and don't have. My blue pair of panties with daisies on them is gone.

I dive into my car one last time and turn it upside down, but I can't find them anywhere. A nasty feeling creeps up on me when I think that maybe the creeps who broke in took them. Is that possible? I clench my jaw at the thought. The very idea makes me nauseous. No. Nonsense. Impossible. Who the hell steals dirty underwear? Those panties must have fallen out of my bag. I shake off the jitters and turn my attention to my traveling companions.

Frey is coloring and Isa is reorganizing the contents of her closets. After the break-in and our flight away from the fire, we had haphazardly stored everything. Her posture seems a little less tense, but maybe that's wishful thinking.

"I think I'll go into town alone for a while then, if you don't mind," I say. Even though I no longer have to answer to anyone for what I do and don't do, it's still ingrained in me.

"Oh, really?" She seems disappointed. "So, what are you planning to do there?"

I shrug. "I don't know. I haven't done any research. But since I'm here, in Lisbon, I at least want to soak up the atmosphere."

She nods and bites her lip. Her eyes flash from Frey to me and back to Frey. "You know, maybe you're right," she says. "I mean, what could happen? Remco can't know I'm here, right?"

I shrug again. I don't know the man. No idea what he's capable of, but I'm sure Isa would have recognized him if he had been at that campsite, too.

Isa must think the same because she gets out of the van. "Okay, let's do it. It'll do us good."

"You're sure?"

"Yes. Come on, before I change my mind. Frey, we're going on an trip, honey! Go find your shoes," she says, hiding her hair under a cap and putting on big sunglasses.

***

It's so nice not to be on the road alone anymore, to get on the bus together to drive to an unfamiliar big city.

On the bus, I notice posters of the Océanario: the biggest indoor aquarium in Europe, according to the speech bubble that comes out of the mascot's mouth. We decide to visit it. Isa is so kind to buy my ticket, and Frey falls completely in love with a gigantic octopus. I keep staring fascinated at the sharks for minutes, wondering if a big blue shark may be responsible for the dismembered body on the beach. I try to ask a caretaker for an explanation in several languages, but I keep running into the language barrier, so I give up.

The Océanario is a magical world, away from everything. The dark corridors, the colorful aquariums, the different shades of blue, the sounds reminiscent of a tropical rainforest. It all contributes to what both Isa and I needed so badly: to escape reality for a while.

The only slightly unsettling moment is when Isa stands mesmerized watching the amphibians being fed. Her mouth is grim, her jaw set tight, while her gaze remains fixed on something in the dark.

"What is it?" I ask worriedly. But she doesn't answer; in fact, it seems she hasn't heard me at all.

I follow her gaze and see that the reptile is consuming some large insect with relish.

"Ugh, what's it eating?" I ask. Isa almost sticks to the glass, so absorbed is she in the scene. Frey gets impatient and starts pulling her hand. That seems to bring her out of her trance.

"Huh? What?"

"What's that creature eating?" I ask again.

"A dragonfly," she replies.

"And you find that interesting because…"

"I don't like dragonflies." She shrugs. "Shall we go for lunch?"

As if we hadn't just witnessed a scene that would turn the stomach of any normal person.

In the afternoon, we take the bus to Belém, a well-known district of Lisbon, next to the Tagus River. Along with many other tourists, we stand in line for almost an hour to buy the world-famous *Pasteis de Belém*, a delicious custard pastry that you can only find in one place. The weather is beautiful, so we walk to the *Jardim Botanico Tropical* which is near the bakery, and eat our pasteis there. We sit on a bench under a tree that looks like it has been there for centuries. With branches that reach to the ground and are so thick they look like pillars or bars of an exceptionally large cage for a giant monster. Frey intently studies the booklet she got in the souvenir shop of the Océanario.

Isa sighs blissfully as she stretches her tanned legs forward. She's wearing turquoise slippers, with a gold tassel.

"I wish I had legs as tanned as yours," I say.

"Huh, what?"

"Your legs, they're so beautifully tanned," I say with a glowing face. I don't know why I blurted that out.

"My legs? My stumps, you must mean. Tsss, if anyone should be jealous, it's me!"

"How so?" Now it's my turn to look baffled. "You don't want to trade with my white stilts, do you?" I ask incredulously.

"Sure, and right away. I would kill for such beautiful long legs," she grins.

I laugh shyly. Is she kidding? *Matchstick, matchstick,* echoes through my head. If there's one thing, I hate more than my flaming red hair, it's my skinny legs. Not feminine at all, just long and strident.

"I, um, can't say I share your opinion," I reply sheepishly. "But you know, the grass will always be greener on the other side."

"It actually is," she replies.

"What do you mean?"

"It's true the grass is always greener on your neighbor's property than on your own. From your perspective, that is."

I stare at her and she laughs. "I'm not joking, mind you. A study has proven that if you look over your garden hedge at your neighbor's grass, it looks greener than your grass. It's because of the angle and the light and so on. Matter of perception, then."

"You're serious," I laugh.

"I'm serious. Everyone must deal with their share of shit, but when we compare our shit to someone else's, it seems the other person has golden shit, which of course they don't. Everyone has a cross to bear, you know."

I nod. Like me, Isa has accumulated a nice mountain of 'shit'. One that is quite a bit higher than mine.

"My plan was to clean up some of my shit and return home a little lighter and cleaner," I say.

She nods. "That's a nice plan." She looks at a couple walking by, hand in hand. "Is there someone waiting for you at home, Michelle?"

"What do you mean?" I ask, although her question was obvious.

"A husband, friend, roommate?"

"No, not really."

"Do you live alone?"

I sigh. "Not quite, no. Let's just say I'm in between places. Can we talk about something else?" I don't feel like telling her about William or my mother.

"Oh, yeah, sure. Sorry."

The look in her eyes makes me feel guilty. "No, you don't have to apologize," I sigh. "It's a subject I don't like to talk about. Just like you'd never have told me the story about Remco if your van hadn't been broken into."

"And if I hadn't soldiered on with that bottle of wine," she grins. "I get it, though. You're not on the road alone for nothing, right?"

"Right."

"Do you know where you want to go?"

I shrug. "Nah, just somewhere. Anywhere. I'm on a road trip," I answer evasively.

"Yeah, okay, I got that," she says, laughing. "But on a road trip whereto?"

I think for a moment. "My final destination, you mean?"

She nods. "Yes, where are you going?"

I hadn't thought about that at all. "To tell you the truth, I don't have a clue. Nowhere, I guess."

"There must be a place you'd like to see before you go home again, right? Or a place where you can leave that "shit" of yours?"

"I don't know, not really. I've barely thought about it until now. As long as I'm on the road, I'm fine."

"Do you want to see other countries?"

"I'd like to, but I don't have enough time for that. I have to work again in September." At least, I hope so.

Isa nods and eats her *pasteis* in thought. "I know a nice end goal for you."

"Which is?"

"The end of the world."

I laugh. "I don't want to drive that far!"

She laughs along. "No, no, not really the end, but that's what they call the place. It's in Sagres. It's the most southwestern point of Europe, the Cabo de São Vicente lighthouse. They call it The End of the World because people used to think that the world stopped there."

"That sounds cool," I say.

"Yeah, look it up," she says as she gets up and wipes the crumbs from her skirt. "Shall we go?"

Before we get back on the bus, we buy a newspaper. Together, we try to make sense of the article about the corpse on the beach, but it's still gobbledygook. I learned at the Océanario that shark is *tubarão* in Portuguese, but to my great relief, we don't find that word in the text. So, it is unlikely that a shark attacked the man.

The rocking of the bus is soothing. I feel my eyelids getting heavy. Frey has fallen asleep on her mother's lap; Isa is absently stroking her daughter's blond hair. That she trusts me, even with Frey, is obvious. But now that I know what she's on the run for, I see how wary she is, and how often she checks her cell phone. Moreover, she hasn't taken off her cap all day and those big sunglasses look like they're stuck to her nose. Still, I feel that knowing I'm monitoring her does her good.

I am not sure yet what to think of Isa, and of her decision to go on the run with Frey. It doesn't seem healthy for Frey to be trekking through Southern Europe with a mother who sees danger everywhere. What particularly concerns me is how much she drinks, even to my standards. Is she trying to keep her nerves under control? How stable is her state of mind really, I wonder?

It's these concerns that make me decide to travel with them for a few more days after all.

Chapter 20

This is the last day we will spend together; tomorrow Isa and Frey will once again drive inland, heading north. I will continue to Sagres in the south, as Isa proposed, to the most south-westerly point of Europe, at the Cabo de São Vicente lighthouse.

'The End of the World'. I can't imagine a more appropriate destination. It sounds like a pilgrimage destination, for my personal quest.

Last night we arrived in Sines, where we can spend the night for free in a parking lot next to the ocean. There are plenty of other campers here, most of them surfers. They look so relaxed; they don't seem to care about anything. I even start to recognize some of them, and they me. Once in a while, as I peer out at the ocean from the beach, sheltered by my sun hat, I think I see those two girls again, the ones who were arguing with Daniel, but it always turns out to be someone else.

I have a lot of time to read, and my Eat Pray Love book is beginning to grow on me now that the protagonist has left Italy and traveled to India. I can relate to the questions she asks herself: 'Who am I?' and 'Why am I here?'

Can I interpret this 'why' however I want to? Where will my path lead me? Who will walk next to me? What makes me happy? What gives me joy? I've been pondering these questions a lot, and one of the things I've decided is that I want to learn how to surf.

Watching the surfers day in and day out makes me itch to give it a try myself, and Isa has promised, by way of farewell, to give me a basic lesson. She claims she learned it as a child on the French coast, where she grew up, and is excellent at it.

"Maybe it will help you build confidence. You're stronger than you think, Michelle," she said at dinner yesterday. "And Sines is known to be an ideal place for beginners. It's now or never."

She knows by now why I travel alone in my car. She knows that my mother taught me to distrust people and that my ex has managed to embed that belief even deeper in me. That I keep making the same mistake of clinging to the people I trust, like a goose barnacle, which ultimately causes them to reject me and thus confirm my belief. Deep inside, I know that not everyone is like that. I am eager to learn to trust people, like Daniel, who helped me when I needed it. But it's hard. So hard.

"To trust others, you must first trust yourself," Isa told me. Although the irony of taking advice from someone on the run doesn't escape me, I rented a surfboard this morning, and I am looking at Isa jump up from the board into a squat.

"See? Like this, hop! And you stand up," she shouts as her petite body flips up like it's nothing. "Now you."

I've covered my milky-white limbs with a thick layer of sunblock, my hair is tied on top of my head, and I'm terribly aware of my big ears sticking out as I stand next to the board. I know Isa is right; this is probably the only chance I'm going to have on this trip to learn how to surf because I would never do this on my own. This is my Eat Pray Love moment, I think to myself. This is my chance to rewrite my story. Groaning, I lie down on my stomach.

"So, you paddle with your arms as you see the wave coming up behind you, and from the moment you feel it lift you, you paddle two more times with all your might and then put your hands down and push your elbows up and put your right knee down. Yes, like that," Isa says, as I follow her instructions." And then, hop, you pull your left leg in, put your foot down, turn… No! Turn! Like that, yes. And you stand! Good. One more time."

This goes on for twenty minutes until I can do the movements in smooth succession while safely on the beach and my body is covered in a layer of sweat and fine sand. "I think I'm ready now, Isa," I say as I dust myself off. "And I could use a dip."

"Okay, give it a try. The plus of this spot is that you don't have to go too far into the ocean, you pick a small wave and just let it carry you. Small steps." She raises her thumb. She would make a good teacher.

With the board under my arm and the strap around my ankle, I walk into the water. Isa and Frey remain standing in the surf.

"When I say 'go' you start paddling, okay?" Isa yells.

I nod and raise my free arm. With each step I take, further into the deep, I try to increase my confidence. I imagine the seawater giving me strength like Obelix falling into the druid's cauldron of magic potion.

I can do this.

There are countless people in the ocean. Young and old, fat and thin. It's not just athletes surfing, but whole families. Fathers, mothers, children. When I've gone deep enough, I lie on the board on my stomach and wait for Isa's signal. She stands with her hands above the flap of her cap, peering at me. Frey has her arms wrapped around her mother's leg. From this distance, they look so carefree. So normal. But, isn't that always the case with what you see from a distance?

Chapter 21

I can't believe I saw you. It was so hard not to run to you, take you in my arms, squeeze you all over, kiss you everywhere, like before. It just made the pain worse.

Why did you let me down, Belle? Why?

You knew I couldn't go on without you. You knew it! How could you do this to me? You torment me so... I thought I was feeling grief more than anything, but only now do I realize how angry I am with you.

It's all your fault, you know? Of course, you do. Since you're gone, my life has been spiraling downward into the abyss. I'm turning and swirling deeper and deeper. Like Alice in Wonderland.

If you were still with me, were mine, I would live in light and love. Not in the dark caverns of pain I feel every day. The pain that I try in every way possible to erase, to kill, to drink away.

This anger exhausts me. It makes no sense. I can't hate you. Never. My love for you is too great for that. But I don't want to let you out of my sight again this time. I will never let you go.

Never again.

Chapter 22

Floating in the water, my thoughts drift back to William. I didn't have feelings for him right away. The first time I saw him, I was only twenty-five. I had graduated but was still living with my mother. Since that time on the ski trip, I had not dared to leave her behind. The thought of finding her lifeless in bed again made my stomach turn. Now and then I felt the urge to spread my wings, but every time I even considered moving out, I was immediately overwhelmed with feelings of guilt. She didn't stop me, though. Not literally, at least.

"If you believe you'll be happier by leaving me, Michelle, then you should," she said. Or something else along those lines. But to be honest, the prospect of living alone was not so appealing that I wanted to take the risk.

Since my friend Heleen had left for the United States to study, I didn't have anyone to talk to. At school, my colleagues were good company during lunch, but most of them had families and the conversations were often about their partners and children. There was no one I clicked with or who I could meet with outside of school.

It wasn't all bad, by the way. There were good times. Once a week, I would get Chinese food, and Mom and I would watch Cops or The Voice together. Me sprawled out on the couch with a pillow stuffed under my head, and my mother in the recliner. Me with a glass of red wine, Vera with sherry.

Oh yes, I called her Vera. She had suggested that herself when I turned eighteen. How mature of her. I was content, or at least I thought so. My mother was well-off. Her parents had owned a well-known antiques business and had been avid art collectors. After they died, most of the art was sold. I barely

Barbara De Smedt

remember my grandparents; they both died before I turned six.

Our regular family doctor, Dr. Van Capellen, had been with us for so long that my mother addressed him as "Robert". At least once a month, she would drum the man up. For palpitations, hair loss, strange lumps, and overwrought nerves. Again and again, the small, balding doctor came to her rescue. Dressed in his uniform of brown pants and a plaid jacket with elbow patches in dark green velour, he stood at the door, his leather doctor's bag in hand.

When I was younger, I didn't quite understand why my mother didn't just go to the practice like everyone else. Only later did I notice the subtle flirting: the lip gloss that was suddenly on Vera's lips, the cloud of perfume that hung in her bedroom. The compliments she paid the timid doctor so that his cheeks turned as pink as the dressing gown that hung loosely around her body. At first, the realization made me crawl away in shame until I realized that Dr. Van Capellen was only too happy to play the role of savior.

But that day, when Vera called the practice, Dr. Van Capellen was not there. The good man had been hospitalized with a heart condition; the secretary told her. He would be absent indefinitely. Would Mrs. Deckers perhaps like to come to the practice to consult the replacement? Mrs. Deckers certainly did not want that, so the replacement came to her home, just like his predecessor. And that was the day I first came face to face with William.

***

Unlike Dr. Van Capellen, William was neither small nor balding. On the contrary. He was tall, even by my standards. His dark hair was neatly coiffed in a side parting and not a stubble could be seen on his cheeks. From behind his glasses, a bright pair of eyes looked at me kindly but distantly.

"Mrs. Deckers?"

Since my mother had failed to mention that Van Capellen would not be coming, I had been off my game for a moment, causing me to stare at him for a few seconds too long. He repeated his question with a smile.

"Mrs. Deckers? You needed a doctor? I'm William Vermeersch, the replacement for Doctor Van Capellen."

"Oh, yes… No, I'm not Mrs. Deckers. Or… yes, I am, but not the one who requires a doctor," I stammered. "Please come in."

My head had turned bright red by now, and he followed me with an amused look. I showed him the way to my mother's empire and left him there. In the bathroom, I splashed some cold water on my heated face and then looked at myself in the mirror.

My parents had never married, and because my father had fled the scene, I had my mother's last name. On our doorbell, it said V. Deckers, and below that M. Deckers. Two old spinsters.

Except for Doctor Van Capellen, no one ever came into our house. No one. And especially no man.

A young man.

It was as if our house reacted now that there was a stranger in it. As if it sniffed the unfamiliar odor and folded itself to the newcomer. The atmosphere changed completely, and I looked at myself through the eyes of someone who was seeing me for the first time: a tall, thin woman with a pale face, fiery red cheeks and straight copper hair that no product could add volume to.

I fixed my white blouse, ran a comb through my hair, and went to the kitchen to make a pot of tea. My heart was still beating much too fast. My body kept sending out strange signals.

Later, William would claim that what I felt then was love at first sight, but I think it was just my natural reaction to the first strange person who stepped into my world. I had once read that a hatching duckling is genetically programmed to consider the first creature it sees, to be its mother. Whether that be a duck, a dog, or a human. Or a newly graduated family physician named William. I wouldn't be surprised if I had that gene too, aside from the goose barnacle one.

When I heard Doctor William come back down the stairs, I waited for him in the hall.

"Can I have a word with you?" he asked gravely, which caused a range of possible scenarios to march through my head. Ranging from a terminally ill mother and the resulting flood of guilt that idea brought, to a marriage proposal.

"Of course, I made tea. Can I offer you a cup?"

"Yes, that would be nice," he replied. I walked ahead of him to the kitchen, where he put his doctor's bag — which was much cooler than Doctor Van Capellen's, more like a backpack — on the floor next to the kitchen table.

"I examined your mother," he continued, pouring the tea. "And I've also gone through her file."

A silence fell as I handed him the sugar and watched him drop two lumps into the amber liquid. His long fingers had nails that were neatly trimmed short. Unconsciously, I looked at my hands, which looked a lot less feminine than his.

"Your mother is in fine health; her cholesterol may be a little too high but other than that, I can find absolutely nothing." He had his hands wrapped around his cup.

I imagined we were a married couple and sat like that at breakfast every morning. It was not an unpleasant thought. "So, that's good news then?" I asked.

"Hm... She was, how should I put it, rather disappointed because I wouldn't prescribe her any medication."

"Oh, that's what it's about. The pills."

"Yes, well, I was wondering... I didn't find any prescriptions in her file, although she says she gets medication from Doctor Van Capellen for sensitive nerves." At that last word, he blinked his eyes for a moment. His eyelashes were thick and black.

"Well, that's true. She does indeed get pills from him."

"Do you happen to know which ones?"

I shook my head. "No, they are little yellow pills."

"Do you still have a wrapping, perhaps? So, I can see which ones they are? There were none left in your mother's room. She said they were out, and she desperately needed new ones."

"I can have a look for you if you like?"

"Yes, please."

I walked to the bathroom and rummaged through my mother's medicine cabinet, but found nothing. Damn. She took those things so often, surely there had to be a box somewhere? Doubtingly, I looked around. I didn't feel like going to her bedroom and turning it upside down. My eye fell on the trash can. With any luck, there was still an empty package in there. With the handle of an old toothbrush, I rooted through the trash and... bingo. The jar was of clear plastic with a handwritten label stuck to it.

As I walked back down the stairs, I wondered why Doctor Van Capellen was giving my mother medicine for which she didn't have a prescription. He was always so nice, he wouldn't be cheating or deceiving her, would he? Was he poisoning my mother and was that the reason she was sick so frequently?

Concerned, I handed the empty jar to the new family doctor and stood beside him, a little insecure. He studied the label with a frown, only to stand up as he held out his hand.

"Thank you, don't worry," he said, shaking my hesitantly extended hand. Then he turned and walked out of the kitchen.

I remained perplexed for a moment and then ran after him to open the front door. "Do you know what pills they are?"

"No." He shook his head. "But I do have an inkling. In any case, nothing to worry about, your mother is in good health."

I remained standing in the doorway. Even more puzzled than before. "What do you mean, in good health? So why was she taking pills?"

Because of the small steps that led to the front door, I was at eye level with him. Although I didn't ask my questions out loud, the question marks in my eyes didn't go unnoticed. I must have looked downright distraught.

He apologized. "I startled you. That was not my intention. Give me your phone number, and I'll call you as soon as I know more," he said kindly.

If I had had any experience with the ins and outs of the world, bells should have been ringing by then. Any normal doctor would have asked me to contact him myself. But I didn't know that.

Chapter 23

It was on a Friday night, after school. He called me and asked if I could come to the practice. He received me in Dr. Van Capellen's office, where the smell reminded me of the countless times I had been there as a child looking for relief from the unbearable cramps in my legs that later turned out to be growing pains.

Ill at ease, I sat down opposite him, acutely aware that my hands were still full of paint from the Christmas project I was working on with the preschoolers.

He followed my gaze and smiled. "You must be very creative."

"I'm a kindergarten teacher," I replied, my cheeks burning. "I just came from school."

"Ah, nice." He leaned back a little in his chair, his relaxed posture the opposite of mine.

Would he have children? I suddenly wondered. How old would he be? About thirty, maybe?

"I found out what was in those pills," he interrupted my internal ramblings. Since I didn't answer right away but continued to stare at him, he continued, "They were regular vitamins."

"Vitamins?"

"Yes, only that."

This I had not seen coming. "But why did Doctor Van Capellen give vitamins to my mother if she needed pills for nerves?"

He didn't answer and left me to think for a moment myself.

"Oh," I said, as the truth hit me. "She didn't need those pills at all, according to the doctor?"

He nodded. "I think Van Capellen wanted to help your mother by making her believe she was being medicated, a sort of placebo, so to speak. Was she ever hospitalized?"

"What do you mean? For an injury?"

"No, I mean whether she has ever been admitted to a psychiatric clinic before. Or is she in therapy?"

At first, I shook my head but then realized that she had been. "Yes, therapy, briefly. But that was a long time ago."

After the ski trip incident, Vera had to see a therapist. It was mandatory. But after two sessions, she refused to go back. She didn't need a therapist; she had said. She wasn't crazy. It's been so long, almost ten years, that I don't remember it all clearly.

"Does she require therapy, you think? Or to be admitted? I don't quite understand…" I felt my face burn again. What was this man trying to tell me? That my mother was crazy? Or that she would try to kill herself again?

"I don't want to rush to a diagnosis, but I would like to refer her to a psychologist," he replied, still in his relaxed attitude. He was irritating me.

"But why then? From what do you infer she needs one?" Although my mother had her idiosyncrasies, I felt I would benefit far more from therapy than Vera Deckers. Her only problem was poor health.

"Because apparently, she calls this practice several times a month for a home visit but is never sick. And she's been doing that for years."

I bit my lip. And every time, Dr. Van Capellen came and gave her yellow pills that did absolutely nothing. Slowly it dawned on me: my mother was not sick, never had been.

"But then why does she do it?" I said more to myself than to him. "Why was she pretending to be sick?"

"That's something a therapist should discuss with her; I have no idea. Why do people do what they do? Or why don't they do what they're supposed to do?" He shrugged and looked at me kindly, but I felt he was observing me at the same time. Was he wondering why I was still living at home at twenty-five? No, of course not. Why would he care, right?

***

He did care. The following week, he called me again, supposedly out of interest in my mother's health.

How was Vera doing? (Good.)

Had she made any moves to see a therapist? (No.)

And how was I doing? (Um.)

Another few days later, he asked me out to dinner. That same night, we kissed for the first time. Before I knew it, I was in a relationship. Not because I was so in love with him, but because it was so damn nice to have something all mine for once. I kept my secret hidden for as long as possible from my mother, who still demanded a visit from her family doctor. Since he knew his way around, William first walked to Vera's bedroom to give her the yellow pills, and then he snuck into my room.

Chapter 24

"Michelle! Now!"

With a jolt, I find myself back in the present, feeling a wave lift me. Like a woman possessed, I start paddling with my long arms, which are now splitting through the water. The wave lifts me, and I put my hands down, just like Isa taught me. Then I get up on one knee, pull my other leg up and turn my body, so I'm crouching on the board.

"Ohmygodohmygodohmygooood!" I exclaim, as I extend my arms horizontally beside me and am propelled forward along with the wave toward the beach. I'm surfing! I am doing this! Alone! My legs start trembling uncontrollably. On the beach I see Isa and Frey jumping up and down. My heart nearly explodes. Washed away is the memory of William, drowned is the image of my mother. I am surfing the waves of the Atlantic Ocean. The feeling of freedom is indescribable. When I'm approaching the beach and the board slows down, I dare to stand completely upright.

"Woohoo!" I shout, my arms spread in the air.

"Woohoo!" shouts Frey back.

"Woohoo!" shouts Isa, "Again?"

I drop into the sand laughing, allowing Frey to crawl all over me. "Give me a moment to recover," I say, still gasping for breath.

"That was superb though, for a first time. Next time, try to get up a bit earlier, I have a feeling you can do it."

"Beginner's luck," I say, but the compliment makes me smile even more. What a wonderful feeling this is.

After a short rest, I jump up and run back into the water. This time I start paddling too early at the first wave and am exhausted when it finally catches up with me. At the second,

I am too late and have to watch another surfer take it. By the third, I'm up. Fast and powerful. Completely balanced. The sun on my face. When I come to a stop in the surf, I can't wait to paddle back out into the deep. The experience of the surging wave beneath me, how the ocean and I work together to lift me, is just too beautiful. So, I let myself get carried away, again and again. Each time I stand up quicker. Each time I paddle further, where the waves get higher and I can't see the ocean floor anymore.

And then it goes wrong.

The swelling wave is a work of art that looks like glass, so clear. I paddle as if my life depended on it. I brace my hands, get my legs into a crouching position, and just as I'm about to stand up, I glance sideways at something I see flash by out of the corner of my eye: a surfer has caught the wave just in front of me and is coming quickly and deftly towards me. I know I have to get out of the way, Isa explained the rules to me, but when I see who the surfer is, I forget to react. The surfer shouts something and then skims past me, causing me to lose my balance. At that moment, the wave breaks over me, and from then on, there is only swirling dark water. Above me, below me, in me, and on me. Water everywhere. I desperately gasp for breath and get a big gulp of brackish seawater in my mouth. In a panic, I flounder my arms and legs, looking for the surface, but I keep spinning around. After what seems like minutes, I finally manage to get my head above water. With a silent cry, I breathe oxygen, finally.

In a split second, I see the surfer again, bobbing on her board. She looks straight into my eyes, and then her gaze flashes briefly to something behind me, and before I realize what's happening another wave lands with a thump on top of me and I spin around once more. My surfboard has become detached from my ankle, and my body feels heavy, like a sponge. I have no strength left. Can't breathe. Thoughts of my mother flash by, of William and Marie, of Heleen. Of the surf girl. I spin around my axis, my mowing arms feel limp, they don't seem to belong to me anymore. My chest explodes. I have to gasp for oxygen. Where is above? I don't know, I can't wait any longer, so I open my mouth and let the salty water flow in. The last thought I have is: You see, Michelle, it's dangerous out there.

Then a hand grabs my arm and pulls me to the surface. I see the sky, the clouds. I want to take a deep breath, but I can't. My lungs seem to shut down. I am pulled along by someone, using a surfboard as a life preserver. The ocean pushes us to the beach. I lie on my back in the warm sand. A shadow falls over me, soft lips on my mouth. My nose is held shut, and the strange mouth blows air into my lungs. An icy wave wells up from my insides. I cough out the seawater, gratefully sucking in the oxygenated air, my hands clawing at the sand searching for a hold. When I open my eyes, I look straight into those of the surf girl. Brown, with green specks.

"Are you okay?" she asks. Her voice sounds hoarse like she's been in a bar all night.

I nod, my throat aching and feeling swollen, my chest still rising and falling. Slowly, I get up, supporting myself on my elbows. The girl helps me up. Her nails are chipped to the skin. In her dark hair are some fine braids. Running feet approach over the sand, I see Isa with Frey in her arms.

"Michelle! Michelle!" shouts Frey.

I raise my hand, so they know everything is okay. Because it is, thanks to the strange girl.

"Your name is Michelle?" The girl smiles. She has a small gap between her front teeth. Then, she sings: "*Sont des mots qui vont très bien ensemble*". Her French pronunciation is perfect. "It's a French name. Did you know that?" she asks.

I nod shyly. "Yes, my mother loves everything French, but my name is written the English way," I rasp.

"Nice to meet you. I'm Aline, *enchantée*," she says, followed by a deep bow.

I feel my cheeks getting hot, but am saved just in time by Isa plopping down on the sand next to me and grabbing my shoulders. "Jesus, Michelle, you scared me. Suddenly, you disappeared underwater, and your surfboard washed up without you! Are you okay?"

"Yes, I'm fine. I swallowed a bathtub of seawater but otherwise, I'm okay. Thanks to Aline here."

"Thanks to?" replies Isa, a frown on her face.

"Yes, she pulled me out of the water. Didn't you see that?"

"Hm. Yeah, I guess."

"Didn't you?"

"I didn't see it properly, so I will not comment on it," she says stiffly. Her eyes avoid those of Aline, who doesn't understand a thing we're saying in Dutch, shrugs her shoulders, and takes her surfboard back under her arm.

"Bye, Michelle," she says. "Are you staying here in the parking lot tonight?"

I nod. My last night together with Isa and Frey.

"Okay, we're having a campfire, here on the beach. You're welcome, just bring your own drinks," she says, before walking to her blonde friend, who's watching from a distance.

When she's gone, I knock the sand off my body. My hair is completely covered in it.

"There's a cold shower in the parking lot, you'd best rinse off there," says Isa, who also gets up.

"What was that about?" I ask.

"What do you mean?"

"Why didn't you look at Aline? You're avoiding her like she has a dirty disease."

"Am I?"

"What's wrong, Isa? Why are you acting so weird? She might have saved my life. Just a little longer and I would have drowned."

"Hm. What happened? Why did you go under?"

I don't want to tell her that the sight of Aline fixing me with her speckled eyes upset me so much that I forgot I had to paddle. "Misjudged the timing, I guess."

"It went well, didn't it, before?"

"Yeah. But really, why did you react like that? Don't you trust her? You can tell me."

She sighs. "I don't know. I've run into her and her friend before and... I just have a weird feeling about that kid. She reacted very late, by the way, from where I was standing. She could have helped you much earlier."

"Jesus, Isa, you do see ghosts everywhere!" I say, still hoarse.

If I didn't know better, I would suspect Isa to be jealous. I drop the subject, and together we walk to the showers, Frey holding my hand tightly. The girl must be shaken, I realize, and I give her an encouraging squeeze.

While Isa and Frey return the rented surfboard, I let the ice-cold water of the beach shower flow over my body. Sand mixed with salt sticks in my hair, and I feel my cheeks burning. By now it is noon and the sun is shining brightly. I urgently need to get into the shade, but want to bask in this feeling a little longer.

Because I am alive.

What does it matter that I will soon be burnt red? Who cares if I can never get the knots out of my hair again? I'd never admit it to Isa, but it's true that only half an hour ago I was convinced that my last hour had struck. And that the last thought that went through my head was a sneer from my mother. Imagine if I had drowned, then the first time in my life where I had felt happy, surfing on the waves, would also have been my last.

I push one more time on the shower button and let the water flow. I open my eyes and look at the clear blue sky. A dragonfly buzzes by. Everything is so clear and pure, even my thoughts. From now on, I will only listen to my own voice.

Chapter 25

Oh, Belle, today I felt so close to you.

Do you remember, when we were just getting to know each other, we took a bath together, and I washed your hair? You used to enjoy it so much, with your eyes closed, your muscles completely relaxed. You were like butter in my hands.

When I lie on my back in the dunes, the dune grass tickling my arms and legs, the sand warming my back, I close my eyes and try to imagine that it is your hair that I smell. I have to restrain myself not to jump up and call out your name loud and clear.

Because I can't do that. I can't show who I am. Who I really am. Even though I feel it's getting harder to stay under the radar.

There is a competitor on the horizon, Belle. She has the power to ruin everything. That cannot happen.

But don't worry, I have everything under control. Soon, all will be well again.

Chapter 26

I have parked my car at an angle with Isa's van to create a cozy spot out of the wind where we set up the table.

The days are getting shorter, we enjoy the setting sun together, a spectacle I can never get enough of. As long as the sun sets in the evening and rises again in the morning, everything will be fine, I tell myself.

The van's windows spread their soft light. A citronella candle makes its flame dance in the hope of discouraging the mosquitoes, though that hope will again prove to be vain this evening.

I can't pitch my tent on the concrete of a parking lot, so I will sleep in my car. Although Isa has invited me to put my sleeping mat on the floor of her van, which I refused. In my mind, I have already said goodbye and I know myself: staying overnight is only going to make it harder. I want to leave tomorrow morning before Isa and Frey are up.

Since it's my last night, we cooked dinner together. Frey's lips and chin are smudged with spaghetti sauce. I make a pot of tea, while the girl pulls the game box out from under the camper bed. I hope Isa switches to tea too, she has already emptied half a bottle of red wine by herself.

"Quartet or Memory? Michelle gets to choose!" shouts Frey.

"Memory sounds great," I laugh.

Despite Isa's story about her ex, I hope we'll see each other again someday. According to Isa, the chances of her going back to Belgium are slim, but I don't know. Now that I have spent a few days with them, I have experienced no threat. It has even crossed my mind that Isa may have made up the story, or at least exaggerated it. Although it is unclear to me why she would do that. Maybe to make herself more interesting? People have done stranger things. Look at my mother.

Isa has tried to persuade me to stay longer and travel together, but although the idea is enticing, I have rejected it. It's time to move on. Being on my own was the entire point of my trip. I quickly shake off thoughts about what comes next — going home, confronting William, and facing my colleagues. I'll worry about that later.

We hear people laughing. It's coming from the beach below us. In the distance, I see fire flickering. If I'm honest, I'd like to go to the campfire. Be among the surfers. After all, I'm one of them now. But I'm going to wait for Frey to go to bed, so I can say goodbye.

Isa reads my mind. "Are you still planning to go to that campfire?"

"I am, actually," I reply as I pour the tea into mugs. "But not yet. It's only just getting dark."

"Hm, just be careful, okay? You don't know these people."

"Isa, you sound like my mother. Do you believe I can't take care of myself? I've been doing it for almost three weeks now, you know," I reply in irritation.

"Of course not. I'm just saying you should be careful. People aren't always what they seem."

I remain silent and sip my tea. I can't argue with her. If Isa's story is true, of course, she's right; what she has been through would make you suspicious of anyone and anything. But what are the chances this hippie group of surfers and backpackers would include another lunatic like her ex? And besides, I wouldn't be alone. Aline and her blonde friend will be there too.

We continue playing for a while, letting Frey win often enough so that she's happy. Then I put on my woolen cardigan.

"Do I get a goodbye hug from you before you go to bed, Frey?" I ask. I don't think she realizes that this may be the last time we will see each other.

She comes over to me, snakes her arms around my neck like a little monkey, and presses her warm body against me. I do realize it, of course, and feel my eyes getting moist. I hate saying goodbye and have become increasingly attached to Frey over the last few days.

"You know what?" Isa says suddenly. "Frey and I will walk you to the campfire. If, for some reason, you decide it doesn't feel right after all, you just come back here with us, okay?"

I roll my eyes but am secretly glad that the goodbye is postponed. "You are overprotective." I smile through my tears. "Why don't you bring something to drink and cozy up by the fire with me? I think I hear guitar music."

"Guitar!" shouts Frey. "Then we can sing songs!"

Now it's Isa's turn to roll her eyes, her curly hair hangs loose and for a moment she runs her hands through it, her gaze fixed on the dark beach. After a few seconds, she gives in. "All right then, we can stay a little while. But not too long because you have to go to bed, Frey." She puts her cap on her head as always and tucks her hair under it.

***

The beach and parking lot at Sines are barely lit, so it's pitch black. I look at the mass of stars in the sky. "Look, Frey, the Great Bear! And that's the North Star," I say pointing to it. A bat flutters past right in front of us and Frey lets out a squeal.

The smell of smoke meets us, along with the clear voice of a woman singing accompanied by guitar.

"How idyllic," I say, with just a hint of sarcasm directed at Isa who hums back something unintelligible from under her cap. I already regret taking her with me. If she didn't want to come along, she should have stayed in her van. I honestly don't understand why she's even here, dragging Frey along when she doesn't want to. Is she truly doing it out of concern for me? But I'm not the one on the run, am I?

I don't know whether to be flattered or irritated. Or scared.

About twenty people are sitting around the big fire. They don't notice us right away because they are looking at the singing woman. I have a few seconds to observe them and immediately spot Aline. Her face is glowing in the orange flames, her eyes are shining feverishly. Her blonde friend sits next to her and is the only one who is not looking at the singer but at the fire. She has a strange expression on her face. Empty. As if only her body sits in the circle around the fire, but she is somewhere else. The sand feels cold on my feet and sends a shiver down my spine. Maybe we'd better go back after all? Isa is right. We don't know these people.

Too late.

"Hi, Michelle!" Aline has spotted us. "Come, we'll slide over, come and sit here!"

Uncomfortably, we squeeze in between Aline and an older man with a beard. I sit down next to Aline, Isa next to me with Frey on her lap, who looks around curiously.

"Have you recovered from your near-death experience yet?" asks Aline grinning.

I turn bright red, but in the glow of the campfire, I hope it doesn't show. "Yes, thanks," I stammer.

Aline's body presses against mine. What a strange effect this girl has on me. My entire body shudders under her touch.

She bends over me to Isa. "Hi," she says, to which Isa replies with a short nod. If Aline is at all offended by the cool response, she doesn't show it. "Your daughter?" she asks with her gaze fixed on Frey, who claps her hands along with the rest of the group when the song is over.

"Her daughter. I don't have any children," I reply, with the old familiar stab in my stomach. Only then do I realize that Aline implied with her question that Isa and I are together, and again I turn crimson. "We're not a couple, you know. I'm not… I'm married. To a man. We got to know each other on the road. Tomorrow I'm continuing on my own again." My cheeks get extra heated by the fire and I rub a few hairs out of my face.

"Okay," Aline replies, a bit uninterested. "This is Trixi," she says, pulling the blonde girl towards her with one arm. "We travel together too, don't we, dear?"

Trixi, shooting awake from her trance, produces a faint smile. Either she's dumbfounded, or stoned, which is quite possible because I've been sniffing a spicy scent in the air. Maybe it wasn't such a good idea to bring Frey here after all. I reach for the cans of Coke I brought and offer Aline and Trixi one.

"Coke? Don't you want a beer?" asks Aline.

"No, thanks," I say, pulling open the can.

"You?" Aline asks Isa.

Isa shakes her head. I sense that she feels much like leaving and raise my eyebrows questioningly, but she avoids my gaze.

"Cheers," I say to the girls, holding up my Coke.

"To life," Aline replies, tapping her beer against my can. Trixi seems to cringe at those words, but I don't have time to wonder why because at that moment all hell breaks loose.

Chapter 27

Hanging over me, Isa grabs Aline's wrist, causing the latter's beer bottle to fall into the sand.

"Where did you get that from? Where?" Isa screams, her face distorted with anger.

"Isa!" I shout back. "Let go of her! Are you out of your mind?" What's got into her all of a sudden? "Get a grip!"

But Isa is unstoppable. "That bracelet! Where did you get that bracelet?" she shrieks like a madman.

Aline has a leather bracelet on her wrist, nothing special, as far as I can see. Frey, who has crawled away from her mother, widens her eyes and starts crying.

"Isa, stop it! You're scaring Frey." This is anything but how I imagined our last night to be.

The group around the campfire has fallen silent and everyone is staring at us. Aline tries to pull her wrist loose. "Let go of me, bitch," she hisses. Her eyes look like smoldering coals. Her blonde friend Trixi looks shocked at Isa. No, not shocked. Terrified.

This is bad.

I sit like a buffer between the two and instinctively step back, pulling Frey towards me. I have to get the girl out of here. Has Isa lost her mind? What mother in her right mind acts like that? In front of her daughter! I hold the sobbing child tight.

Aline jumps up and tries to pull herself loose from Isa's grip, but she doesn't let go and pushes her down again, causing Aline to fall backward onto the sand.

"Tell me right now where you got that bracelet, or I'll slit your throat, you hear?"

At last, the rest of the group awakens from their apathy, and a few of them spring into action. "Hey, leave that girl alone!" someone shouts. Two boys run toward Isa and pull her away from Aline.

Fuming, she fights back. "Let go of me, goddamn it! Let go of me!"

Aline scrambles to her feet. For a single second, time stands still, and she stares at me, then she grabs Trixi by the wrist and yanks at her arm until she gets up. Before I realize what has happened, the two girls are gone.

"Let go of me!" Isa shouts again, but the two boys are pinning her against the ground, where she remains floundering. "I'll find you! Just you wait, you won't get away with this!" she screams at no one, for the girls are no longer visible in the dark night.

With a pounding heart, I press Frey's face against me. I grit my teeth in anger. The child will never forget this. I wish I could throw the memory of her mother's face, disfigured with rage, into the ocean to be swallowed by the waves. Softly I hum "Somewhere over the Rainbow," rocking Frey back and forth. I feel how her little body, which just a moment ago was tense like a feather, relaxes against mine.

A few meters away, Isa also calms down, her panting breathing slows, and her hands stop clawing at the sand. The young men let her sit upright between them. Her shoulders droop. I feel my anger dwindle when I see tears rolling down her cheeks.

"That was not cool, I think you better go," one of the guys tells her.

Isa doesn't answer. She shakes her head. Her cap has fallen off, her ponytail is loose, and her curls hang in front of her face. She turns to me and sees Frey in my arms. The look in her eyes tears me apart. She might as well have stuck a knife in my belly. Seeing the bracelet on Aline's wrist has caused her to freak out so badly, it must have something to do with her ex, I realize. How impossible that may seem.

I get up and lift Frey, who is breathing heavily, on my shoulders. "Come, Isa, this little one has to go to sleep." To my relief, she stands up willingly. "Sorry, enjoy your evening," I mutter to the group, then begin the trek to the parking lot atop the dune.

The weight of the child is like lead, but Isa doesn't ask if she should take her from me. I don't know where her mind is, but right now, her daughter is no longer the priority she was before.

After I put Frey in the enormous bed, I stay with her for a while, stroking her blonde hair. Isa doesn't say another word. She grabs a bottle of wine from the van and sits down on a folding chair outside. The urge to ask her what just happened gets stronger every silent minute, but maybe I don't want to know.

Indecisive, I remain on the bed. To be honest, I'm relieved that I can close this door behind me. That I don't have to breathe the suffocating air of Isa's fear and pain all the time. I have my own pain. On the other hand, I realize in frustration that I can't just leave at a time like this. With a sigh, I lower myself from the bed, tiptoeing out of the camper, facing the inevitable conversation with Isa.

But the chair is empty, an empty bottle of wine stands orphaned beside it.

"Isa?" I say in a half-whisper. An oppressive feeling settles in my chest. Where has she gone? Perplexed, I sit down on the chair. It still feels warm. She must have gone for a pee, I think hopefully. But when my mobile phone beeps from within my bag, I know immediately that something else is going on. I hastily dig it out. Its battery is almost empty. On the screen, I read: *I need to do something; I'll be right back.*

Angrily I throw the phone back in my bag. What now? What on earth is she up to? I want to scream, but of course, I can't, so I grind my teeth in frustration. If only I knew where the surfing girls' camper was, I could go and check it out. Because I don't doubt for a second that Isa has gone there. What I can't figure out is why. What is so important about that bracelet that she goes there in the pitch dark and leaves her traumatized daughter behind with — come on, let's be honest, I laugh hoarsely—a strange red-haired woman?

I have to know why she attacked Aline like that. Why was she upset about a cheap bracelet that every teenage girl has in her jewelry box? That she's supposedly on the run from her ex and doesn't let her daughter out of her sight at any other time of day makes her actions even stranger.

I start pacing back and forth between the van and my car. The parking lot is so dark I can't see anything, but I'm quite sure there isn't a single empty parking spot left. That means there are about fifty cars and vans parked here. I can't go knocking on all those doors and leave Frey alone, so there's no other option for me but to wait for Isa to return.

With a sigh, I get back into the van and drop my bag on the passenger seat. Frey is sleeping peacefully. I check the time on my mobile: almost eleven o'clock. My eyes drift to the many photos of Isa and Frey and I move a little closer to the wall to get a better look at them. The glow of the colored bulbs provides just enough light to see them, but not to study details. Still, I notice that in many of the photos, Isa has a leather bracelet on her wrist. Was Aline wearing that same bracelet? Impossible. There is no connection between the two. Besides, a bracelet like that isn't unique.

My anger turns into pity again. Poor Isa. She must be seeing ghosts. I stretch out my arms, I'm suddenly so exhausted, my body feels so heavy. Was it only this morning that I surfed the waves of the Atlantic for the first time in my life? It seems like an eternity ago. An eternity in which I almost drowned, no wonder I'm worn out.

With a suppressed groan, I lie down on the bed next to Frey, my slippers dropping from my feet with a thud. I pull a corner of the blanket over me, up to under my chin. As soon as Isa gets back, I'm out of here.

For good.

I yawn so wide it makes my jaw pop.

Chapter 28

I'm not a cold-blooded monster, you know that, right? Then why are dead bodies piling up around me?

After that first corpse – Matthew – a second one quickly followed.

Yes, Belle, indeed: my second corpse was the one you know all about. That was not my fault either.

The third one may have died because of me, but without me wanting it. That was an accident. A terrible accident that I'd rather not think about anymore.

But the fourth... that was my first real murder. And for good reason. Deserved. Although, again, no one will probably understand that but you.

I am not convinced that makes me a murderer. Like any other animal trying to survive in the wild, I will only kill when I have no choice. And that was the case this time. I just didn't expect it to be so easy.

I'm not the same person anymore, Belle.

Chapter 29

Sometimes your body knows that something terrible has happened before that information reaches your brain. The persistent buzzing in her head, the cramping muscles, the pounding heart: she registers it even before her consciousness returns. Cautiously she opens her eyes. Sharp pangs of pain shoot through her head, and flashes of light dance through her vision like fireflies on speed.

Where am I?

She lies on her stomach, the floor beneath her feeling cool. She doesn't recognize the smells that enter her nostrils. Again, her body reacts first: a sob escapes her throat involuntarily. Only then does she realize: *my daughter!*

She raises her head from the floor, trying to find support with her hands. She opens her eyes wide and her pupils dilate in an attempt to dispel the darkness. The pains become more intense, and she feels nauseous, but she must find out where her daughter is. Whether she's safe. Her heart thumps against the floor at lightning speed. Panic spreads through her body and takes her breath away.

Why isn't she here? She's always with me, I never let her out of my sight.

She can't use her hands to push herself up, something is wedged in her fist. Something that feels heavy and sticky. She tries to focus her gaze on it, but the image remains blurry. Confused, she looks around, scrambles to her feet, and leans her back against… what? A wall? Her eyes begin to get used to the dark. She sits on the floor of a cramped space. A container? She can hardly fit into the space, although she is not a tall person.

Why am I here?

She closes her eyes and tries to conjure up images, to remember something.

Dragonfly is the first word that comes to mind, followed by the image of a plastic cutlery drawer. A cutlery drawer? She opens her eyes again, and vaguely sees the outline of that same cutlery drawer right before her. And then, as if someone has called out "action," the film of what has happened starts playing on her retina. One by one the images come back: how she walked to the van in the dark and saw that the door was slightly open. How she first knocked on the door, but when nobody answered decided to go inside. How she then, on impulse, started to pull open all the cupboards and drawers, looking for what she needed. How, to her dismay, she found something else, carelessly discarded between the knives and forks, rubber bands, and old crown caps.

She reaches for her pants pocket with her free hand and immediately feels it there. Tears of relief roll down her cheeks. She has found it again. She found *him* again.

"Now I'll never let you go," she whispers.

Again, her attention shifts to the object in her other hand. She raises her arm slightly, trying to catch the light on it, but to no avail. Then she remembers that she has her handbag with her. She puts the heavy thing down and lets both her hands search the floor until she feels the familiar shape of her leather bag. The light on her cell phone springs on, and she aims the beam at the strange object. She screams.

Chapter 30

Dazed, I open my eyes to slits. What time is it? I grope for my cell phone but can't find it right away. Where am I? Not in my tent, not in my car. I look through my eyelashes and see wooden slats on the ceiling. Right, I'm lying on the bed next to Frey, in Isa's van. The girl is still sound asleep on her back, with her arms wide, and her mouth open. As carefree as a sleeping child can be. It would be a beautiful scene if I didn't realize at that moment that Isa hadn't come home last night. She's not here.

So, what did I wake up from?

I hold my breath. I hear something, a scraping sound. It's coming from the van door. Silently I lower myself from the bed. I'm still fully dressed, fortunately. The shutters are closed, so I can't see what's happening outside. I hear it again, but now something is rattling too. Keys. Isa is back! But why is she taking so long to come in?

I shuffle to the door in the dark and open it as softly as I can, so as not to wake Frey.

"Isa?" I whisper, my hand still on the door, so I can quickly slide it closed again if necessary.

A groan in the dark is the only answer I get. My heart pounds faster.

"Isa? Where are you? I can't see a thing," I say, a little louder now. Where's that stupid phone of mine? Something rustles near my knees and slowly my eyes get used to the darkness. Isa is crouched in front of the van door.

"What the hell are you doing sitting there?" I'm getting irritated. Is she that drunk that she couldn't get the key in the lock? I crouch at her level, immediately flinching away again. "What's that smell?"

"Michelle, I…" She holds out a hand to me, which I grab in a reflex. I pull her upright.

"Are you drunk?" I whisper. I still can't see her clearly, but she's upright now, so I let go of her hand. A sticky goo remains on mine.

"No, I… Oh, Michelle, oh no, you have to help me!" To my dismay, she starts sobbing.

"What is it? Did something happen? Did you go after those girls?" I wish I could see what's going on with her, and what that sticky stuff is.

She leans her body against the van and grabs her head.

"Are you hurt?" I ask.

"Yes, the back of my head."

So that stuff is blood. "Shit, Isa, come in quickly. Let me take a look."

"No!" she says in a loud whisper. "Frey can't see me like this, and there's no time."

"What do you mean, no time?"

She cries again, softly. "I need your help, Michelle. For Frey." Her breathing sounds agitated.

"For Frey? What happened, Isa? Did you go to those girls' van?" I ask again.

"I did a stupid thing, Michelle, so stupid."

"How so? Tell me!"

"That bracelet on Aline's wrist? I was sure it was mine. You remember I told you about it, right? The one I'd gotten from Remco. The one he had stolen from my apartment? At least, I was sure of it. Now I'm not so sure."

"You went there for that bracelet? And you fought over it?"

"No, no. I only remember going to that van and seeing that the door was slightly open, but no one responded when I banged on it. I went in and pulled open some cabinets and drawers, looking for my bracelet." Her voice trembles and falters in her throat.

"And did you find it?" I ask impatiently.

She shakes her head, reaches into her pocket with her hand, and pulls out something shiny. "No, not the bracelet, but this." A faint smile plays around her lips as she shows me the silver pendant in her bloodied hand. Her father's ashes.

"So those girls are the ones who broke in here?" I whisper in dismay. The image of my underpants with the daisies shoots through my head and I swallow heavily.

"Yes, I knew I couldn't trust them, Michelle. I knew it. I am so glad to have Dad back with me. But right after that, everything went black, I must have gotten a blow to my head." She takes her hand to the back of her head and a grimace draws across her face. "The next thing I remember is waking up on the floor of that van, with my head pounding and…" She starts sobbing again, and I hold my breath, afraid of what else she's going to say.

"Oh, Isa," I say, but she holds up a hand and silences me.

"…and I had a bloody knife in my hands…"

I inhale sharply. "You didn't…"

She shakes her head. "I have no idea what happened. There was a lot of blood, the knife was covered in it too. In my panic, I dropped it, but now my fingerprints are on it. I only just realized that."

"My god, Isa! Did you stab those girls?" I say in horror.

"No! At least, I don't think so. I don't remember! I really don't! There wasn't a body anywhere. And why would I do that? It makes no sense, Michelle. There was nobody there when I got there. I am being set up. Someone put that knife in my hands, I have no other explanation."

"Who then?"

"I think Remco is behind this, I can't think of anyone else who would do something like this. With me out of the way, he has free access to Frey, then there's nothing to stop him. That's why you need to leave with Frey now. Immediately."

"I... what?" I exclaim.

"I will call my brother, Jacco. I'll give him your number; he'll call you to make further arrangements. It's the only way, Michelle. You know I can't trust the police. There's no time to lose. You have to leave with her now."

"Have you gone mad? You must turn yourself in, Isa. Remco doesn't have that much influence, at least not here, in Portugal."

"Please! I'm begging you! If I had any other solution, I would do it. I told you what kind of person Remco is. If the police pick me up, what will happen to Frey? He can't get his hands on her, not again. Please, Michelle!"

Chapter 31

Three weeks ago, I could barely decide where to fill up my gas tank, and now this.

I can't do this alone; I don't want this. I want to leave, away from Isa and her problems. I have nothing to do with this, so why do I feel so torn? Why do Daniel's words keep running through my head?

When I see someone in trouble, I help that person. And I hope the reverse is also the case.

Isa is in trouble, but am I helping her by running away with Frey? More importantly, am I helping Frey by doing so? The only thing I know for sure is that I would never leave a child in need. Never. So, what should I do? Suppose Isa is arrested later, what then? What happens to Frey then? I need time to think about this, but I don't have that luxury.

Isa stares at me pleadingly. According to her Frey is safest with me. Is that so? If there's one thing I can do, it's dealing with small children. It's the only thing I'm good at. I clench my jaws in frustration. She presents me with an impossible dilemma; I have no choice but to accede to her request. It's simple: whether or not that guy Remco is after them, I'm the only one who can take care of Frey. There's just no one else.

So, I give in.

Isa disappears into the dunes to give me the chance to wake Frey up. The beginning of my insane mission.

"Frey, we're going on an adventure, you and me," I chirp.

"On an adventure? With maman?" she asks, rubbing the sleep out of her eyes.

"No, not with maman. Maman needs to go away for a while, and she's asked me to take you to your uncle Jacco."

"Zja-Zja!" cheers the child. "On the farm!"

"Yes, on the farm. But we must be quick, so I'll give you a bag and you'll put your stuffed toy, your favorite dress, and your Game Boy in it, okay?"

Frey nods excitedly and from the drawers under the bed, I pull out a small sports bag. "Everything is going in here. I'll count to a hundred and then you should be ready. Deal?"

"Okay!" Frey starts throwing stuff into the bag like a little madman, and I count out loud. But I can't shake off the fear of what I'm about to do. I'm terrified, but must not let it show.

"One hundred!" I shout. Frey proudly shows me the stuffed bag. She's put cookies in it too, I see. Wise kid. I open the mini fridge and take out a can of Coke. On my way out, I quickly snatch the pictures of Frey and Isa and put them in the bag, too.

I install Frey snugly on the back seat of my Volvo, with some pillows and my sleeping bag, and start the car. Isa is nowhere to be seen. Will she see her daughter again? I swallow a lump. I feel dirty and tired. My teeth desperately need a brush. A glance at my mobile phone tells me it's only half past six in the morning. Everyone is still asleep.

At a walking pace, I drive past the parked campers to avoid attracting attention. We leave the bumpy parking lot and turn left onto the road. Not even a hundred meters further, I almost get a heart attack for the second time that morning when I see flashing lights on the side of the road. There is another parking lot. One that is slightly less popular because it doesn't lead directly to the beach but has more privacy. With a jolt, I realize that the flashing lights are coming from an ambulance. As I drive by, I see police ribbons stretched around one of the campers. It's a white van with a horizontal blue stripe. It is shielded from the public and next to it is a white tent. Just like back then on the beach.

Pale-faced, I focus on the road ahead.

"There wasn't a body anywhere," Isa had said.

Was she lying? All that blood… Only now do I realize what it means. Or rather, could mean. What did Isa do? Or Remco? Who's in that tent? Who is dead? I want to scream, but instead, I breathe in and out, my hands shaking so badly that my steering wheel jerks. I can't turn back now; I have Frey in the car with me. It's going to be okay; everything will be okay. This is all a big misunderstanding, and soon it will all be over; I'll drop Frey off at her uncle's house, and then I'll finish my trip towards the south. As long as I stay calm and take care of Frey, everything will be fine.

Slowly, my breathing becomes regular again.

Think, Michelle.

Which direction should I go? Surely, Isa didn't mean for me to drive all the way to Bordeaux, in France, where Jacco's farm is? The man hasn't reached out to me yet, as she had promised.

I check the GPS and decide to drive to Lisbon. With a heavy heart, I leave the south behind me. Will I be able to finish my trip? The tiny amount of money I have been so frugal with will not last me long now that I have to drive hundreds of miles along the highway. Not to mention the gallons of gasoline my ecological disaster of a car swallows. Please let my paycheck be deposited today, I pray.

In the rearview mirror, I see Frey's blonde head, her eyes closed, half a sticky cookie still in her hand. The chaotic morning has taken its toll, not only have we not been able to wash ourselves but, moreover, we have not had breakfast. We'll have it later, at the first refueling. I let the miles of asphalt shoot by under my Volvo, making the distance between Isa and us bigger and bigger. I focus on the white painted lines on the road and try to keep my mind empty, it's the only remedy I have to stop a panic attack. I'm not a hero. I'm just Michelle.

My phone pings, I received a voicemail message, but I haven't missed a call. I curse softly. The coverage is probably poor, and my mobile didn't ring. I clamp the phone between my shoulder and ear and listen.

"Michelle, listen carefully and delete this message as soon as you hear it." A male voice pronounces the words with great effort. His English has a fat French accent. I clamp the device closer to my ear and check in the mirror that Frey is still asleep. "My name is Jacco, I'm Isabelle's brother. I'm deeply sorry you got involved in this, Michelle, but unfortunately, there's no other way. Isa says she trusts you... thanks for wanting to help her. Remco is very dangerous, so don't talk to anyone, don't trust anyone. Not even the police. Especially not the police. Please drive Frey towards Salamanca, in Spain, as fast as you can. I am leaving Bordeaux now, and I will meet you there. I will call you again later today to agree on a meeting place. Be careful."

I throw the phone down on the passenger seat and bite my lip. So, the story about the ex is true, at least that's something. I change the destination on the GPS to Salamanca: three hundred and seventy miles. At this rate, we won't arrive until late tonight, if I ever find my way. I can only turn on the GPS for a few minutes because it's almost empty and the car cigarette lighter doesn't work. Everything appears to be empty: my mobile phone beeps warningly and my petrol gauge is also dangerously in the red, but the next petrol station is still miles away. My pay should have been deposited, but it can take hours for it to arrive in my account. I'm keeping my fingers crossed that it gets there in time, or I'll be in even bigger trouble. Why didn't I buy a road map while I still could? How am I supposed to charge my phone now? Even if I buy a new charger, which I should have done by now but didn't, I can't plug it into a broken cigarette lighter. It seemed less important when I was traveling with Isa and could use hers. It's incredible how quickly I seem to fall back into that old pattern, how quickly I put my fate in someone else's hands instead of doing my thing. In any case, I am being punished for it. If I had traveled alone as I had planned, I would not have a child in the back seat now, and I would not be on the run from some psychopath, but I would be on my way to Sagres. By myself.

I slow down to a boring pace of fifty-five miles per hour, where I am allowed seventy-five, but the fuel gauge continues to drop dramatically. It's a hot day and since I have no air conditioning in my old Volvo, I open all the windows.

Frey wakes up from her nap. "Are we almost at Zja-Zja's?" she asks.

We haven't covered a quarter of the way yet, but I don't say that. "Not yet. Shall we play 'I spy with my little eye?'" I suggest. That way I keep her occupied for the next fifteen minutes and suspend the latent anxiety about Isa.

My stomach rattles, and my mouth feels dirty. I need a shower and clean clothes, but Jacco's imperative words echo through my head again and again: "Don't talk to anyone, don't trust anyone. Drive Frey towards Salamanca as fast as you can."

I'm terrified, but I need to pull over at some point. Without gas, we won't get anywhere. And we need to eat.

Much to my relief, I see a sign appear which says: gas station — 3 miles. Not a mile too early, according to the gauge. When I give it a firm tap, it drops another millimeter deeper into the red. We drive on at a snail's pace.

"We're about to stop, Frey, will you put your slippers back on?"

153

"Are we there yet?"

"Not yet, I'm going to fill up with gas, and then we'll buy something yummy. What are you in the mood for? A croissant?"

"And orange juice!"

The thought of a strong cup of coffee lightens my mood a bit and a little later I come to a halt next to one of the pumps. With a frightened heart, I insert my debit card. I cross my fingers. Please let the balance be sufficient, I silently pray.

When the tank is half full, the gauge turns off automatically. Darn. So, my paycheck still hasn't arrived. I reach for my wallet and see what I have left in change. It should be enough for that cup of coffee and the croissants. I park, close all the windows, and walk with Frey into the store.

We are near Lisbon, and it's high season, so it's a coming and going of people. In front of the bathroom, there is a long line, but we have no choice. I have to go, so does Frey, and I want to freshen up. While we wait, I stare at the television set hanging on the wall. It's eleven o'clock and a rerun of the morning news has just started.

I stare at the screen and remain nailed to the floor as a picture of Aline's blonde friend Trixi appears. The camera shows images of the van with the blue horizontal stripe and the white tent behind it. Nervously, I strain my ears. With my poor knowledge of Portuguese, I can only understand that Trixi is from Germany, her German license plate also appears in the picture. So, it was her van. But I have no clue whether she's dead, missing, or merely wounded. They don't say a word about Isa or Aline. That's a relief. Imagine Frey seeing her mother's face plastered on TV. I do need to be more careful. Immediately after the item about Trixi, the news continues with an item about the dismembered body. The police still don't know who the victim is.

After our bathroom visit, I look around the small store to see if they happen to sell external batteries for my mobile phone, that would buy me a few hours, but alas no. Not that I have the money for it.

My hand trembles as I help myself to a cup of coffee from a vending machine. If my cell phone dies, Jacco won't be able to reach me. Then I'll never find him, nor be able to call for help if I get into trouble.

Shit shit shit. Michelle, you are such a dumbass!

I blow on my hot coffee and try to think of a plan, but my mind is a blank page. There's nothing I can do but just drive on and pray my phone holds out long enough.

"Michelle?"

The familiar voice jerks me out of my slumbering panic.

Chapter 32

I turn around, Frey's arms wrapped around my leg.

"Daniel! What are you doing here?" I say relieved.

"Refueling, of course, just like you." Frey looks at him curiously. "And who may you be?" he asks her.

"I'm Frey," she replies with her broadest smile and her mouth full of croissant.

Daniel looks at me questioningly, but I'm not sure how to explain the girl's presence.

"Frey, um, she's a friend's daughter, and um, I'm watching her for a while," I stammer. Blushing, of course. I can't pretend Frey is my child. Daniel knows she isn't.

"I thought you were traveling alone?"

"I was," I say quickly. "But I got to know her and her mother on the way." I'm so bad at lying, please don't let him ask too many questions.

"After we met?" he asks.

"Um, yes?"

"Wow, then that friend must have a lot of faith in you to let you look after her daughter so soon."

If only he knew. "Well, some people have faith in other people," I say with a wink. "By the way, weren't you the one who gave me a lecture on trust not too long ago?" My shrewdness amazes and delights me.

He chuckles softly. He doesn't strike me as the type to ever laugh effusively; it seems to be something he doesn't do, something he's never really learned and has yet to practice.

"Touché." His voice sounds warm, and frankly, I'm glad to see a friendly face, one I know, even if it's only superficially. He has his fishing hat on again and this time he is not wearing a wetsuit, but white linen pants and a ditto shirt. Long sleeves again. He has also generously applied sunblock to his pale skin. I want so badly to tell him what I've gotten myself into, but once again the words "don't talk to anyone, don't trust anyone" drone through my head.

I pay for our breakfast with the change in my wallet.

"Come along, Frey, we have to go. Bye, Daniel," I say. He raises his hand, similarly to when I left him on the side of the road a few days ago. That reminds me of something. "Hey, wait a minute. What was in that bag the other day?"

"Excuse me?"

"The day I had a flat tire, I saw you give a dripping bag to a man in the beach bar. What was in it?"

"Ah, that. *Percebes*."

"Percebes?"

"Yes, goose barnacles. A real delicacy. I hunt them."

For a moment, I am too bewildered to answer, but then I realize that there is no way, no way at all, for him to know that I have been calling myself a goose barnacle for days.

"You hunt for goose barnacles?" I repeat.

"Yes. You find them here on the coast, on the rocks. That's how I make my living."

I wince slightly, hoping he doesn't see it. Then I remember he knows Trixi and Aline too, and before I realize that I would have been better off keeping my mouth shut, I say, "By the way, did you see the news?"

"Of that girl who was murdered?" he asks.

"So, she's really dead?" I whisper in shock. Even though I knew it somehow, I'm still shocked.

"Yes, I just heard it on the radio. Stabbed."

Oh, God, Trixi is dead. She was stabbed to death. I feel the blood draining from my face, my heart hammering like crazy.

"Is everything okay, Michelle? Did you know her?"

"I... no, I didn't. But you knew her, right?"

He looks surprised. "How do you know?"

"I saw you guys that day; you were arguing with her and her friend," I say, scrutinizing his reaction.

"Oh, then. Yes, indeed." His facial expression grows grimmer. "It was only a matter of time before those girls got into trouble."

"How so?"

"The break-ins. On me, on you. The others. I knew they did it, but I couldn't prove anything and those two were so slick. In your face all kindness and social chatter, but behind your back they would steal everything you owned."

My legs go limp. If those girls are responsible for all the thefts, I realize, then it's not too far-fetched to think that Isa wasn't mad and that Aline indeed had her bracelet on her wrist. The only problem being the bracelet was in Remco's possession. He had taken it from Isa's apartment before she embarked on her journey. If Aline and Trixi found the bracelet during one of their burglaries, then Isa has been right all along: Remco is following her and has been robbed by Trixi and Aline along the way.

So, he is coming after his daughter. And now, he's coming after me, too.

"I'm guessing they messed with the wrong person," Daniel continues. "Someone will have caught them red-handed and took his revenge. Or hers."

He has no idea how close he is to the truth.

"They picked up a suspect, didn't they?" he goes on. "A woman who was found with blood on her clothes near the van. At least, that's what I heard."

So, Isa has been picked up. I can hardly breathe, that's how scared I am.

"Michelle, is everything okay? You look like you've seen a ghost." Daniel looks at me with concern, and I don't know what to do. Up to this moment, this strange trip to Salamanca was part of a bizarre adventure. But this changes everything. Remco is now after me, looking for his daughter. I have to get Frey to safety.

Now.

Another thought shoots through my head: what if Isa is responsible for Trixi's murder after all? Then I'm helping a murderer while being chased by her psycho ex. Bewildered, I think of what my mother would say about this. How on earth did I get mixed up in this?

"Michelle?" repeats Daniel.

Frey begins to whine.

I stagger toward the exit; I need to get to my car. Daniel comes up behind me. "Are you sure everything's okay? You're acting weird."

I need to get to my car. One by one, new insights are demanding my attention: Trixi and Aline also broke into my car. So not only was it them who stole my panties, I realize to my horror, but after that, Aline rescued me from the ocean and invited me to the campfire, straight-faced. All this time my dirty underpants were in her possession.

I'm getting nauseous. The few feet between the small, crowded gas station and my car are scorching hot and sweat drips from my body. I drag Frey behind me and Daniel follows. When I open the door, I feel the boiling hot air blowing past me. I open all the doors except the broken one. Meanwhile, I try to think. The most sensible thing would be to go to the police, but that's just not possible.

I look at the blonde head of the child standing next to me. Without a mother, without a father. If she knows this Jacco, she might be safe with him. The responsibility weighs

160

heavily on my shoulders and there is no one to help me, I have to do it alone.

Unless…

Chapter 33

Belle, you are the only one to whom I will ever admit this. There is nothing quite like manipulating someone's fear with just your fingertips. To make her so afraid that she becomes oblivious to everything around her with a simple press of a button. So afraid that she no longer trusts anyone.

Up and down, I make that button move. When I want her to, I make her think she's safe. I love that part. I let her trip and hop, under the delusion that her nightmare is over. Until I intervene with my button and watch her face slip into a mask of despair and fear. That's when I feel alive again, Belle.

Is that bad? Yes, you probably think so. You were always a better person than me, even though you claimed not to be. What does that mean, anyway, being a good person? My mother did what she did to give her children a roof over their heads, is that so bad? I don't know. The distinction has never been clear to me; maybe that's why I've always felt so different.

Anyway, my fifth and sixth corpses are now a reality. The fifth was again an accident, unfortunately. I'm sorry about that. The sixth I'm not sorry about, even though it's not what I wanted. It never is. But this time I knew very well what I was doing and also why: she gave me no choice, unfortunately. What I don't understand is why I enjoyed it so much. Sorry, Belle, but watching the light extinguish in her eyes was the most intimate moment of my life. Except for my time with you, of course. I felt so close to her, holding her hand as she rasped out her last breath. Light red bubbles appeared on her soft lips, resembling glistening fish eggs, and then burst.

Remember when I wrote to you about that competitor on the horizon? I told you I would take care of it, right? Well, I did. The coast is clear once more.

Chapter 34

I turn to Daniel and start talking in a whisper, so Frey can't hear us. "Listen," I say. "Frey's mother is in trouble, and she has asked me to take her child to her brother. He's on his way from Bordeaux and we'll meet in Salamanca."

Daniel frowns but remains silent.

"The problem is I still can't charge my phone and your GPS is pretty much dead too because my car cigarette charger doesn't work. So, when that guy calls me later with the address of our meeting place, there's a good chance I won't receive his call. I desperately need one of those external batteries or some other way to charge my phone, so I can drop Frey off safely."

Daniel peers into my car at Frey's belongings scattered here and there in the back seat. "You sure managed to get yourself into trouble, didn't you?" he says. I can't tell whether he means it funny or not. "So, where's the kid's father? Can't he pick her up?"

I glance at Frey, trying to make him understand she mustn't hear what I'm saying. "Her father has a restraining order," I mutter through my teeth. "It's all rather complicated."

Because the shadow of his fishing hat falls across his face, I can't see his eyes. Even so, I can tell a grim mask comes over his face. He seems to weigh his words, his fists balling. Something I said has upset him. He pulls his cell phone from his pocket and taps the keys until he finds what he's looking for. "This is what we're going to do," he begins. "A few miles further on is a DIY store. They sell those car cigarette chargers you need; I'll have it replaced for you in no time. It costs almost nothing. Way cheaper than a battery. And they sell telephone chargers too."

"Great!" I exclaim with relief, but he still has that dogged pull around his mouth.

"Hm, yeah. Just follow me. I'll show you the way."

Quickly, I reattach Frey in the back seat, flip open the windows, and wait for Daniel to pull up in front of me. I'll have to ask him to lend me some money, I realize. How lucky to have run into him. I wouldn't know what to do otherwise. I start the car and drive behind him, back onto the highway. At the first exit, he gets off again, and I heel him. He's driving slowly, probably to avoid losing me. We drive through a village, and I expect to arrive at our destination at any moment. Each time I see his blinker light working, I think we have arrived. He had said "a few miles" hadn't he? It is much quieter here than on the busy highway. I can hardly imagine that there is a DIY store here.

Then my phone rings — a Spanish number.

"Hello?" I say breathlessly.

"Is this Michelle?" The heavy male voice speaks English with a French accent; it's Jacco.

"This is she!" I reply with relief.

"Did you get my message?"

"I did."

"Are you on your way with Frey?"

"I am. I mean, I might be. How do I know I can trust you? And why couldn't I leave her with the police?" I don't know why I'm asking him questions I already know the answer to, maybe because I still need to convince myself that this was the right decision.

A sigh on the other end of the line. "I understand that this must all be rather strange for you. It was for me, too, when Isabelle showed up at my door with her daughter. Completely panicked. I suggested she stay with me, but she didn't want to. The risk was too great, she said, that her ex would find her."

My mobile beeps for a moment. "I'm sorry, but I don't have much time, my battery is almost dead," I say hurriedly, meanwhile trying to follow Daniel's van.

"Okay, I'll keep it short. Michelle, you should know that Remco is an ex-policeman, these guys protect each other, so please don't trust anyone. Especially not the police, even in Portugal."

I am not happy to hear that again. All my life I have been taught that the police are my friend, not my enemy. Something in me fights with the idea. "But that restraining order? They can pull up the information in Portugal too, can't they?"

"Sorry Michelle, we can't count on that. You must bring Frey to me as soon as possible before Remco finds her."

"But how do I know she's safe with you?" I whisper in frustration. "Doesn't Remco know where you live? You're Isa's brother!"

"No, he doesn't. Besides, we've never met in person. Listen, I get that this is not your fight, but nothing will happen to you, as long as you come my way with her."

"Is it true that the police have picked up Isa?"

"I'm afraid so."

My mobile beeps again.

"Can you at least tell me what this ex of hers looks like?"

"He may have changed his appearance, but there's one thing that sets him apart: he has a large tattoo of a wolf all over his right arm."

Wolf. Check. Sounds like a mega creep.

"Michelle, Isa is counting on you. I'll be waiting for you and Frey in Salamanca, in front of the entrance to the cathedral."

Before I can ask how to reach him, my phone cuts out. Empty. Shit, shit. I toss the useless thing onto the passenger seat and keep my gaze on Daniel's van in front of me. Like a virus, distrust spreads through my body. Don't trust anyone. So not even Daniel? Oh, come on, if he happened to be that infamous ex of Isa, Frey would have recognized him immediately, right? Wouldn't she? I have no idea when she last saw her father. How long has Isa been on the road with her? I only realize now that I don't know. And Isa had no pictures of him in her van. Frey might not have any memories of her father. No, that's insane. Too farfetched. I'm already starting to get as paranoid as Isa. Although come to think of it, Frey is very light. Her hair and her eyes are so unlike her mother's.

But very much like Daniel's.

I shake my head. Impossible. I would have noticed a big tattoo like that.

Wouldn't I?

With a jolt, I realize that I have never seen Daniel's bare arms. Not then at the beach, in his wetsuit, and not at the side of the road when he had a long-sleeved T-shirt on, and not today because even now, his shirt has long sleeves while it is almost thirty degrees.

My mouth is dry and I lick my lips. I had noticed it before, but only now do I wonder why he never shows his arms. One by one the pieces of the puzzle fall into place: he told me himself he suspected Aline and Trixi of having broken into his van... So, Isa's bracelet must have been there! And of course, it was no coincidence that I ran into him just now at the gas station; he had simply followed us. Who knows for how long already?

Oh, God.

He even said that he hunts goose barnacles. And now I'm driving behind him through a deserted landscape, like a lamb being led to the slaughterhouse. He didn't even have to try hard to make me follow him. Cold sweat breaks out on me now that I realize I am in danger. I am responsible for a child, damn it. I was asked to do one thing: don't trust anyone.

And what did I do?

Chapter 35

I grip the steering wheel tightly with both hands. I need to get back to civilization as soon as I can. How lucky Jacco called me, at least now I have a chance.

I turn the GPS back on and peer at the map. We are driving straight towards some kind of industrial area. There are a few houses here and there, but vast fields dominate the view. I can see the mountains in the distance. The landscape here is not as hilly as I was used to in Portugal.

How could everything have gone so wrong? In Galicia, I was still so hopeful, so full of good cheer that I would return home as a better person. And now... now I don't even know whether I can ever go back if I don't escape from this madman soon.

"Frey, is your seat belt fastened properly?" I ask when I see a twist in the road looming.

"Yes!"

"Okay, I have to brake hard now, hold on tight, okay?"

"Okay!"

When I see Daniel's van turn around the bend, I take one last look in my rearview mirror. Damn, someone is driving behind me. In the split second I have, I decide to do the maneuver anyway. The other car is still a long way behind me. I hadn't even noticed it because of my fixation on Daniel. I hit the brakes, throw my steering wheel to the left, almost drive into the shoulder but correct just in time by driving backwards for a moment and then dash back to where we came from as fast as my old Volvo can handle.

I hope Daniel doesn't look in his rearview mirror, so I can make it to the intersection we just passed. It's a road where you're only allowed to drive fifty miles per hour, but I must be going about seventy-five. I skim past the car that was just behind me and deliberately keep my face averted. Maybe I should put on a cap too, like Isa. My red hair doesn't help to blend into the crowd, it's blowing in all directions now that I'm driving so fast with the windows open; my throat is constricted from fright. It would only take one inattentive driver coming out of one of the narrow side roads, a tractor for example, and we are all dead.

At the crossroads, I want to turn right, back toward the highway, but of course, that's the way Daniel will go too, so I impulsively decide to turn left, deeper into the vast country. One last look in my rearview mirror tells me there is no one there. Again, I accelerate and take the first side street I come across.

Crisscrossing I drive on, once to the left, then right again, until I have no idea where I am, but I'm quite sure I have lost Daniel. Frey thinks it's all great, it's a game to her, but I'm furious with myself. How could I have put her in such danger? I've only trusted the wrong people so far: Aline is a thief; Daniel is called Remco and is a psychopath, and Isa... I tell myself all the time that she couldn't have killed Trixi, but how sure can I be?

I'm exhausted. Empty. The adrenaline from my escape is wearing off and tears are burning behind my eyes. This trip was supposed to change my life for the better, not for the worse. I should have discovered where my strengths lie. I should have learned to stand on my own wobbly legs, no matter how shaky they are. So why can't things work out for once? Will I prove my mother right again? Would I have been better off staying home, with her? As stifling as life was in my old bedroom, with a bottle of wine as my only escape route, at least it was safe there. And every attempt I made to get away from her came to nothing.

What does that mean?

I'm not religious, but I almost suspect that there are higher powers at play that don't want me to spread my wings, with — until today — my failed marriage being the low point.

***

William and I had so much fun in the beginning, though. He spoiled me with cinema visits, surprised me by picking me up from school when he had some time off, and had flowers delivered to me for no other reason than pleasing me. I was living on cloud nine.

For my birthday, he took me to a B&B in the Flemish Ardennes, where we sat cozily by the fire after a long walk to let our wet shoes dry; me with a glass of amaretto and him with red wine. He had quasi-abducted me that Friday night, very much against the wishes of my mother, who pretended to have severe flu.

William was the first man I slept with. The day I told him I was a twenty-five-year-old virgin, he reacted incredulously at first. But once he realized I was telling the truth, it was like he got to unwrap the best Christmas present ever. And if he was happy, so was I. Although I never truly enjoyed it myself, making love to him. Not the way I saw other women doing it on TV while they were writhing on the bed. But it was never really unpleasant either, not counting the first time. William was always careful and sweet, and I was good at pretending. As soon as I discovered it made him happy I made little sounds of pleasure, I did it every time. After a few months, he suggested I take the pill, which he prescribed for me, and that's when things went wrong.

Unlike my mother, I was not used to taking medication. I often forgot to take a pill, which I then "caught up" later.

One rolled into the sink and I couldn't catch it. I didn't think it could do much harm because we rarely got around to doing the deed, anyway. After all, I still lived with my mother and she demanded my full attention. As nice as William's company was, for now, he came second. He wasn't too pleased about that, but I didn't have the strength to tear myself away from my mother. Even when I knew her illnesses were not real, the guilt I felt still weighed me down. She was lonely. I was all she had and vice versa.

I remember exactly how the panic took hold of me when my period was late. I didn't even dare to take a pregnancy test. In retrospect, you might think that I unconsciously got pregnant deliberately; that it was a tactic to get away from my mother, making it look like it wasn't my own free choice. You might say that's why it took me so long to tell William about what I suspected to be true. But I wasn't that calculated. I was just terrified.

Anyway, after the initial shock, William was overjoyed that we were expecting a baby. And because he was happy, so was I. When I felt the baby kick a few weeks later I experienced a feeling of intense happiness for the first time in my life. What I wouldn't give to be able to experience that feeling one more time.

***

I pull over on the shoulder of the small road we are on. With both hands, I reach for my belly. I want to scream but realize in time that Frey is with me. I may not have been able to protect my child, but this child I will not abandon. This time I don't need my belly to protect it, only my head.

It's a second chance. A chance to do something useful with my life. To make a difference for someone in this world after all. This is not about me, or my fear, or my lack of confidence, but about Frey. I am responsible for her; right now, she has no one else. I glance at the little blonde girl who looks at me questioningly from the backseat, who senses unerringly that she needs to keep quiet. No child in my classroom could make herself so invisible, it's as if she realizes it's in her best interest. I inhale deeply through my nose and blow the air out again through my mouth.

"Shall we get out and have a picnic?" I suggest cheerfully.

She nods enthusiastically, and I grab the bag of croissants and the bottle of water I bought at the gas station. I reach back and pull Frey's cup from her bag. With our arms full, we reach the shade of a tree and sit down on the dry grass, where I've laid out a bath towel. It hasn't rained for weeks and the fire hazard is high. Witness to this are the trees on the other side of the road, with their blackened trunks, which seem to be staring at us.

I break off a piece of a croissant and give it to Frey. She chats away about the children in her class, apparently not wondering where Daniel has suddenly gone.

"Tell me about Jacco's farm, what animals live there?" I ask when she has exhausted the subject of school.

"Chickens!" she exclaims. I make her imitate every possible animal sound until she starts yawning. I let her pee behind the tree after which I strap her back into the back seat, a new coloring page on her lap. Only when I start the car I realize I forgot to turn off the GPS while we were parked. The thing doesn't respond to my repeated attempts to make it work. The screen remains grimly black.

I have no idea where I am, much less which way to go. I reach for my mobile phone, in the vain hope that it has miraculously risen from the dead, but alas. Resigned, I slump down. Now what? It is already getting swelteringly hot in the car, if I don't want us to end up like boiled lobsters I have to start driving. I have to get back on the highway, but how?

Desperately, I stare ahead of me. I force myself to stay calm and think. There's nothing to it but to choose a direction haphazardly. At some point I'll come across a sign that sends me on the right path, I reassure myself. In my panic, I may have driven a little too far into the deserted interior, but I'll get there. I can always orient myself to the sun, right? It's in the south now, and I need to go north. Simple.

With clammy hands, I drive on, but my first attempts to go north end in impassable dirt roads. You never know here, a paved road can turn into an unpaved one and vice versa, or end in a field.

I'm losing precious time. I know that. Besides, I can't call Jacco. How long will he keep waiting in front of that cathedral? The realization that I still have many hours to drive before I reach my destination brings tears to my eyes again. I am already devastated by the fear and all the other emotions I have had to deal with since yesterday. But I have no choice, I must move on. So, I keep driving and turning back until — finally! — I see a sign with the redeeming text: A6 - 5 miles.

Chapter 36

You are mine and mine alone. I won't let anyone take you away from me. Now that I have you in my sights, I won't let you go. Never again will I let you go, Belle, my beautiful dragonfly[1].

You were the only one who understood me. Who saw who I was, and who knew what I had done. With you, I didn't have to wear a mask, our love was as pure as the clear spring water in my water bottle. I remember the softness of your skin, the freckles on your nose. And your scent. But I also remember that other smell, of death.

Yes, Belle, I am not crazy. I know that I have lost your body. That I will never hold you in my arms again. You, my second corpse. But your spirit I continue to carry with me, forever. Did you know that I have immortalized you on my skin, in indelible ink? The most beautiful dragonfly is now on my shoulder, if I turn my head a little, I can kiss her.

We are inseparable, dearest Belle.

---

[1] In Dutch and French, the word for dragonfly is « libelle »

Chapter 37

After we got over the initial shock, William and I decided to move in together. That is, I moved in with him. I was also the one who insisted on getting married, by the way, so that the baby would be sure of a father and would also bear William's name. What I had gone through — not knowing who my father was, a lifetime of searching for answers—I didn't want to do that to my child. For William, it was fine; I think he was genuinely happy with me.

Our wedding was simple, neither William nor I wanted a church wedding, and we went to a fancy restaurant with his parents and my mother. My Mom held her own, although she regularly sighed about how beautiful a church service would have been, how lonely she had been before I was born, that we didn't need to worry about her, she would survive without me, which was accompanied by a tear that she theatrically wiped away. William's mother put her hand on hers, she seemed like a sweet woman. It must have been a bizarre situation for her and her husband that their son was expanding their family so suddenly. At least I was reassured that William came from a warm nest and that our baby would have a set of normal and loving grandparents.

When I told my mother the baby would be a girl, she seemed genuinely happy. I promised her that I would pop in to see her several times a week until the baby was born. I didn't have much else to do anyway because as a kindergarten teacher, I had to stop working immediately, and I still didn't have any friends.

That day, my mother and I went out shopping for the baby. After three hours of trying out every possible type of baby carriage, I was exhausted. I don't know what possessed me to take my mother along; she questioned every decision I made. She even managed to buy a supply of powdered milk, while I was planning to breastfeed.

"Yes, that's what you say now. Just wait until your nipples bleed through your T-shirt, then you'll be glad you have an alternative. Mark my words," she said.

I was completely fed up with her and longed to go home, to the peace, the quiet. But I had promised her we would have lunch together at her favorite bistro. I remember I struggled to eat a bite of the vol-au-vent with fries on my plate. The nausea of the first few months might have passed, but that day the baby pressed so heavily on my stomach that it made me feel sick. With my hands on my big belly, I sat back.

"Are you all right, Michelle? You look a bit pale," my mother said.

I mumbled something and drank a few sips of Coke, hoping to ease the heavy feeling, but it only got worse.

"I think I'd better get some rest, Mom."

To my surprise, she didn't protest but immediately beckoned the waitress and paid the check. My car was luckily parked nearby. The Volvo was already an old lady when I bought her, and my mother couldn't hide her disdain for my means of transportation.

"Can't William buy you a new car? Soon you'll be transporting a baby, that's not safe, is it?"

"Volvos are the safest cars in the world, Mom, don't worry about it now," I said. When I still lived at home she never protested about my car, back then it was good enough to serve as a cab.

I dropped her off at the door of my old house. Before she got out, she flipped open her makeup mirror and touched up her lips. For whom or why? No idea. My mother never set foot outside the door without her brightly colored mask and a cloud of floral scents. She stepped out, said goodbye to me, and straightened her jacket before putting the key in the door. The door behind which she lived all alone among her antique furniture and paintings from a glorious past.

By now my stomach was as tight as a drum skin and I hurried home. William had bought an old mansion that he had completely renovated before we met. It still felt uncomfortable to settle down on the couch in the living room and feel at home. I sometimes felt like someone was going to come in and chase me away. To tell me I didn't belong there, like when you were walking into an expensive store in your sneakers. Not that William's place was so fancy, but it just wasn't me. Then again, who or what was I? I had no idea.

I tried to sleep, but the swelling of my belly prevented me from doing so. A pillow between my legs didn't provide any relief either. It was getting worse and worse, at times I even had trouble breathing. I went to the bathroom, took a stomach tablet, and lay down again. That seemed to help a little, and I must have dozed off because it was already dark when I woke up again.

When William worked late, he had a big lunch so that a simple sandwich at his office would do for him in the evening. As I didn't have to cook for him, I decided not to bother at all. I still couldn't get a bite through my throat anyway. I sat up, the sleep still in my eyes. Immediately the bloating increased, but at the same time, I felt great pressure building up, as if I urgently needed to go to the bathroom. My digestion was playing tricks on me, I thought. Perhaps the sauce from that vol-au-vent had gone bad? I stumbled to the bathroom but even before I could reach it, I knew something else was going on. A fluid flowed down between my legs, soaking my cotton maternity panties.

After that, I don't remember much.

That William came home at that precise moment and drove me to the hospital. That I was put on a bed and rolled through a long corridor. That I got an oxygen mask pushed on my face. But of the delivery itself: nothing.

Maybe it didn't take that long, I don't know. William had to decide everything alone that day; I couldn't get a sensible word out. The doctors asked him if he wanted them to start intensive care for the baby or not. Only later did I realize how slim her chances were and that William had to make a very tough decision completely on his own.

Let her go gently, or try to save her life, with no guarantee of a happy ending.

Our little daughter, Marie, lived for one more day. To this day, I still feel her tiny hand in mine. She was so minuscule, so incredibly small in her big plastic incubator that had to do what I had not been able to. That plastic thing had to keep my daughter alive but was as unsuccessful at it as I was. Nobody knew why my body decided after just under six months of pregnancy that it had had enough. And no one was prepared for it. One day I was still pregnant, the next I was not, without becoming a mother.

I had nothing to take home except an overnight bag full of shattered dreams.

I shouldn't say I was on my own because William did his best to be there for me. And although I couldn't dwell on it then, he must have grieved too.

My grief took up too much space. I mourned raw and hard; he mourned soft and quiet. Besides, he had to go back to work almost immediately; he was unable to abandon his patients.

"What about me?" I said. But of course, I had to go back to work too, after a while. And yes, that was a blessing because sitting at home alone doesn't make your grief go away. But working doesn't make it go away either. Grief just doesn't go away. Ever.

Maybe it would have been different if I had had a safety net of friends and family, but there was no one. The children in my class and their parents were well-prepared for my return. The principal had informed them, and they had made sweet drawings for me. Some came to hug me. My pupils provided the distraction I needed not to think too much about why.

Why? Why?

But not everyone knew what had happened. And no matter how well-intentioned, every "Oh, back already! And? Boy or girl?" cut through my soul.

***

"Done!" shouts Frey.

She has been coloring all this time. What a great kid. Proudly, she pushes the result of her hard work between the chairs towards me: a colored drawing of Belle and the Beast. She has given Belle bright red hair.

"That's you," she says with a wide grin.

"How beautiful! Thank you," I say.

We are still driving on the A6 towards the Spanish border. My plan was not to stop before we reached Spain and look for a way to charge my phone there, but I can't wait any longer. I'm unable to reach Jacco, and he can't reach me either if my mobile is empty. Besides, there is no way I am going to get to Salamanca today before it gets dark. I will not stand there in front of the cathedral in the middle of the night waiting with a toddler.

I suspect Jacco was calling me from a phone booth or a gas station. It was not a mobile number that appeared on my screen. So, what now? He should call me, but he probably already has.

At the next gas station, I pull over. I quickly take Frey to the bathroom, where it smells like bleach and toilet cleaner. I spot an ATM. If my salary hasn't been deposited by now, I'm in big trouble. The odds are better now that it's the afternoon.

I swear to myself that I'll order a credit card as soon as I get back home. Prepaid, of course, with my meager salary.

With trembling fingers, I insert my card into the slot.

"Please, please, please," I pray. "Don't make me have to call my mother to beg for money. Please, please, please." I key in my code and press the button to see the balance. My fingers crossed.

"Yes!" I shout. Four digits smile at me. Hallelujah! I am saved! Relief washes over me like a warm wave.

"Yes!" imitates Frey next to me, the little monkey. She has no idea what wasp's nest we are in.

I grab Frey's hand and hop back into the store with her. Finally, I can find a solution for my phone. We buy another bottle of water and a bowl of fruit salad so that we have something healthy in our stomachs today.

"Do you also sell car cigarette chargers, by any chance?" I ask the sales clerk. I explain with body language that I need it for my old Volvo, but the man shakes his head. He doesn't sell an external battery for my mobile either. He tells me in poor English that the nearest AKÍ is in Mérida, just across the Spanish border. According to him, I would find everything I required there.

On a map, he shows me how to drive. I'm a disaster at map reading, but as far as I understand, I need to deviate from my planned route and take a different highway. A detour is not ideal, as we'll arrive in Salamanca even later, but as long as I can't be reached, I'll be driving around like a headless chicken. So, there's no other option but to make the detour anyway.

I thank the man, pay for the map, the fruit, and the water, and step outside again. I am hyper-aware of my surroundings. I keep expecting to see Daniel's green fishing hat. What did I tell him about my destination? In my mind, I run through our conversation. Did I tell him that I'm taking Frey to Salamanca? Right before I reach my car, I stop, slam a hand to my mouth, and suppress a cry.

Oh, God. Yes, I did!

What an idiot I am! What's the point of taking winding roads when my pursuer knows exactly where we're going? He'll probably even get there before we do! I need to speak to Jacco as soon as possible and agree to a new location.

"Damn it, Michelle!" I mutter to myself. Then a shadow falls over me.

Chapter 38

"*Boa tarde, Senhora.*"

My heart skips a beat at hearing the low male voice.

"Yes?" I squeak, turning around. Fear immediately hits me around the throat. Two men in green uniforms are standing before me; two others are leaning against their car a little further. Police! One of the men says something in Portuguese that I don't understand.

"*Inglés?*" I try.

"Your name and documents, please," says the other officer, after exchanging glances with his colleague.

"What, why do you need them? What's going on?"

"Please," he repeats, holding out his hand.

Confused, I search for my bag and grab for my wallet. With trembling hands, I fumble out my passport and hand it to the young policeman. Meanwhile, my thoughts bounce around. They know. They know I'm on the run with Frey.

They will take me into custody; throw me in jail. My mother will have a heart attack and William will be ashamed to death of his criminal wife. After all, we're still married. It feels like there are thousands of stones gathered in my stomach.

"Are we leaving?" Frey tugs at my T-shirt.

"Just be quiet," I hush. "I need to discuss something with these men here."

The officer studies my passport and consults with his colleagues. "Michelle Deckers?"

I nod affirmatively.

"I need to ask you to come to the station with us, please."

"Now?" I stammer.

"Yes — now. The Polícia Judiciária wants to ask you some questions about Mrs. Durieux."

"About whom?"

"Mrs. Isabelle Durieux."

"Isa? Why?" So, Isa is called Durieux, I had no idea. I don't know anything about her except that she's from France, was a dental assistant, moved to Belgium for Remco, and is now on the run from him. My brain is working at lightning speed. I have to pretend I don't know what happened, which is partly true. I don't know what happened to Trixi. Or to Aline. But if Isa is suspected of murdering Trixi, they might consider me her accomplice.

"Did something happen to her?" I ask as innocently as I can.

"Mrs. Durieux is fine, Mrs. Deckers. Come with us, please, and we'll get this over with."

With trembling hands, I want to pull open my door, but one of the men stops me.

"No, you're riding with us. Leave your car here."

"But… my things?"

"It's safe here, Mrs. Deckers."

"Then may I at least take her Game Boy for a moment?"

"Make it quick."

Bewildered, I get what I need out of the car and, holding Frey's hand, I follow the policemen.

Damn, this is precisely what Isa wanted to avoid. I look down at Frey's blonde head. This is terrible. Do they know Frey is Isa's daughter? My gut says they don't. They barely glanced at her. I have to keep pretending she's mine.

Oh, the irony. If God exists, I think he or she will think this is hilarious. The thing I've wanted for so long, a child, is being forced upon me at the worst possible time. I feel a bit reassured that the men are not behaving hostile, though. With

Frey next to me, I take a seat in the back of the police car, very much aware of the prying eyes of bystanders.

We drive into a small parking lot paved with cobblestones. "GNR" I read on a building with green stripes. The Portuguese military police. The older policeman stays behind the wheel; the other one gets out and opens my door.

"Come with me. This way, please."

I follow submissively, with Frey by my side. In the narrow hallway, there are a few chairs against the wall, and he orders us to sit down.

"Is Mommy here?" asks Frey.

"I don't know, doll, soon we'll know more," I try to reassure her, as the policeman disappears behind a door. Fortunately, no one here understands what we're saying when we speak Dutch. Another officer approaches us and kneels in front of Frey. Without a word, he conjures a lollipop from his pocket, which earns him a wide smile from her.

A door opens, and a plainclothes officer wearing a blue body warmer beckons to me. Confused, I look at the lollipop man.

"I'll stay here with her, don't worry," he says in impeccable English.

Although I am immensely worried, I do as I'm told and step into the interrogation room. Two men, both wearing the same blue body warmer, take their seats at a worn wooden table and order me to sit across from them. *Polícia Judiciária* is written on their chests. Nerves are pumping through my veins. A glass of water is placed before me and, gratefully, I take a sip. A third person enters, a young woman in jeans and a T-shirt who introduces herself as the interpreter.

"Okay," begins the elder of the two, a man with graying temples and a stubble several days old. "Mrs. Deckers, can you tell us where you were last night between nine o'clock and midnight?"

I put down my cup. "If you can first tell me why I'm here and what's going on with Isa." I sound a lot more confident than I am.

The two men look at each other. On the younger man's upper lip sits an immature little mustache that tells me he will not easily give up. He puts his hands folded together on the table.

"The lifeless body of a young woman was found last night in a parking lot in Sines."

I put my hand in front of my mouth. "Isa?"

When you have lived all your life following someone else's agenda, as I have always done, you do learn how to lie. It just makes life easier. Today, this talent comes in very handy for me.

"No, the victim is called Trixi Dreher, of German descent. Do you know her?"

I automatically shake my head while my thoughts jump in all directions. Trixi Dreher... so that's her name.

"What happened?" I ask breathlessly.

Mustache shakes his head. "I can't give you any details. So, you don't know her?"

"No, not really. At least, I did see a blonde woman named Trixi last night, but I didn't talk to her or anything. And I don't know if she's German," I lie again glumly. "But what does Isa have to do with this?"

Again, the man shakes his head. "As long as the investigation is ongoing, I can't give you any details. Where did you see this blonde woman?"

I tell him about my near-death experience yesterday morning in the ocean, about how Aline rescued me and then invited me to the campfire where Trixi was too.

"Was Mrs. Durieux also present at that campfire?"

I nod.

"Did you see if she talked to Trixi Dreher?"

"I don't think so, no." I feel the familiar glow rise to my cheeks. I'm not lying. Isa didn't exchange a word with Trixi by the campfire.

"Did anything else happen?" he toddles on. "Anything unusual?"

Whether Trixi was killed by Isa or by Remco, or someone else, I don't know, but I'm not about to lie needlessly to the police, so I tell them about the clash between Isa and Aline.

"Trixi Dreher didn't intervene?"

I shake my head.

"Can you describe what this Aline looked like?"

"Did you not find her? Wasn't she with Trixi?"

"No, but we suspected Mrs. Dreher was not traveling alone."

I remain silent, confused. Then where is Aline? Has she fled? Is she dead? I'm afraid to ask, I don't know if I can trust my voice. The less I say, the better.

"And you have no idea why Mrs. Durieux became so angry?" asks Mustache.

"She thought Aline was wearing a bracelet that had been hers. But that's all I know."

"You didn't ask her?"

I swallow. "No, when I wanted to ask her, she had disappeared." That's the story I agreed to with Isa. That I just went to sleep, along with Frey, when Isa stormed off.

"What time was this?"

"I don't know exactly, but she sent me a text message, so I can take a look if I can just charge my mobile?"

Old guy nods and I hand him my mobile and charger. He plugs in the dead phone and waits for it to come back to life, then lets me type in my access code. After a few seconds, the screen lights up. With sweaty hands, I wait to see if a message from Jacco comes in, but it doesn't. Then I show Old guy the last message from Isa. He writes down letter by letter what it says and shows it to the interpreter.

Finally, it's becoming clear to me what's going on: Isa is indeed suspected of Trixi's murder, and witnesses probably told the cops we were traveling together. Someone must have been clever enough to pass on my license plate. But I don't understand where Aline is. And do the police believe Isa could kill someone for a bracelet? But then why would she kill Trixi, who had nothing to do with it, and not Aline? Or maybe Remco killed Aline too and her body is still hidden somewhere? I'm totally confused.

"Can I leave it to charge in here for a moment?" I ask, turning my mobile to silent mode. Mustache nods and I sit back down. Old guy rejoins us as well. He confirms that the message from Isabelle Durieux was sent at ten to eleven last night.

"How well do you know this woman?" he asks.

"Um, not that well, as it turns out. I didn't even know her last name." I explain that I met Isa at a campground, that we traveled together for a few days, and that I would be moving on with my daughter today. My ears feel hot as barbecue coals, but they don't seem to question Frey being mine.

"How would you describe her general state of mind?"

I think of the first outburst I witnessed when Isa thought she had lost Frey. Of her total meltdown in response to the break-in. Of her strange behavior in Lisbon, and finally of her unforgivable action last night. The policemen almost certainly see the doubt in my eyes; I sincerely don't know what to do. If I tell them all this, I might as well hang a noose on a tree for her. So, I answer, "No, nothing out of the ordinary."

"Did she look happy, in your opinion?" asks old guy.

I puff up my cheeks. "Happy… I don't know. I've only just met her." I keep playing dumb. "One meets so many people on the road, with some you click a little better than others. I clicked with her. That's all I can tell you."

The men talk among themselves in Portuguese. Old guy jumps up and leaves the room. My mobile phone vibrates on the floor, but I don't dare pick it up. The humming breaks the silence of the interrogation room. Mustache is thoughtfully sipping his cup of coffee and the interpreter is tapping away on her phone with a bored expression on her face. The humming stops, and I take another sip of my water.

Old guy comes back in. He takes the seat next to his colleague and mumbles a few words to him.

"According to Mrs. Durieux, you are traveling to France with your daughter, is that correct?" he says.

I swallow. 'My' daughter. With every fiber in my body, I force my limbic system not to blush, but it doesn't listen. I can't think of anything but coughing uncontrollably, as if my life depended on it. Tears spring to my eyes and I reach for the glass of water that is being pushed closer towards me by Mustache. Gratefully, I take a few sips.

It is said that in moments of great stress; you see everything clearly before you. In an impending car accident, everything moves in slow motion, so you have time to react. Your consciousness heightens, and you use your brain capacity to the full. But I feel none of that, quite the opposite. My brain seems frozen, like the test picture on an old TV that someone other than me holds the remote control of.

Before I fully realize what I'm doing, I nod my head resolutely and say, "Yes."

Immediately, the panic sets in. I'm lying blatantly to the police. Instead of simply telling them how things are, I'm playing along with Isa's dangerous game. But what if I don't? What if Frey's father is indeed on his way? What if the child is not safe with the police? This is Isa's way of letting me know her daughter is in danger. My heart begins a solo dance and I hide my face behind the glass of water. What will they do when they find out I've been protecting a murder suspect? Will I be considered an accomplice? Like a speeding train, I feel the panic attack approaching.

"Okay, we have your contact details. You may go, thank you for your cooperation," says old guy as he gets up.

Stunned, I look at the interpreter. Did she translate that correctly?

Mustache coughs briefly during the silence that follows. "You can go, thank you," he repeats in English.

They let me go? Just like that?

Quickly my mind adapts to this new turn of events. Yes, of course, they are letting me go, I'm not a suspect at all. I'm just a casual passerby. A mother with a child. Innocent.

With as much control as I can muster, I grab my bag. Old guy goes ahead of me and holds the door open for me.

Frey is still sitting in the same chair, with the Game Boy on her lap and the police officer next to her. She looks at me expectantly and says, "Is Mom coming now?"

I give her my widest smile while trying to hide my panic and say, "Just a minute, come along now!" as I grab her hand which is still sticky from the lollipop.

The policeman gives me a short nod. "I will take you back to your car, *Senhora* Deckers," he says.

I can't believe it. The need to sort out everything that has happened is enormous, but first I have to get back to the gas station without revealing the truth. Back to the car. On towards Salamanca.

"*Obrigado*," I say, and we get into the back seat. I pull Frey close to me, but she seems unconcerned, bending over her Game Boy again.

My head doesn't stop spinning. What is Aline's part in this story? The police know of her existence, but will they go looking for her? I don't have much time to think, the clock is ticking, and I've already lost precious time because of the interrogation. The police car slows down and drives into the parking lot of the gas station, my Volvo is still neatly parked where I left it. I continue to rummage around in my bag when the officer stops, but not until I'm sure no suspicious people are hanging around do I get out with Frey.

When I get back behind the wheel, panic tears roll down my cheeks. I ignore them, start the Volvo, say "Ready to go?" to Frey, and leave the gas station behind me.

Chapter 39

Have I gone mad? Do I not know what is real and what is not anymore? Am I chasing a phantom? A ghost?

Maybe. Even though my head knows you're not here anymore, Belle, and never will be, my heart tells me that's not true. It doesn't matter that I watched your eyes stare into nothingness. Or that I felt how your body stopped responding to my touches; how it turned limp like a rag doll. I know you're not gone, not really. You're just not here anymore in this particular place, in that body. You are not the body that betrayed you anymore.

Instead, you are everywhere.

I feel you in the swell of the ocean and the warmth of the sun. I see you in the drops of dew that glisten on the grass in the morning. I taste you in the sweat on my upper lip. And every time I see a dragonfly, I know you are watching over me and showing me the way.

There is a reason she came my way. You sent her. I know that for a fact. Just as sure as I know why you did it: so we could be together one last time. Not like the togetherness we have in my dreams, but really together. Skin to skin.

I have to be careful, though, I know. I must handle this properly, and wait for the right moment. I can't rush because then I'll scare her off and never see her again. I have only one chance. This time, I won't let it get out of hand, Belle, I promise. I'm as patient as a falcon that keeps circling high in the sky, invisible to the naked eye. Invisible to her.

Chapter 40

I shake my head in wonder as I focus on the road ahead. How is it possible that I got out of that interrogation unscathed? They only questioned me as a possible witness, like they probably did with other campers. Only I was the closest to Isa, but thanks to her testimony, she drew the suspicion completely to herself and kept me out of it.

My cell phone only managed to charge ten percent at the police station. The missed call turns out to be from my mother, she also left a message, but I'd rather not listen to it now for fear of missing a call from Jacco. He still doesn't know we can't meet at the cathedral. Another big obstacle I have to overcome is the border. Even though we're in the EU, a customs check is always possible, and I have a child with me who is not mine, I realize all too well.

My heart shoots into my throat and then straight into my shoes when I see the long-awaited sign: Espanha - 2 miles. Moments later, with a visibly pounding chest and a face that burns fiery red, I cross the border. Nobody pays any attention to me, and I can continue my journey without any problems.

This time, my map-reading skills don't let me down, and I reach Mérida without any issues worth mentioning. I have no trouble finding the shopping center and drive into the large parking lot. I almost clap my hands with joy when I see that there is not only an AKÍ but also a Worten where they sell all kinds of phone chargers. Being lucky is a welcome change.

"Burger King!" shouts Frey.

"If you're a good girl and go with me to these two stores, you'll get an ice cream from Burger King," I promise. I think about how quickly children recognize logos. Because, of course, Frey can't read.

With her small hand firmly in mine and my old broken car cigarette charger in the other, we step into the AKÍ. It takes a while before the friendly boy with the nose ring pulls out the right one.

"Iz old car," he says with a wide grin.

I nod, smile back, check out, and step cautiously outside, but there is no Daniel to be seen. And yet... They say you can feel it when someone spies on you. Well, I can swear someone is watching us. But in the crowded parking lot, it's impossible to tell.

In the Worten, we again have to wait a long time for help. I am aware that I look anything but relaxed, with my jaws clenched and eyes darting back and forth. Eventually, I buy a phone charger and ask the salesman at least three times if it will fit the car cigarette charger, which he confirms. When I read the time on the wall clock behind the cash register, I see it's already four o'clock. But we can't leave without giving Frey her ice cream, as promised.

"Vanilla, chocolate, or strawberry?"

"Vanilla!"

Again, we stand in line, and again I feel something tingle at the back of my neck. I should have followed Isa's example and put on a hat. I'm standing here like a signpost, so to speak: look at me, the tall red-haired beanpole who is completely out of place. Look, she's holding the hand of a kidnapped child. Right here!

"Michelle, our turn!"

"Oh, sorry! *Vainilla por favor*," I order. I want to get out of here as soon as possible, we're attracting too much attention.

I take Frey to the car and let her eat the ice cream there while I try to replace the cigarette charger. It takes me fifteen minutes, but it works. Which, in my opinion, is a small miracle.

Look at me now, William. Look what I can do.

Then I plug in the phone to check if it's charging. Yes, it is. I see my mother's voicemail message blinking again. I don't want to think about her now, first I will take Frey to her uncle, and then I'll have plenty of time.

I pull the phone out again so I can plug the GPS into the charger, just for a moment, so I know which way to go. From where we're parked now, it's at least another three hours of non-stop driving to Salamanca. I bite my lip. I have no choice but to keep driving that way until I talk to Jacco, so I pull out the GPS, plug my phone back in, and drive out of the parking lot while keeping a close eye on whether we're being followed, but the stream of cars driving in and out of the parking lot is endless. It's as if a colony of giant ants has descended.

When we get back on the highway, I turn on the radio. Not too loud, so I can hear my phone. I zap through the radio stations and get stuck on Radio Flashback, a Spanish station that plays music from the eighties and nineties. We sing along to the "Macarena" and a moment later Frey falls asleep.

My thoughts wander back to Marie. What would she have looked like if she were still alive? A six-year-old with red hair, like me, or dark, like William? Would she sing along with the radio, like Frey, and not stop chatting, or would she be rather quiet and withdrawn? She would surely be tall, as both of her parents are. Maybe she would play the piano or do ballet. Or be a chess prodigy.

Oh well, why torture myself? My fantasies are pointless because Marie is dead. My body is defective; it failed to grow a human inside it. I had stopped trying to understand, but now, here, feeling lonely while driving on the hot asphalt in the Spanish inland, I ask myself again: why did my body get pregnant so easily if it could not finish the task? A thousand nights I lay awake thinking about it, but it still makes little sense.

When you bake a cake, the hardest part is mixing the right ingredients in the correct proportions, right? The oven does the rest of the work. As long as you don't turn off the oven, or take the cake out too early, you're set. So how is it possible that the right ingredients didn't produce the desired result for us? Why did my oven malfunction? William's fertility was fine. Technically, so was mine. The problem was in the subsequent phase. As soon as it started to grow, my body rejected the embryo. And to this day, I don't know why.

The first time I got pregnant again, after we lost Marie, I miscarried, but didn't understand what was happening. We were so happy with the positive pregnancy test, but because of what had happened, we were reluctant to share our joy with the outside world, even with our parents. We wanted to be sure that the baby was healthy.

When I started cramping on Sunday morning and went to the bathroom, I was shocked. After a splash of water, something "plopped" into the toilet bowl. It looked like a bloodied mini balloon containing a white shrimp. I was eight weeks pregnant.

William took me in his arms, comforted me, and explained I had suffered an early pregnancy loss. He reassured me that many women go through it and that it didn't mean we couldn't have children.

"It's probably for the best," he said. "A mistake of nature corrected in time."

I looked at the amniotic sac floating aimlessly in the white enamel bowl, a bit like those big transparent inflatable balls at the fair, in which children bounce around while floating on chlorinated pool water. But in this case, there was no joyful screaming and laughing.

"What now?" I asked in bewilderment. "What shall we do with it? Bury it? I can't flush it, can I?"

William laughed, which I believed to be a strange reaction, and led me away from the bathroom. "Take a hot shower, get dressed, and I'll take care of the rest."

Was it that naïve of me to have expected him to fish the embryo out of the bloody toilet water and for us to ritually bury it in the garden? I allowed myself to be soothed by a breakfast of chamomile tea with sugar, a croissant, and freshly squeezed juice. But the sound of a toilet flushing has given me goosebumps ever since. It was hard for me to forget the image of that little shrimp, but I had nowhere to turn with my grief. Because when no one knows you were pregnant, no one knows you're not anymore either.

A few months later I was pregnant again. We went for our first check-up, had an ultrasound, and heard the heart beating. A few days earlier, my nausea had miraculously disappeared, leaving me worried. Worries that William laughed away. But I felt something was wrong, and judging by the face of the gynecologist, who was fruitlessly searching for a heartbeat, I could tell that I was right.

"I regret to inform you that the fetus has died. This happens rather frequently in the first trimester," he said. And then, as if I were not still in the chair with my legs wide in the cold stirrups, he turned to William. "I'll prescribe the necessary medication to drive the fetus out then you can try again at the next normal cycle." To which William gave him permission with a brief nod and paternally squeezed my hand.

What neither gentleman told me that day was that this medication would cause me to have cramps that were as painful as contractions and that I would bleed for days.

I was in my classroom when it started. Break wouldn't start for another half hour, and a kindergarten teacher couldn't leave her classroom. Ever. With clenched jaws, I tried to call my principal so she could replace me, but she didn't answer the phone. Through the classroom window that looked out onto the playground, I saw she was busy talking to the handyman who was fixing a leak in the roof. When I felt blood seep down my legs, through the sanitary pad I was wearing preventively, I realized that I had no other option; I had to get out of there. It would traumatize my young pupils more to see their teacher bleed out than to be left alone for a few minutes. So, I grabbed my handbag, held it in front of me and said, "Guys, Mrs. Deckers needs to go to the bathroom for a minute, everyone stay in their seats until I get back, okay?" To which they nodded angelically. "Jens, you too!" I called out before I ran out the door.

In the bathroom, I washed the blood off my legs as best as I could with balls of toilet paper that I held under the tap. Fortunately, I was wearing a long skirt and as far as I could see, it had not gotten bloody. I replaced the soaked sanitary napkin with two new ones that I laid on top of each other and put on a clean pair of underpants. I had, of course, expected some blood loss; I had become experienced in losing embryos by now, I thought grimly. I swallowed down a painkiller with some water, wiped away my tears, gritted my teeth to ignore the cramps, and ran back to my classroom.

But even before I got back to the hallway, I could hear from the commotion that things had gone wrong.

Chapter 41

Ready to raise my voice and call my class to order, I swung open the door. Jens was lying on the floor, groaning in pain, there was blood on his forehead that ran into his eye.

Instinctively, I ran towards him. "Jens! What happened?" I exclaimed. Only then did I see that the headmistress was sitting on the floor next to him. Her eyes shot fire as she looked at me.

"Mrs. Deckers! May I ask you to stay in your class and not leave it, not even for a second, while I take this young man to the infirmary," she barked.

Too startled to respond, I nodded in agreement, my cheeks burning with embarrassment. It took me a lot of effort to calm the kids down after the incident, and since I kept having cramps, it was one of the toughest days of my career. In between singing songs and reading to them, I tried to think of what I would say if the headmistress called me to her office after school, which she undoubtedly would. Should I tell her the truth or was it better not to?

In the end, I told her that I had probably eaten something bad.

That's the problem with secrets. Once you start hiding stuff in a box that only you have the key to, opening it will have consequences. If I had told her about the pregnancy loss, she would not only know about my pregnancy but also that William and I were trying to have another baby. I didn't want that, partly out of shame and partly out of self-protection. People are nosy, and I didn't want to hear their advice or sympathy, no matter how well-intentioned. I wanted to stay under the radar as long as I could. Besides, the less my colleagues knew about it, the less I had to admit my failure.

Jens had luckily gotten off with a scare. He had climbed onto his table in an overconfident mood, and it had capsized under his weight. One of the legs had hit him just above his eye, on the brow. It wasn't as bad as it looked, thankfully. He didn't even need stitches. After I had apologized to his parents, I got a big warning and that was the end of it.

I did not immediately become pregnant again. This was not due to my body or William's, but to the simple fact that we barely made love to each other. He worked hard, was often home late, and I only wanted to have sex when I ovulated. So those times were scarce but I stubbornly persisted. I didn't want to believe that we wouldn't succeed.

My desire to have children had taken disproportionate measures; it was all that mattered in my life. I became pregnant again, the third time, and my hopes flared up, but this time too my world collapsed. God's will. Whatever.

After that third one, William started talking about surrogate mothers, and adoption, but I had no ears for that. I was furious with him for giving up, for not wanting to believe that we would succeed. I blamed him for not wanting it, not like I did. I yelled at him that he didn't love me, that he had only married me because I was pregnant.

"You must be sorry now!" I spat in his face." If only you had known Marie was going to die, you could have saved yourself the trouble!'

He gave in and we tried again. Meanwhile, I was undergoing further tests, but there was no physical reason why it shouldn't happen for us. Therefore, there was no cure either. I was racking up miscarriages, one after the other. After the fifth time, William wanted to stop. He threatened to divorce me if I got pregnant again. But I managed to convince him to try one more time.

One more time.

I had a good feeling about it, I said. And he gave in, as long as I promised it would be the last time. I did. Cross my heart.

That day, I stepped out of the house to go to school. I knew I was pregnant again; my breasts had been yelling it for a while. Out of superstition, I hadn't taken a test. This time, I was going to do things completely different.

If you want the outcome of a sum to change, you have to change the terms first. Everything I did was different. Whereas before, I used to keep and treasure the positive pregnancy test, now I disposed of it immediately. I kept drinking coffee every morning so that William wouldn't get suspicious. When he wanted to order sushi, I didn't strain a muscle. I just pretended not to be pregnant. I figured that the longer I waited to admit it to myself, the longer I could deceive my body and my mother's God. As long as no one knew I was pregnant, I reasoned, they couldn't change it either. Thinking about it now, I can see I was really out of it.

William had left early in the morning. It was a morning like any other. I had showered, had breakfast, and packed my school things. The moment I reached for the car door, I felt a stab of pain so severe that I collapsed on the sidewalk, where I remained groaning. I remember seeing flashes of light shoot past my eyes. Never before had I been in so much pain. The strange thing was that I did not panic at all. I never thought for a moment that the pain had anything to do with the pregnancy because it came from a wholly different place than usual. I felt no contractions this time, no tension in my uterus, no back pain.

Appendicitis, was my first thought. Yes, that had to be it. It didn't matter, I could have had a stomach tumor as far as I was concerned, as long as it wasn't a miscarriage. And this wasn't one, I was very sure of that. Then I lost consciousness.

In the neighborhood where I lived with William at the time, everyone knew us. Me as Mrs. Michelle the kindergarten teacher and William as Doctor Vermeersch. When I collapsed that day, several people rushed over to help me. They supported my body, called William, and waited for the ambulance. That whole part has been erased from my memory. I only remember a blissful peace. No stress, no fear, no sadness. I was floating around on a peaceful cloud where no one wanted anything from me. Whatever was wrong, it would be all right. I was truly convinced it would. Only later did I realize how close I had balanced on the edge of death. How close I was to Marie that day. An ectopic pregnancy had caused internal bleeding that could have killed me in half an hour, but it didn't. My neighbors saved my life that day, and for a long time, I was unable to forgive them for that. My right fallopian tube was removed, and my gynecologist advised me to give up my wish to have children. He might as well have told me I was terminally ill. For me, my life was over.

***

Frey is still asleep, the traces of her ice cream still visible around her mouth. I feel a strange sensation come over me, my body begins to tingle, and my neck becomes warm. I could forget the whole Jacco plan and drive into the Spanish inland with Frey. I could be her mother. We could rent a small house; I could homeschool her. We could keep chickens and goats. I could protect her. I have no one, she has no one. If I can believe my mother and Elizabeth Gilbert, God has my best interests at heart. So, who's to say it's not in His grand plan for me to become Frey's mother? Why else did she come my way?

My thoughts make me blush. I shake my head in embarrassment and replay Jacco's message, which I have not yet deleted. Please let him call soon, I think, as the asphalt shoots under my Volvo mile after mile.

If not, I might start doing stupid things myself.

Chapter 42

"Michelle, whereabouts are you now?" It's Jacco, at last.

I tell him the names of some Spanish villages I've just passed, I'm not that far from Salamanca anymore. "But something happened," I say, "I think I saw him."

"Remco?"

"He calls himself Daniel."

"Are you sure? Did you see his tattoo? What did he look like?"

I briefly tell him how I met Daniel, what he looks like, and why I suspect he is Remco, without alerting Frey in the back seat.

"Hm, Remco is also light-skinned, indeed. It could well be him. How did Frey react to him?"

"She didn't give any sign of recognition, even though he addressed her directly."

"Well, that's strange. I don't know how well the memory of young children works. Do you? Isa has been on the run for a long time. Can it be that she has forgotten about him?"

"I don't know. It's possible, she's only a toddler."

"And you're sure he didn't follow you?"

"I don't think so. At least I haven't seen his van again, but to be honest, I have the feeling sometimes that someone is watching us."

"That's not surprising. Isabelle has put you in a difficult situation."

"Yes, she has. I'm probably just paranoid, just like her."

"I don't blame you. Anyway, just to be on the safe side, we won't be meeting here at the cathedral anymore," he concludes. "I'll come and meet you. You will soon see the exit for a village called Martinamor. If you take it and then turn left immediately, you will arrive at a small hamlet with some restaurants. One of them is called *Mesón Viejo del Jamón*. It is very well known among truckers, and you are never alone there. Can you order something to drink there and wait for me?"

"Okay, great!" I stammer. This is it. I'm almost at my destination!

"Good. I'm heading there now. You're almost there, Michelle. You did well."

He disconnects before I can ask him how I'll recognize him, but of course, I don't have to. He knows Frey, right? And Frey him. My ordeal is almost over. A few more miles and I can deliver her safely. If Frey shows the slightest hesitation at the sight of her uncle, I'll go to the police myself, I decide. But something deep inside me says that won't be necessary. It almost feels like a symbolic act: the one child I could save. It may not be my child, but that doesn't matter.

Tears spring to my eyes when I see the exit as promised. Martinamor. Are they tears of joy? Of relief? Or sadness? I blink them away and keep my gaze fixed tightly on my rearview mirror. Just as I get to the junction where I need to turn left, I notice a gray Citroën driving some distance behind me. Have I seen this car before? It's possible, I'm not sure. Nervously, I turn left without using my blinker. And sure enough, the Citroën also drives to the left. Shit. The car is too far behind me to see who's behind the wheel. I step on the gas, wanting to be in the village, among other people, as quickly as possible. As soon as I see the sign for the restaurant *Mesón Viejo del Jamón*, I turn right. The square is now right in front of me. It is indeed crowded, and I breathe out in relief. There are several cars and trucks in the large parking lot, people walking in and out. Apart from the restaurant, which has a covered terrace at the front, there is also a *mini-mercado*, a supermarket, where people walk in and out. I park my car as close to the restaurant as possible and stay put until the Citroën also enters the parking lot.

"Are we there?" asks Frey.

"Just a little longer, dear, we'll be getting out in a minute." My facial muscles are so tense they make my jaw hurt. The car door opens, and a blonde woman with big sunglasses gets out. She lights a cigarette. Immediately, I feel my body relax at the sight of the unknown woman. False alarm. I do have a lot more understanding for Isa now I know how it feels to be on your guard day and night. In my case, this has only been for a few hours. And with a child who is not mine. Isa must have gone through hell.

I drag Frey with me to the restaurant. First, we go to the bathroom one more time. I comb my hair with my fingers and throw some water in my face. I also take care of Frey's little face; the ice cream is not just around her mouth. When we are cleaned up again, we pick a table. The interior of the restaurant is simple, but cozy, with wooden tables on which lie green tablecloths.

"What can I get you, ladies?" The waiter appeared out of nowhere.

Oh, what I wouldn't give for a glass of wine and the relaxing effect alcohol has always given me. Yes, I've more than earned a glass, but I refuse to give in to the urge. I've managed without alcohol for so long, I'll manage for a while longer. Besides, my mission isn't over yet, so I order juice for Frey and Coke for myself and since we're both starving, I ask for the menu right away. When the waiter brings our drinks, and I take my first sip of Coke, tingling with ice cubes, I can barely suppress a groan of pleasure.

Just a little longer, just a little while, and then this stressful mess will be over.

We order fish sticks for Frey and a slice of pizza for me. I keep my cell phone on my lap the whole time, in case Jacco calls. He could be here any minute, so I keep watching the parking lot through the window. The gray Citroën is still there. I let my eyes wander, looking for the blonde woman, but I don't see her. Not in here, that is.

"What does Jacco look like, Frey?" I ask.

"Old," she replies.

I smile. In my experience with children, this answer may situate the man's age between thirty-five and ninety-five.

"Is he taller than me?"

She shrugs and sips her juice.

"Does he have gray hair?"

She nods.

The waiter comes back with our food and Frey is temporarily distracted by her fish sticks, which I cut into small pieces for her. A young couple sitting diagonally next to us look at her endearingly. They probably think I'm her mother.

I think of Isa, how would she be doing, all alone in a cell? The answer to my question follows so quickly, it seems magic is at play. On the TV screen – they seem to hang in every restaurant in Spain — the seven o'clock news starts with a picture of Isa. Instinctively, I position my body in front of Frey so she doesn't see her mother. I hear and understand nothing of what is said about her, but it is clear that she is associated with Trixi's murder. Trixi's photo also appears. Then, to my dismay, the image jumps to a picture of Aline. How did they get a picture of her? Did they find her? Or maybe they got it from Trixi's mobile? Damn, I don't understand a word of Spanish. My heart is in my throat. I strain to hear what is being said, but alas.

"That one must have fled," a man says out loud. It's two truckers who sit at a table in front of us, their backs to us.

"Yeah, I heard it was a fight between lesbians. Jealousy, probably," says the other trucker.

"They don't know what they're missing," his mate replies, followed by a greasy laugh.

I'm getting nauseous; the pizza doesn't agree with me. I take a few sips of my Coke. Is Aline on the run? Was she also attacked, just like Trixi? Or are the police looking for her as a suspect? That makes three of us: Remco, Isa, and Aline could all have killed Trixi. But why would Aline kill her friend? She is the least logical suspect. Deep down, I'm afraid Aline was murdered too, most likely by Remco.

"Frey!" someone shouts.

"Zja-Zja!" Frey chirps.

A large man with the same dark eyes as Isa comes rushing to our table. His graying hair, which must once have been jet black judging by his beard, is long and held together by an elastic band. His appearance is somewhere between a Hells Angel and an elderly hippie.

Frey jumps from her chair and wraps her arms around him. Our eyes meet, and I know immediately that it's okay. Relief and endearment are on his face. He comes to our table with Frey, I point to an empty chair, and he takes a seat with Frey on his lap.

"You must be Michelle. I don't know how to thank you," he begins.

I shake my head. A mixture of pride and relief flows through me. The finish line has been reached. I've done it.

"No one followed you here?"

Again, I shake my head, "I shook off Daniel. Or Remco."

He nods approvingly. "Isabelle is very lucky to have met you. I hate to think how this could have turned out any other way."

I start to blush and he smiles. His front teeth are a little crooked, just like Isa's. I take another sip of my Coke, the last one. "What will happen to her now, to Isa?" I ask.

His smile disappears. "I don't know. It doesn't look good for her. From what I understand, she went to those girls' van because she thought they had broken into hers."

I nod affirmatively. "Yes, that's right. She was all upset when she saw a leather bracelet on Aline's wrist, Trixi's friend."

"Indeed. She got it from Remco before they got married. It is a leather band held together by a silver dragonfly. After their divorce, Remco broke into her apartment and took it, among other things. She must have been convinced that this Aline the police are now looking for had that same bracelet."

I nod again. A dragonfly. So that's why she was acting so strange in the Océanario when that dragonfly was being eaten by a reptile. "She found her pendant with your father's ashes in that van," I explain to him. "Or did you know that already?"

"No, I didn't know that. I only talked to her on the phone very briefly. What else do you know?"

"According to her, the van was empty, the door was open. She was foolish enough to step inside, and that's the last thing she remembers. When she regained consciousness, there was a bloody knife clutched in her hand. That's what she told me. She doesn't remember anything at all about what happened, but she thinks someone tried to frame her."

"Remco," he growls through his beard.

"Yes, but why? Out of revenge for Isa taking Frey? Surely, there are easier ways?"

"Or because he wants to terrorize her in every way possible. Did she tell you how he locked her up when Frey was born? I don't know how he managed not to get convicted, but he's a piece of work, for sure. A restraining order, bah. A joke, it is. He tried everything to deprive Isabelle of custody, the daughter of an ex-colleague of his in the force worked for Social Services. She wrote such a scathing report about Isabelle, the prospect of losing Frey became very real."

We look at Frey, who is unaware of the gravity of our conversation. "I promised I would take care of her no matter what," Jacco says. "But she can never go back to Belgium."

"How will you do that? I mean, you'll have to enroll her in a school. People will ask questions about who she is. A child can't just disappear."

"No? It happens every day, you know. If need be, I'll cross the ocean. I'll think of something. As long as Remco is around, she's not safe. But first I have to get Isabelle released. Someone must have seen something that proves her innocence."

Aline, I think. She must know what happened. If she's still alive.

Jacco puts his hands on Frey's shoulders. "What do you think, little miss? Shall we go to the farm?" Then he looks at me. "If you like, you can come along?"

"No, thanks," I say. I've been thinking about what I want to do for the past few hours. I'm exhausted and want to go home, take a warm bath by candlelight, and have a glass of wine. Tell William the entire story. But I don't have a home anymore, nor do I have William. I don't want to go back to my mother.

I've lost one whole day because of this crazy rollercoaster, but my goal hasn't changed: I'll drive to the end of the world, and only then will I return. Only then will I have proven I'm no longer the old Michelle who can't do anything on her own. Michelle 2.0 is what I'm going for.

So, I wave Jacco and Frey off, start my car, set the GPS, and drive back to where I came from.

Chapter 43

I drive in the dark, focusing on the white-painted lines on the road. I have everything I need: a working GPS, a phone with a charger, a car with a full gas tank. Jacco insisted on pushing a bunch of cash into my hands, as compensation for the expenses incurred and the "lost" day.

I expected to feel relieved, euphoric even. After all, I had saved a little girl, hadn't I? But I feel none of that, quite the opposite. I feel empty and alone. I miss Frey. In those few hours, I had gotten used to her being there. Pretending she was my daughter came naturally. But now she's gone, and my stomach hurts at the realization that I may never be as important to a child as I have been today.

Was this it? Was this my one day as a surrogate mother? It's a meager consolation prize for poor little Michelle, who can't have children.

A moment ago, it seemed like a good idea to continue my journey, but now I'm doubting my decision to drive on.

I miss William, I miss our house. It may not have been mine when I moved in six years ago, but meanwhile, I have more than left my mark on it. I know I have made mistakes. I know he felt rejected. After Marie died, we both hoped that the arrival of a new baby would make our loss less painful and that it would help dry up our grief. But when the baby didn't come, when I started to see sex as a means and not an end, and when I started to see William as a means, he turned away from me. After the ectopic pregnancy that almost cost me my life, I lost him for good.

A part of me knows that this was my fault because I pushed him away. But I do keep asking myself: why didn't he fight back?

I can feel tears rolling down my cheeks again. I seem to have an inexhaustible supply. It's difficult to see anything on the poorly lit roads here as it is, and now I'm making it even harder on myself. I wipe my eyes and swallow. I was so dependent on him; it must have repelled him. That's what I suspect. But then again, wasn't I already a goose barnacle when he met me? I was still living with my mother, for crying out loud, what did he expect?

I have to stop thinking like this because it will lead me nowhere. I can still fix this. If I managed to push him away, I could pull him back too. If I admit my mistakes to him, if I let him back into my bed. Our bed. If only I let him see and feel that I love him. Then he can love me again too. Then he won't need anyone else.

A flash of light in the distance startles me. Thunderstorms can pop up quickly and unexpectedly here and disappear just as fast. Through my open window, I can smell the change in the air, the scent of the eucalyptus trees mixes with the smell of rain, and before I can turn on the windshield wipers, it's already pouring down. A few seconds later, I can see absolutely nothing. I frantically close the window, but can't prevent my left side from getting wet. My wipers can't swallow the amount of water and I slow down as much as I can.

I should have stopped before night fell, but my brooding and pondering have kept me going too long, and now it's too late. I even crossed the border into Portugal without realizing it, that's how distracted I've been driving.

In utmost concentration, I peer at the road, turn on my fog lights, and continue cleaving through the wall of water. At the next gas station, I'll pull over, I promise myself. But I know very well that that could still be miles away.

"Damn!" I shout. "Michelle, you idiot! You should have stopped! Can't you do anything on your own?" I roar at no one.

Not a shred is left of my earlier happiness in accomplishing my mission. The memories have reawakened the old Michelle. The goose barnacle.

Lightning lights up the sky, thunder shakes my old Volvo. The road is badly constructed and if so far I have been able to avoid the potholes, I now absolutely cannot. A few times I bump into a deep one, and I'm afraid I might get a flat tire, which is not a good idea in this weather. Stopping in the dark is not an option, so I grab my cell phone, turn on data roaming and try to search with one hand for a place to spend the night. A small hotel or a B&B would be great now that I have money.

A few options come up on the screen and I choose the closest one, no time to be picky, as long as they have a room available. I am now constantly being passed by other cars, one of them even honks, that's how slow I'm going. Behind me is a string of cars, like ducklings following their mother.

I follow the instructions of my GPS and a little later I arrive at a hotel that looks a lot more expensive than what I can afford. I sit in the car for a moment staring indecisively at the big glass door with the gold letters above it. Now that I'm safely parked, should I just keep looking for something within my budget? I look at the screen of my mobile phone: it's almost ten o'clock. I'll be lucky if I get a room. Besides, it's still pouring down.

Twenty minutes later I take off my soaking clothes and sink into the most wonderful bathtub. I've squeezed a thick blob from one of the jars in the bathroom into the water and foam is growing and towering above me. I flatten it with my hand; otherwise, I can't reach the glass of sparkling wine I've put on the edge.

Yes, wine. Real wine.

The bottle was in the minibar and this time I gave in. I've punished myself enough. Besides, what better way to celebrate delivering Frey safely than treating myself to my first glass of alcohol in three weeks? I've earned this, dammit.

I sink into the foam, sniff the scent of lavender, and go under for a moment, only to surface coughing. My Pretty Woman moment. I smile when I realize I have the same hair color as Julia Roberts. I laugh even harder and pour myself another glass, which I drink far too quickly. Before I know it, I reach for my cell phone and key in William's number.

"Michelle?"

"Hi, William!"

"Michelle! How are you doing? Where are you?"

"Right now? In a hotel. In the bathtub," I say, with a wide grin. I want to take another sip, but my glass is empty. Fortunately, I've put the bottle next to the bathtub. It's a small feat to refill the glass without the bottle slipping from my wet hand or the phone sliding into the bath water.

"Oh. What are you doing there?"

I take a sip. "Just taking a break," I say worldly. "Road tripping is fun, but my holiday is almost over, and I wanted to treat myself before I come back home."

"Home? To your mother's, you mean?"

Another sip. "Maybe. But I was thinking perhaps when I get back, we can talk."

It remains silent on the other end.

"I realize now that I pushed you away, William."

"Michelle,"

"No, let me finish." Another sip. "I know I acted selfishly after Marie died. And that with each miscarriage I distanced myself from you more."

"Michelle, can I just –"

"I was depressed, William. You could see that, couldn't you? You're a doctor, dammit."

"Yes, I saw that." He sounds stern. Measured. Always when I curse. "Didn't your mother call you?"

I start to sob. Why does he start talking about my mother? "All I wanted was a baby, was that so much to ask?"

"Michelle, have you been drinking?"

"What the hell does that have to do with anything? I'm trying to tell you something! Listen to me, man!"

Silence.

"I longed so much for a baby," I continue, "that I didn't see that you were hurting too. I only had eyes for myself. Now I see that. I'm sorry I let it get this far. That I drove you into Stephanie's arms."

Saying William's new girlfriend's name gives me puke fits. Especially when I think of the moment he told me about her.

It remains silent on the other end.

"But we had a good time together, didn't we? We were a beautiful couple. Teacher Michelle and Doctor William."

My tongue plays games with me and I can't pronounce his name very well anymore. "I think we should try again, together, when I get back. Maybe we should consider adoption, as you suggested."

My glass is empty again, but I don't feel like raising myself from the warm water. William still doesn't answer. I can hear him breathing on the other end of the line.

"I miss you," I say. "I miss us."

"Michelle–"

"Hmm?"

"Stephanie is pregnant."

***

I don't remember how I got out of the bathtub onto the bed.

I lie wrapped in the thick hotel bathrobe on top of the bedspread and stare at the streak of light from a streetlamp shining in through a crack in the curtains. The bottle of sparkling wine is empty. I screwed up everything. There is no bigger loser than me. I've driven my husband away by my obsessive behavior. My body fails at the one important function that so many women pride themselves on, and the one child that was entrusted to me by fate, I had almost voluntarily delivered to a psychopath. If Jacco hadn't called me, then...

William... What I couldn't give him, he found with Stephanie. A woman who went to Uni, does her own thing, is fertile. Who doesn't have a barren, unwelcome womb. Whose oven won't stop working prematurely.

I smother a cry in one of the thick pillows on the bed and unabashedly surrender to a hefty dose of self-pity.

Why do I exist? If I am no longer here, who will mourn me? My mother? Yes. But besides her? William certainly won't. I haven't seen Heleen in years, since she moved to the US. My colleagues probably won't even notice I'm gone.

I want nothing more, except to forget that I exist. If that could just be possible, if that could just be...

There's a loud bang on the door.

Chapter 44

If the police find out who I am, they'll know what I've done. But they won't. Yet. They are still looking for me as a possible victim. They combed the woods behind the parking lot looking for me, or my dead body. There was a lot of my blood in the van, I made sure of that. How long will they continue to believe in the victim theory? They are coming closer to the truth. My time is running out, no question.

But it's okay, Belle, I'm at peace with it. I think I'm ready. The circumstances are perfect, better than I would have dreamed. Now that she thinks she's alone, now that she's lowered her armor, my time has come. She will be my seventh corpse.

Belle, she reminds me so much of you that it hurts. I've been trying to muffle the pain under a blanket of drugs and alcohol for years. It's the drugs that drive me crazy sometimes, that make me do things I don't want to. You know that.

Like, when I saw her fighting for her life in the ocean. Her eyes, Belle, I will never forget her eyes. How they were wide open, every time she came up for a moment. The agony that could be read in them was mesmerizing. Hypnotic, almost. She was so beautiful in her struggle that I almost reacted too late.

There are gaps in my memory. Some things I remember razor sharp, others not at all. For example, there's the head. Where did I put the head? Did I burn it, along with the other limbs? Or bury it? I don't remember, I only remember the rage I felt when he tried to tear off my bracelet. My dearest Belle, no one will take you from me. No one. Soon we will be together again. But first I want to feel your warm skin against mine one more time.

Chapter 45

With my robe pulled tightly around me, I stumble from the bed to the door. I peek through the peephole. An unknown woman is standing in the hallway. She has half-long blond hair and wears a large pair of sunglasses.

"Yes?" I ask.

"Michelle? It's me!"

I recognize the voice, the smoky husky sound, the accent. I look again, but can't match what I hear with what I see. Baffled, I open the door. "Aline?"

"The one and only. I come with gifts." She raises a bottle of red wine as she pushes me aside and steps into my room. I'm too bewildered to react. And under the influence of the bottle of wine I just emptied after weeks of abstinence.

I close the door and lean against it. Aline makes herself at home and walks straight to the minibar, grabs two wine glasses, opens a bag of nuts, and places everything on one of the nightstands. Then she sits down on the bed and taps the mattress with her hand.

"Come, sit! We have a lot to catch up on."

I walk carefully to the bed, doing my best to walk in a straight line. It is Aline, but she's cut her long hair and dyed it. Or she's wearing a wig. She is unrecognizable, but the attraction that emanates from her remains unchanged. As if by an invisible hand, I am pushed towards her and sit down next to her. Why is she here? Why in disguise? I want to process what's happening, but my brain is temporarily paralyzed, and I accept the glass of red wine she hands me almost mechanically.

"Finally, you and me, together," she says, clinking her glass against mine and taking a big sip. Her slender neck bares itself. Her skin is so dark that her white blouse seems fluorescent, and her scent… Confused, I take a sip too.

She studies my face; holds her hand right next to my cheek, I feel the warmth she radiates, but she doesn't touch me.

"You've been crying." It's not a question, but an observation.

I nod and bite my lip. Her fingertips touch my face agonizingly slowly, examining it, and I feel my skin tingle. I can barely move, but I know I have to do something. That she's here, in my hotel room, is not only very strange but also impossible.

"I don't understand," I say. "How did you know I was here? Why are you here? The police are looking for you. Trixi is dead! What –"

"Hush," she interrupts me, stroking my cheek and wiping away a tear that was still hanging in the corner of my eye. "None of that matters anymore, we're going to have a good time together, you and me."

Her hands caress my hair, she's curling it with her fingers, twisting it, something I do too when I'm reading a book or concentrating on something. My throat is dry, my head spinning and spinning.

"Who killed Trixi?" I manage to utter. "Where were you that night?"

She takes the glass from my hands, sets it on the nightstand, and gently pushes me back on the bed. Her hand slips under my robe, my breath falters, and I find neither the strength nor the will to stop her.

"I was on the run," she whispers into my ear with her warm breath.

My eyes fall shut, my muscles slacken, but I want to know. "From whom?" I whisper.

"From myself," she replies.

She sets aside her glass as well, gets up from the bed, and rolls my body to the middle. Through my half-closed eyelids, I see how she comes to sit astride me. My robe hangs wide open, and I try to lift my hand to cover myself, but it doesn't work. My limbs no longer listen to what I want. She must have put something in my glass, I can't be that drunk. She bends over me and starts kissing me all over. I feel goosebumps growing all over my body.

"Oh, Belle," she moans.

This can't be true; I think to myself. She has gone crazy. I am deeply ashamed of how my body reacts to her touches. What has she drugged me with? Rohypnol? I am way taller than her and yet here I am, helpless and naked, like a goose barnacle without a shell. I want to say I'm not who she thinks I am, that my name is not Belle, but out of my mouth, only a soft moan sounds.

"I missed you so much, you have no idea," she continues.

Missed you? I think.

"I followed all the signals you sent me and now here we are, together again, you and me."

Together, again?

"The police are on my heels. If they find me, they'll know what I've done right away. This is our last chance, Belle."

I swallow. My throat feels thick and swollen. I feel like I'm about to lose consciousness. I do not know what she's talking about. "What did you do?" I finally manage to ask.

She takes my arms and puts them over my head. She ties my wrists together with something. My eyelids are so heavy. The temptation to let myself sink into oblivion is overwhelming. This is what I wanted, right? To forget, to disappear. Letting myself drift away on this soft cloud. Never waking up again.

Aline's arms are close to my face now. She wears a leather bracelet with a silver pendant on her wrist. I know this should mean something to me, that it is important, but don't remember why.

In the nightlight's glow, the pendant shines brightly in my eyes. I try to focus on it. I must know what it looks like. I just have to. But my brain resembles cooked porridge, and no sensible thought floats to the surface.

"You know what I did, and also what I'm going to do, Belle." She says.

I keep focusing on the pendant and then, suddenly, I see it clear as water: a silver dragonfly holds both ends of a leather strap together with its delicate wings.

A dragonfly.

Belle. *Who is Belle?*

"I'm not Belle, I'm Michelle!" I want to shout it, but nothing more than a hoarse whisper comes out of my throat.

"Michelle, ma belle," I hear her laugh. "Sont des mots qui vont très bien ensemble, très bien ensemble," she sings, her voice hoarse and high, just like yesterday at the beach.

I know the song by The Beatles; it's not the first time someone has made the association with my name. But it is the first time someone has subsequently started calling me Belle. I don't know what exactly is going on, but Aline somehow confuses me with someone she knows or has known.

Something wet drips onto my face. Is she crying? Everything is blurry and the world spins. My hands are bound, but not attached to anything, so I can still move my arms. I try to refocus my eyes and to my horror, I see Aline is now at my feet, her upper body naked.

When did she take off her blouse?

I think I'm falling in and out of consciousness.

It is not Aline who is crying; it is me. I feel the tears streaming down my cheeks, but I can't fall apart. I must stay alert and control my emotions. She caresses my legs, my thighs. Is she going to tie my legs together too? What is she up to? I must stay awake, there is something important I must do.

What?

It's that bracelet. That was the reason Isa went to Trixi and Aline's van that night. The bracelet Remco stole from her. Which was then stolen from him by Aline. But when Isa got to the van, she got hit on the head. *You know what I did.*

"You... Did you kill Trixi?"

A hoarse laugh. "You know I did, Belle."

Her warm hands keep sliding over my body, stroking, caressing. Sometimes she calls me Belle, other times Michelle. As if she can't decide who she wants me to be.

Did she just confess she killed Trixi? That means Isa is innocent. Neither she nor Remco killed Trixi. I have to call the police. They have to release Isa so she can take care of her child, so Frey can't be claimed by her father. They have to... but I can't do anything. There's a killer on top of me. I'm tied up, naked. I'm screwed. She's going to kill me.

Maybe if I can keep her talking, I can find a way. This is not how my life should end. Not now, not yet. I feel myself sinking into nothing again and force myself to come back.

"Why?" I whisper. "Why did you kill Trixi? She was your girlfriend."

"My dear beautiful Michelle. I have no friends. I am alone, just like you. But now that I've found you, I will no longer be."

While Aline explores my body, I keep my gaze fixed on her tanned back and try to shut off from the feelings her touches arouse. I stare like a madman at a spot on her right shoulder that, on closer inspection, turns out to be a tattoo. With great difficulty, I get my gaze focused: it's a dragonfly. Again.

I feel as if I must finish one of those numbered drawings where you draw a line from one point to another, but in this case, the points are too far apart, and I get lost in the white nothingness in between. The picture just won't become clear.

I continue to stare at Aline's back and see her panties protruding a little from her jeans. Blue panties. With daisies. I'm past bewilderment now. I did know that Trixi and Aline had stolen my panties, along with my money. But that Aline is wearing my panties knocks me out. A thought shoots through my head: has Aline been targeting me all along? Is this not about Isa or Frey, but about me? I see Trixi's blank stare again before me, the night before last at the campfire. Who was she to Aline? They were lovers, I thought, but now Aline acts like she meant nothing to her. Is it my fault that Aline killed her?

"Why did Trixi have to die?" I ask again. I need to know. If I die soon, I want to know what happened and what I had to do with it.

"She was going to betray me, Belle, she was too weak. I had no choice. She was going to ruin everything. But I spared the mother of that child, didn't I? She only got a tap on the head, that's all. That woman wanted to steal my bracelet, she's lucky she got off so cheaply."

Isa had not lied, then.

"By the way, you should choose your friends better, Michelle. That woman, that Isa, she's nuts, you know?" Aline continued imperturbably. "And you know what's funny too? You only really get to know people when you break into their lives. You have no idea what you'll find, you have no idea."

I try to focus on what she's saying because I sense that it's important, but I can't. Only bits and pieces seep through. The only thing that remains crystal clear is that my life is in danger. Aline killed Trixi. Who knows what else she's capable of?

I'm sinking much deeper this time. Air bubbles escape my mouth and dance around me, I feel peaceful, my body cleaving through the azure blue of the ocean. Is this what it feels like to be dead? Although I am alone, it doesn't feel like I am. It's as if the billions of water molecules around me all know me. I feel carried.

A white silhouette, a phantom it seems, looms in the distance in front of me, growing larger and larger. I know who it is, even without being able to focus on her, and do not feel threatened, quite the contrary. It is the mother shark, searching for her child. She comes swimming towards me, her pupils are big and black, I can see her sharp teeth blinking, but still, I am not afraid. She comes swimming beside me and I put my hand on her dorsal fin, letting her pull me along, deeper and deeper. I tell her that I was with her baby and that I sang to her. I tell her that I too lost my baby and we understand each other. We swim even deeper. It gets so dark that I can't see anything, not even the shark. I don't feel her anymore and I claw my hands through the water, but she's gone. I, too, begin to disappear, or rather, I am no longer me.

I am everything.

Suddenly, I'm brutally pulled to the surface, pain shooting through my body as if I've been branded by thousands of hot rods. The peaceful feeling is gone, I am back in the hotel room.

Fight back, I see flashing before my eyes in large letters, a flickering billboard created by my subconscious. I smell the metallic scent of blood but don't know whether it's mine or Aline's.

Fight back. Now.

With all my might I try to keep my eyes open. In the distance, I hear Aline talking, singing it seems. She has a knife in her hands; there is blood on the blade.

Somewhere deep inside me, something wakes up. Something that wants to live, something that is done with being passive, with being lived. Done with the grief for my unborn children, done with my mother's narcissistic behavior, and done with William's betrayal. It's as if my body knows exactly what to do, as long as I don't stop it. Without thinking, I reach with my bound hands for the heavy lamp next to the bed. I feel like I'm stepping outside my body and watch in a daze as I swing the object toward Aline's head, which is hanging halfway down my thighs. I roar a primal scream as I let the foot of the lamp come down.

She doesn't see the blow coming, and falls sideways, off the bed, onto the floor in the small space between the bed and the window. For a moment, I keep looking at her in amazement, her wiry dark body, her head with the blond hair that has shifted a bit – so it's a wig, after all — and reveals shorter dark hair underneath it. A brown stain is beginning to form beside her.

Trembling, I slump backwards on the bed, my chest heaving up and down. There is blood on my belly, it burns badly. Adrenaline foams through my veins like an ocean in stormy weather, helping me along with the pain to stay awake. Exhausted, I reach for my phone to call the police. I don't know what number to dial. What country am I in again? What is the international emergency number?

I hear shouting. Then a loud thump, followed by a male voice. It comes from outside my room, down the hallway. In a reflex, I pull the robe over me as best I can and with my bound hands, I reach for the lamp.

My nightmare is not over yet.

The door flies open. This time I'm ready to defend myself. I'm not giving up anymore. I must fight. Frey and Isa have only me to uncover the truth.

A man storms towards me, hollering. I can only see his silhouette outlined against the light rectangle that forms the doorway. I swing the iron lamp base back and forth in front of me, but he grabs my bound wrists with one large hand and pushes me onto the bed with his knee.

Chapter 46

"Where is she?" he roars. "Where's Frey? What did you do to her?"

The lamp falls from my hands to the floor and I try to wrestle myself free from his grasp.

"What have you done with Frey?" he shouts again.

Now I see who he is: it's Remco, the man I know as Daniel, the goose barnacle hunter. My legs are trapped under his heavy body, and I try to wriggle free, but no matter what I try, I fail. I don't have a speck of strength in my legs; the attack on Aline has taken everything out of me.

"Let go of me!" I shout as loudly as I can. Surely, someone must hear the uproar and call the police? We're not bloody alone in this hotel! "Help! Police! Policía!"

"Don't worry, the police are already on their way. I called them myself," he says.

His light blue eyes are ice cold. He looks at me with undisguised disgust. There is blood on his shirt. My blood?

Oh, crap, I think. Of course, the police are on their way. He's an ex-cop. I'm in trouble, although I can't imagine being accused of anything. That I took Frey to her uncle's is not a crime, is it? Aline is the one they want, not me.

"I did nothing wrong," I say gruffly, but my voice trembles.

"No? Then why did you run off this morning when I wanted to help you? You were clearly on the run. That doesn't exactly qualify as innocent behavior," he spits in my face.

"I ran off because I didn't trust you! And rightly so," I spit back. I look at him furiously; he's still hovering over my half-naked body. Then I think of Aline, lying on the floor next to the bed. "You'd better focus on her, she's the one who committed all those thefts, and she confessed to killing Trixi!" I say triumphantly.

He holds me in check, meanwhile looking around. "Aline? What are you talking about? Where is she?"

"Right here, on the floor, next to the bed," I say, nodding my head.

He loosens his grip slightly to get a better look at the spot I pointed out between the bed and the window. I want to wriggle myself free, but he tightens his grip again.

"Stop playing games, Michelle. There's no one here. There's no one in this room but you and me," he replies.

What? "You can't be serious; she was just here! Who else do you think tied my hands and carved my stomach with a knife? Me?"

Furious, I look around the dark room. Aline must have taken advantage of our struggle to crawl away on her knees and make her way through the open door.

She's gone.

The only evidence that someone besides me was here are the two wine glasses and a brownish stain on the floor. I curse heartily, and then I hear an uproar in the hallway.

"Police are here. Please tell them what you did with Frey. Don't make this any worse," he says, and seconds later several uniformed officers storm in.

Daniel lets go of me and starts rambling on in Portuguese. Two policemen pull me off the bed violently and I scream.

"Let me go! I haven't done anything! You must take him! He's a stalker, a psychopath." But they don't understand me or don't want to hear what I have to say. Daniel is led outside, and the officers make a move to do the same with me. They can't just take me outside, in a dressing gown, can they? But they can. A few minutes later, I'm in the police car with my hands tied, and we drive off with sirens blaring.

Chapter 47

She was no match for you, ma belle. Her hair may be just as red, her skin just as fair, but her scent is not yours. Her softness feels different, her voice is wrong, she is wrong.

For she is not you.

I wanted so badly to be close to you one last time. I miss you so much. Would things have turned out differently for me if you had lived? You were the only one I ever told what my mother made me do. The only one with whom I could let my tears flow. You never judged me. You loved me for who I was.

I'm not that person anymore, Belle. That seventeen-year-old girl who ran away from home, straight into the arms of the commune to which you belonged.

Damaged, but not lost, I was then. The cracks could still be glued. You were that glue. My time together with you was the most beautiful I ever had. I am grateful for every day, every hour, every minute we spent together. Never have I been happier than I was then.

Until you died in my arms.

What reason did I have left to keep living there, in the commune, among those hippies? Among the people who called themselves your "family" and then let you suffer and die. It's their fault that you didn't go to the hospital, like any normal person, when you got the first symptoms. Those spiritual idiots left you to rot, with their ceremonies, stinking herbs, and "conversations with the other world". They kept doing so until your body was completely consumed by the cancer inside, and it was too late.

But I made them pay, Belle. I made their caravans and tents burn to the ground, that very night. Did you see the smoke billowing upwards, to you, Belle? Did you smell the stink of burnt mattresses and rubber tires? I still do sometimes.

I don't regret it, you know. Even knowing now what I didn't know then. I don't regret a thing. I mean, how could I have known that Jinelle wasn't home that night and had left her four-year-old daughter alone in their trailer? With the lock on the door? Who does that? No, I couldn't have known that. Little Summer was my third corpse.

After your death, I left Toulouse, the city that had taken away my youth and my greatest love. Getting a lift was never a problem; I always carried my knife close to me. I only had to use it a few times, as a threat mostly. Meanwhile, the cracks were too big to be glued, Belle. I missed you so much.

The ocean drew me to her like a blue magnet. When I arrived in Biarritz, I met a group of surfers. They also formed a kind of commune. It was winter, so I was happy to lie next to a warm body, Belle. They needed me, and I them.

And then I met Trixi. Sweet, silly, scared Trixi. She looked at me the way I always looked at you, remember? Her eyes followed me everywhere, I could feel them burning on my back. Like a little dog, she walked behind me. She paid for my food, gave me beer, and let me sleep with her. She even taught me how to surf. Oh, Belle, how you would have loved to be swept along by the waves. Floating between the blue sky and the golden beach. Your red hair lit up fiercely by the sun's rays.

But no, you are no longer here.

When Trixi's money ran out, she wanted to return home again, to Germany. She asked if I would go with her. She would take care of me, she said. She was going to get a job and rent a flat in Berlin. I could live there too, she said. Work in a bar.

You know I can't do that, Belle. Everything being the same, day in and day out. I told her to go without me, but she didn't want to. We had no money left to eat, nor for petrol. So, I suggested we rob some tourists. Can you believe how easy that is? They leave their stuff as soon as they go to the beach. Surfers are the best prey: they just leave their car keys on the beach. There is always a spot where they think no one will look, and I would always find it. Soon we had so much money that Trixi didn't have to go home anymore, and we were living like royalty.

Until everything went south.

Chapter 48

I seem to have a déjà-vu. Here I am in the same interrogation room, with the same detectives sitting across from me. Old guy and Mustache have a lot to talk about before they finally turn their attention to me.

I am exhausted but sober. The stuff with which Aline has intoxicated me has almost worn off. I had only taken one sip of the wine, fortunately. I don't want to think about what else she might have done to me. With my body. My belly is full of scratches and cuts, some superficial, some deeper. It burns like crazy.

I nodded off in the police car but didn't sleep. The memory of Aline's hands all over my body makes me shudder. Fortunately, I am dressed now. One of the agents brought in my suitcase, and I was given a few minutes of privacy in the restroom to change. Then a female officer helped me tend to my wounds.

I rub the fatigue from my eyes and reach for the cup of coffee in front of me. I feel resigned, lifeless. I hate that I don't understand anything the men say. Then, finally, the door opens, and the interpreter we were — apparently — waiting for comes in.

"Okay," begins Old guy. "You have a lot of explaining to do, Mrs. Deckers. For starters, can you tell us why you abducted a child and smuggled her across the border into Spain?"

I gasp. "Do you think I kidnapped her? That's not true!" I shout. That must be Daniel's version, of course. That bastard told them I ran off with Frey.

Mustache raises his hand. "Calm down, Mrs. Deckers. If you didn't kidnap her, why did you and Isabelle Durieux make us believe Frey was your daughter?"

There we are. I should never have gone along with this. But I'm not going to hang for Isa, I've already helped her enough. It's in my interest that I play dumb. They must be grilling Isa now too. "I um... I didn't know... Isa told me she was in trouble and asked me if I could take her daughter to her brother. I didn't mean anything wrong by it, I just wanted to help. I didn't know then that Trixi had been killed," I say.

"And that's normal behavior for you? Driving the child of a woman you barely know — as you just admitted — hundreds of miles and delivering her to a man who is a stranger to you? You don't think that's suspicious?"

"No," I lie. "Besides, Frey was delighted to go to her uncle. So, I didn't see any harm in it."

"But why didn't you tell us this yesterday?" asks Old guy.

"Because you started talking about murder! I was afraid you would want to keep Frey here, but then what would happen to her? I figured she'd be much safer with her uncle. What does it matter to you where the child is? Nothing, right?"

Old guy sighs and rubs his eyes. "Mrs. Deckers, it may be so that you think it doesn't matter, but your actions made you look very suspicious. I must tell you that it wasn't wise to lie to us. I suggest that from now on, you stick to the truth."

I nod. "This is the truth, I just wanted to get Frey safely to her uncle, at her mother's request. That's all I know." I wonder what Daniel told the inspectors, and whether Isa was able to prove that he has a restraining order, but I can't ask, I'd be exposing myself too much. Strange, though, that the cops don't bring him up. After all, he is Frey's father. Is that creep sitting in an interrogation room somewhere near me? I shudder.

"Right, let's talk about last night again. So, you claimed during your arrest that you know who killed Trixi Dreher. Can you tell us from the beginning what happened? How exactly did you end up in that hotel room with your hands tied?"

At the thought of how they found me there, bloodied and half-naked, I feel a blush coming on. Reluctantly, I start talking. "I was on my way back from Spain. I had dropped Frey off at her uncle's and was too tired to drive any further, so I stopped at that hotel. Aline must have followed me, probably she had been doing so for a long time."

Old guy takes a sheet of paper from the file in front of him and slides it to me. "You mean this woman?" It's the same picture I've seen on TV before.

I nod. "Only, she's cut off her hair and put on a blonde wig. You haven't found her yet, I suppose?"

Old guy writes something down and shakes his head in the negative. "And you met her at that campfire?"

I nod again. "The day before yesterday, yes, after she saved me from drowning. But I already told you that. I think she started following me when I left for Salamanca with Frey."

"Why do you think she did that?"

I shrug. I don't know. I've been breaking my head over it for hours. "No idea. I think she thought I was someone else, or she hoped so because she called me Belle all the time."

"Belle? And do you know who she meant by that?"

I tell him what I know. I have, of course, made the connection with Isa: Isabelle — Belle — *libelle*, the French word for dragonfly, but I don't see the link between Aline and Isa. I only know that Aline insisted on keeping the leather bracelet with the dragonfly and that she has a tattoo of one, but what this has to do with Isa remains a mystery to me.

"You'll have to ask her yourself," I say. "You'll have to ask her plenty of other things too, by the way. She is the one who killed Trixi. You must believe me. If that psychopath hadn't invaded my room, I wouldn't be sitting here now."

In response, I get a measured nod. Apart from Aline, I'm the only one who knows what happened to Trixi. The only one who can save Isa from the cell. I feel so powerless.

"Fine. Can you tell us exactly what happened? You were alone in your room?"

"Yes, I had just taken a bath and was about to go to sleep when someone knocked on the door." I tell them how I didn't recognize Aline at first, that she then burst into the room and tied my hands after drugging me. That she wounded my belly with a knife while I was unconscious.

What I don't tell them is how she caressed me and how I felt when she did. Still, I feel a blush creeping up from the collar of my T-shirt.

"One moment she called me Belle, the other Michelle." I shrug. "I think she's out of her mind."

"Right. So, you were lying on the hotel bed with your hands tied. You just said that you believe Aline is responsible for the death of Trixi Dreher. Why are you so sure?"

"Aline told me so herself."

"Okay. How would you describe the relationship between Aline and Mrs. Trixi Dreher?"

I blush. "I think they were in a relationship."

"From what do you deduce that?"

"It's just... Aline called Trixi 'darling' and.... I don't know, it's a feeling."

"You're not sure?"

"No," I say. Although I am sure, very sure.

"Did Aline also tell you why she killed her partner?"

I try to remember the conversation with Aline. "She said something about betrayal, she was afraid Trixi would report her to the police."

"What for?"

"I don't know. Trixi and Aline committed several burglaries. Maybe Trixi wanted to quit?"

"Okay. Your hands were tied, Aline made her confession. What happened then?"

"I thought she was going to kill me. She kept carving into my stomach with that knife, I think the pain helped me regain consciousness. Then I hit her on the head with a lamp that was next to the bed. But right after that, this guy stormed in, this Remco, and he overpowered me. If he hadn't, I would have called you myself and Aline wouldn't have been able to escape," I say angrily. "By the way, how did he know I was in that hotel room?"

"Who are you talking about exactly?" Old guy seems confused.

"The man who burst into my room. The one who called you. Remco, Isa's ex."

"You mean Daniel Verellen? He's not her ex."

I look at him with my mouth gaping. Are they messing with me?

"No, you are mistaken! His real name is Remco!"

"Remco who?"

"That, huh, I don't know. But he has a tattoo of a wolf on his arm."

Mustache looks at me strangely, looks at Old guy, then gets up and walks out of the interrogation room. Old guy is clearly struggling with my answer as well.

"Why do you think that man's name is Remco? And that he has a tattoo like that?" he asks.

I feel confused and cornered, still having no idea how much they know. "Isa didn't tell you anything about her ex?"

"No, but we didn't know she had a daughter until now either, thanks to you."

I hesitate. Isa probably didn't dare tell them anything because she was afraid the police were in cahoots with Remco. But now that they know where Frey is, there's little point in continuing to be secretive. So, I decide to tell them the whole story.

"Isa told me she had a restraining order against her ex. She was afraid he would kidnap Frey, so I couldn't trust anyone, she said. But I already knew Daniel, he had already helped me once, so when I ran into him in a gas station, supposedly by chance, I didn't see any harm in it at first. Until I heard that Remco had a wolf tattoo and realized that I hadn't gotten to see Daniel's arms once, even in the hottest weather. I panicked and fled."

Old guy nods. "That's consistent with what Daniel Verellen told us on the phone, only he doesn't have a tattoo of a wolf on his arm, and he's not who you think he is. It does explain why he was convinced that you had kidnapped Frey. Your behavior was extremely suspicious, Mrs. Deckers."

My brain is working overtime again. How can Daniel not be the dreaded Remco?

"Mr. Verellen became convinced by your strange behavior that you had kidnapped the child, so he drove to Salamanca to look for you."

See! I knew he was going to do that.

"When you didn't show up there, he called the police. According to what I understand from your story, this Aline was not up to much good. I think Mr. Verellen did you a great service, although how he could be on the scene so quickly remains a mystery. But we can't ask him that anymore."

Things are getting crazier here. "Why not? Where is he?" I hold my face with both hands, presumably looking like Edvard Munch's The Scream.

Old guy looks deep into my eyes. "There are numerous strange things about this case, Mrs. Deckers. A kidnapping turns out not to be a kidnapping, a suspect not a suspect, and the hero of the day dissolves into thin air. Do you have any idea why Mr. Verellen would not want to talk to us?"

I shake my head speechlessly. I don't know what to think anymore. Old guy is right: nothing makes sense at all. So, Daniel genuinely wanted to help me. But if he's innocent, and he's not Isa's ex, why then would he cover up his arms? And why did he care that I was on the road with a child? It's not normal that he immediately sent the police after me, is it? Especially not when he obviously isn't a big police fan either, because why else would he have run? He must be hiding something.

I try as best as I can to get a grip on the situation, but my lack of sleep prevents it. Then Mustache swings open the door. With determined strides, he walks in, a new file in his hands. His gaze is grim. As he sits down and shoves several pictures in front of me, he keeps his eyes fixed on me. Stunned, I stare at the photos. They have all sorts of things written on them in Portuguese. I see a passport photo of an unknown man and then some blurry photos of a police unit on a beach.

Oh.

And a picture of a tattoo.

Of a wolf.

On an arm.

Confused, I look at both inspectors. "What is this? What's written on it? And whose arm is this?" But as they begin to explain it to me, I realize that I already know. Finally, it becomes clear to me. My mouth dries out as if by magic. Unbelievable. The ultimate proof that Daniel is indeed not the man with the wolf tattoo is in front of me: I am looking at a photo of Remco, also known as "the dismembered corpse on the beach".

"This is the file of the body of a man found on the beach a few days ago. At least, his torso was found. The rest was not," begins Mustache." A few hours ago, one of the man's arms was discovered accidentally, the killer tried to burn the body but must have been interrupted and didn't have an opportunity to dispose of all the limbs, so he buried the arm. The fire department made the lurid discovery during an inspection after a forest fire. Based on the fingerprints and thanks to the tattoo, we were able to identify the victim as Remco De Pauw in the last few hours."

A second light bulb switches on in my head, and I slap my hands in front of my mouth. "Aline!" I exclaim.

"Explain yourself?"

"Aline is the killer you're looking for! I mean, I have no proof of it, but…. That bracelet with the dragonfly! She stole it from him. She's completely nuts. I bet she killed him too, just like Trixi."

A storm of thoughts erupts in my head. So, Isa is on the run from a man who no longer exists. He's fucking dead! And Aline and Trixi had already killed and dismembered him the moment I almost drowned. My stomach turns at the realization of my naivety. So, Isa had been right with her hunch about the girls. Her intuition had told her to stay far away from them. I, on the other hand, flew to them like a moth against a hot lamp. I cozied up with a bunch of killers around a campfire.

"You must find Aline; Isa has nothing to do with any of this. She had simply seen her bracelet on Aline's wrist, and she wanted it back."

Chapter 49

I had seen the man prowling around before. At first, I thought he was a cop because he was clearly observing us, but he left us alone, so then I just thought he was a pervert.

He was such an easy target. We plucked his car keys from the beach, where his towel was. He drove a van belonging to a security company. Of course, that should have set off a warning bell, but Trixi and I had become so seasoned at stealing that we felt invincible. He carried disappointingly little cash, but had a carton of cigarettes that I was happy about.

And then, just as we were about to run off, I saw it, dear Belle, a clear sign from you. Hanging from the sun visor of the car was a leather bracelet with a silver dragonfly.

Yes, I know. When you were still alive, I mocked your belief in ghosts and the spirit world. You saw a sign in everything, everywhere. I was too hardened by life to believe in that. But that day you let me know you were still there, just as I had known all along.

The dragonfly had been your totem, your spirit animal, for as long as I had known you. You firmly believed that this silly, lanky insect was a spiritual guide who wanted to tell you something.

I'm sorry I laughed at you for that. I shouldn't have. That's why, after your death, I had a dragonfly tattooed on my shoulder, with its wings widespread.

Belle, ma libelle. Belle, my most beautiful dragonfly. So, when I saw the bracelet in that man's van, with a dragonfly just like my tattoo, I knew that you had been right there with me all along and that I shouldn't ignore your signs anymore.

I put it on my wrist and Trixi and I took off, throwing the keys inside before slamming the door. We thought we got away in time, but he had seen us. He had followed us. He had waited until dark to come after us, at night, on the beach. He threatened us. He tried to rip the bracelet *off my wrist. He wanted to take you away from me again, Belle. I couldn't let him. I really couldn't. Not when I just had you back. I was so furious. You can go blind with rage, they say, and I can confirm that to be true. My eyes did go black when I stabbed him. And then I did it again. And again. My fourth corpse.*

Trixi screamed and screamed, she was completely covered in blood, and so was I.

I wanted to burn his body, like my mother had done with Matthew. But we couldn't carry him, he was too big and too heavy.

"We'll bury him here, in the sand," Trixi said after she had calmed down a bit. But on the beach, that's no use. The ocean washes everything away; he would be exposed in the surf immediately.

It was my idea to cut him up, so we could carry his body parts separately and burn them. I knew how to do that. So, I began to undress him. He had a tattoo on his left arm: a wolf looking at me with ice blue eyes. I can still see those eyes.

People think it's hard to cut up a body, but it's not. It all depends on the tools you use. With the right knife, properly sharpened, you can cut off a leg. You have to aim right, of course. You can't just cut through a bone; you have to cut through the joint. To accomplish that, you must feel with your fingers exactly where it is and then aim properly. But it's a dirty job, very bloody. Fortunately, we had the ocean on hand to rinse the pieces, just like the Portuguese fishermen's wives clean the fish here, and the sand made sure we could cover our tracks.

One by one we carried his limbs to the van, to be transported. First, we each carried an arm, then we took the legs together, they are so much heavier than you would think. The head, I carried alone; Trixi refused to touch it.

We almost succeeded, Belle, but when we wanted to pick up his torso, I noticed we were no longer alone. A fishing boat was approaching, a glimmer of light on the black water. Although it was dark, we couldn't take the risk, so we fled, leaving the wolf-man's torso right there.

I suggested we burn the rest of him in the eucalyptus forest. Trixi kept crying as we drove there, stupid girl. I should have gotten rid of her earlier, of course. But it was so easy to travel with her, ma belle. I didn't want to be alone.

There in the woods, I made a capital mistake. I realized too late that we were still very close to civilization. The man's bones and flesh did catch fire quickly, but it would take an eternity for them to burn to ashes. We didn't have much time, the chances of someone noticing us, or spotting the smoke, were again too great, so I decided to bury the half-burnt remains. We had to get out of there as fast as we could before anyone saw us. Trixi followed me like a zombie.

It wasn't until the next day that we learned our fire had caused the forest to burn down. It had been very hot and dry, and eucalyptus burns hard and fast.

I can't believe this happened a second time, ma belle. History repeated itself. Just like when little Summer died in the fire I set to the commune, this time several houses were destroyed and a woman was burned alive. My fifth corpse. I'm sorry. I really am.

I think that was the last straw for Trixi. The death of the wolf man had already taken her to the edge, the fire pushed her over it. She wanted no more, she threatened to go to the police and confess to everything.

Murder, Belle. Murder.

The moment they took my fingerprints, they could nail me for everything: the fire in the commune, little Summer's subsequent death, the wolf man, and some other stuff. They'd put me behind bars for the rest of my life. I wouldn't survive that. My freedom is the only thing I own, I won't let them take that away from me. You understand that, don't you?

I talked to Trixi, made her realize she was complicit and would go to prison too. I told her that her future depended on it. That no one had seen us and that she had nothing to worry about, as long as she kept quiet.

I thought it had worked; she stopped talking about going to the police. But when we sat around the campfire that evening, that woman, that French mother, attacked me out of the blue. She, too, wanted to snatch my bracelet from me, my beautiful dragonfly. Ma libelle. Nobody has that right, Belle. No one.

Trixi was hysterical. She was sure we would be arrested; she said that bracelet had betrayed us. She wanted us to turn ourselves in, and when I said I never would, she tried to push me out of her van. She wanted to leave, without me. Little bitch. But I fought back. I grabbed the knife we had cut up Wolfman with and lashed out, but she ran away, out the door. I couldn't risk her alarming the other campers, so I jumped on her from behind and stabbed her, right between her shoulder blades. She fell instantly, pulling me into her fall, and we both ended up on the ground. I dragged her out of sight, behind the van. She lived for a few more minutes, her breath wheezing. I was there, holding her as she died. That's how Trixi became my sixth corpse. I had no choice, Belle.

When that crazy mother came to the door a little later, I was delighted.

I was still lying next to Trixi when I heard her coming. I crawled on my hands and knees and saw how she first knocked and then started banging on the sliding metal door. Reassured that no one was there, she carefully stepped inside. Looking for her bracelet, probably.

I snuck up behind her and watched her rummage around among our belongings.

Oh, Belle, she's very lucky I didn't kill her. I was so angry. How dare she! What mother would leave her child behind for a bracelet, anyway? That's what mine would have done, I thought, pointing my knife at her back.

But thinking of my mom gave me a better plan. I remembered what she had told me so many years ago: if you can't cover your tracks, make sure they lead to someone else. Well, that's what I did. I knocked her unconscious and put the knife in her hands. That stupid cow didn't even see it coming. She should be grateful; thanks to me, her child still has a mother.

What I didn't foresee was that she would wake up again so soon. I wanted to send the police to her anonymously. I had wounded myself with the knife so that my blood would be found in the van. But she turned out to be tougher than she looked and after only a few minutes she stumbled out again. I followed her into the darkness, watching her wake up Michelle. So pure and beautiful. Even in the dim glow of the moon, I could see the glow of her red hair.

I so desperately wanted to talk to you, Belle, to tell you what had happened. But you weren't there, so when I saw Michelle packing her things, I broke into a car, a gray Citroën. When Michelle drove off with the child in that old Volvo of hers, I followed her.

Chapter 50

I look at the screen of my mobile phone. It's seven in the morning, which means I've been awake for twenty-four hours almost continuously.

The police let me go just now. With a paper cup of coffee and a piece of sweet pastry given to me by the officers, I wait in the reception area for my lift back to the hotel. I can't get a bite through my throat.

The hotel manager confirmed to the police that a young woman with dark skin, blonde hair, and a French accent had booked a room ten minutes after I came in and that he had not seen her since.

Aline had checked in under a false name, using a fake passport. Probably one of many she had stolen, together with Trixi. The inspectors let Isa go on the condition that she would stay in the country. They couldn't hold her any longer without charging her, which they were unable to substantiate without evidence. A big manhunt was launched to find Aline.

She is now their main suspect.

I wonder what Isa is doing now. Will she stay in Portugal? Or will she go find Frey, in France? And does she know Remco is dead?

She calls me at that very moment.

"Michelle!"

"Isa! How are you? Where are you?" I almost drop my cell phone in excitement and start pacing around the hall. I can smell myself. The scent of fear, sweat, and stale hair enters my nostrils. I can imagine Isa isn't in much better shape after spending the night in a cell. I envision her with dark circles under red-rimmed eyes.

Her voice is shaking. "I'm free, Michelle, they let me go. Thanks to you. I don't know how to thank you. You saved me. You saved Frey."

"Hey, you would have done the same for me," I say magnanimously.

"No, I mean it. Thanks a million. How did it go? Did Frey behave well? Did she cry? How was Jacco?" She fires off her questions one by one.

"Frey was great. You have a beautiful daughter," I say. "And she's safe with Jacco now. Don't worry."

I step out of the police station, the chances of them understanding anything I say are slim, as we are speaking Dutch, but I would rather not take any. I tell Isa how my day went yesterday. How the police had caught up with us, and that I had pretended Frey was my daughter.

"I was so hoping you would!"

And about Daniel, who was not who I thought he was.

"No, I heard about that. They found Remco murdered," Isa says, her voice thick.

"Are you all right? After all, he was your husband and Frey's father," I ask worriedly.

She blows her nose. "Yeah, I'm fine. It's a lot to take in. I can't believe that he's gone, you know? That I don't have to look over my shoulder all the time, that I don't have to live in fear anymore. On the one hand, I'm so happy that he's dead, but then again, he didn't deserve this. I mean, what did they do to him, Michelle? Cut him up? Set him on fire? It's horrible."

She cries and I feel sorry for her. "Yes, it's horrifying what those two did. And that Aline wanted to frame you for killing Trixi too. But you're still here, and that's what matters. And Frey is, too. Do you have any idea what you want to do now?"

"I'm back in my van, in the parking lot in Sines. A police car just dropped me off here."

I hear her hesitate to tell me the rest, but of course, I know she'll drive to France as soon as she can, even though the police have asked her not to.

"And if you may leave the country again? What then?" I ask, trying to make it easier for her.

I can hear her smile through the phone. "I'm not going back to Belgium, Michelle."

"Why not?"

"Too many memories. There's nothing left for me there."

I nod and understand that our paths separate here. I would probably do the same if I were her, but it still pains me to know that I may never see Isa again, and especially Frey.

"I get it. Will you give Frey a hug from me? You guys take care," I whisper, before putting my cell phone back in my pocket and getting into the cab that takes me to my hotel.

***

The morning sun warms my back. I walk through the glass door of the lobby and nod to the man behind the counter. He smiles at me nervously. It won't be an everyday occurrence, for the police to question him about a hotel guest.

Behind me, the sliding doors open again and a familiar voice calls out to me.

"Michelle! Wait a minute!"

Running footsteps on the marble floor, a hand on my shoulder. Stiffened, I turn around and flinch. "What are you doing here?"

He rests his hands on his knees, breathing in and out heavily. "I... I wanted to apologize," he gasps. "I have been waiting for hours."

I put my hands to my sides, chin up. "It was your fault that Aline escaped," I say angrily.

He lowers his eyes for a moment and then looks straight at me. He's wearing that fishing hat again.

"I know I owe you an explanation and apologies. I'm truly sorry. Do you have time for coffee? I'll explain everything to you. Why I called the police. Please?"

I sigh. "I already know that you thought I kidnapped Frey."

"Yes, but that's not the whole story. Please?"

"All right then, but you'll have to wait. I'm going to shower and put on clean clothes first."

"No problem, of course. I'll wait for you here in the bar." He points with his thumb behind him to the fancy room with velvet chairs and moody lighting where the hotel restaurant is also located.

I nod briefly and walk confidently to my room, where I peel back the clothes I hastily put on at the police station. I still have one clean T-shirt and one pair of clean underpants, so I put them in the bathroom together with a pair of cut jeans that William thinks are too short. But I don't have to worry about him anymore.

I step into the shower and with a contented sigh, I let the water run over my tired body.

Chapter 51

I am exhausted. The hot water reminds me of the last time I was with William. He had told me the night before that he wanted a divorce. He couldn't take it anymore, he said. He didn't recognize me anymore. I wasn't the girl he had married six years before. And he had met someone else.

He had met Stephanie at a convention, where they had had a bite to eat together, and one thing led to another, he had said. He would stay with her for a couple of days, so I had time to pack my things.

His words were so cold, and dry like a desert. It was like he was explaining a prescription to me.

"Pack my things? Then what?" I shouted at him. "Go to my mother's?"

I'd already had a few glasses and my brakes were off. The guilty look on his face said it all, but his decision was firm. I had to leave.

When I woke up the next morning, I could remember what he had said, but not how the evening had evolved after that. When I opened my eyes, I initially thought it wasn't so bad, that I felt quite okay. I couldn't have had too much to drink. That I was lying in bed was in itself a good sign (the weekend before I had spent the night on the bathroom floor).

Carefully I tried to move. I succeeded. I didn't feel nauseous. Maybe this God of my mother's existed after all and took pity on me. I first rolled onto my side, then swung both legs over the edge of the bed and cautiously got up. So far, so good.

My legs felt wobbly, and I staggered to the bathroom, where I lowered myself onto the cold toilet seat. As I let my pee run, I looked around: my jeans lay crumpled in front of the sink, my briefs still in them. I looked down and saw that I still had my T-shirt on, but I quickly realized I shouldn't have moved my head like that. As if someone had pushed the button of a carousel, the bathroom began to spin around me. I lowered my head to my knees and groaned, hoping the spinning would stop. Then the bell rang.

Incredulous, I looked up. It was a Saturday, so it couldn't be the mailman, and no one else came to our door.

I kept quiet.

Again, the doorbell rang.

My mother? She would never come here of her own accord. I always went to her, never the other way around. But maybe something had happened? I got up and immediately lost my balance. On all fours, I crawled across the white tiled bathroom floor to my crumpled pants and wriggled my legs into them, briefs and all. I hoisted myself up on the edge of the sink and repressed the nausea. Foot by foot, I walked from the bathroom, down the hallway, to the front door.

The bell rang a third time, and now I was convinced that there had been a terrible accident. With my mother, or worse: with William. I was prepared to forgive him everything, camp next to his hospital bed for weeks, and feed him mashed potatoes, as long as he stayed with me. I opened the door, expecting to see the police or a concerned neighbor. But standing on the sidewalk was Renée, a little girl from my class who lived on our street. And behind her was her mother, whose smile died where I stood.

I uttered the words, "I — what?" as I sought support from the door frame. Renée stared at me with her big brown eyes, puzzled.

"Mrs. Michelle," she began, and then turned her gaze questioningly to her mother behind her.

"Just ask," the latter soothed, looking at me piercingly. She knew. She had immediately seen that I was having the mother of all hangovers, and she had no intention of letting me get away easily.

"I baked cookies with my Mom, and I'm selling them because we're having a tent camp with our youth group and I get to go. And my brother too!" the child said.

My mind wouldn't cooperate. I felt the blood leave my face and take the little color that was left with it. A cold sweat broke out on me, though the heat of the paving stones glowed. I wanted to answer but didn't know what to say. I had to give money, grab my purse, I realized. Unfortunately, I couldn't move because the nausea had now gotten so bad that I could only stand very still.

"Mrs. Michelle?" asked Renée in her delicate little voice.

Oh, how I hated myself. Her mother's gaze pierced me. I had to do something. I couldn't just stand here. I opened my mouth to do so, but instead, I folded over and vomited out my stomach contents right in front of Renée's little pink slippers.

I will never forget the look on her face, nor her mother's words, "You pathetic drunk! You will never teach those kids again; I'll make sure of that!"

Even when I was in the shower a little later, I couldn't stay on my feet. Sitting under the warm spray that morning, I cried for everything I had lost.

***

But that was then. The shower I'm in now puts me in a better mood. I wash my hair and soap myself gently, leaving the bandage on my stomach, until I have cleared every inch of my body of the smell of the police station.

Curious to hear what Daniel has to tell me, I pack my meager belongings in my bag, so I can check out right after. Then I step into the hotel restaurant, where it smells deliciously of coffee and croissants. Only now do I get hungry. I'm starving.

Chapter 52

Daniel is sitting at the bar and gets up as soon as he sees me. He has taken off his hat and for the first time I see his hair: it's the whitest I've ever seen.

"Is it okay here, or would you rather sit outside? They have a nice terrace," he asks.

I prefer to sit outside. It's a beautiful morning. The terrace looks as luxurious as the rest of the hotel and I tug a little at the hem of my jeans, which may be a little short after all. A girl takes us to a table with a thick linen tablecloth on it and asks if we would like some coffee or tea.

"Cappuccino, please," I say.

Daniel orders a pot of tea.

Together, we walk to the extensive buffet and my mouth is watering. I load my tray with fruit, granola, yogurt, and croissants. Daniel raises an eyebrow in amusement but says nothing. I remain silent as well. I still don't trust him.

"Enjoy," he says, as I gorge myself on my breakfast. I eat like a wolf and occasionally look at his arms, which are again concealed by long sleeves. His chest is broad and his shoulders are muscular. Although last night he freaked me out and overpowered me with his body, I'm not afraid anymore.

"Michelle, I want to tell you my side of the story. Maybe then you can understand why I was chasing you and why I was…"

I mix my fruit into the yogurt and stir in the bowl without looking up. He coughs, clearly uncomfortable, even embarrassed, which gives me a rare sense of superiority. I am in control. I, Michelle Deckers, am the woman in charge.

He removes the tea bag from the pot, places it on the tray provided, pours himself a cup, and begins: "I have a daughter of my own, she's about the same age as Frey."

A daughter? I didn't expect this turn of events. I glance at his hands tersely to see if I can spot a wedding ring, but he keeps his left hand on his lap.

"So where is your daughter?"

"She lives in Belgium." His eyes become moist; he starts turning his mug around in his big hand. "I've done a lot of bad stuff in my life, Michelle, but I'm trying to make up for it."

"What do you mean?"

"I haven't been good to her mother," he says quietly. "It's all my fault. I've done bad things; I realize that now. I've had a lot of time to think about what happened, but at the time I didn't see it."

"What happened?" I ask, intrigued.

He shakes his head. "Doesn't matter. I'm paying the price for it because I can't see my daughter anymore."

"How so?" I ask, confused. "Don't you have that right, as a father?"

"I'm not officially her father. I have a past, you see. Drugs and all that. I went back to see her once, but the risk was too great. If I show my face in Belgium again, a prison sentence is hanging over me. So, I live more or less off the grid."

"So that's why you ran off after reporting me to the police?"

He nods guiltily.

I'm stunned. It seems like everyone I meet on this trip is on the run from their past, just like me. So, the big white teddy bear with the soft voice is a drug addict. I'm the last one to condemn that.

"So that's the reason I freaked out when you suddenly disappeared with Frey. I understood immediately that Isa was the woman suspected of Trixi's murder, and your behavior was so extreme that I thought you were running off with her child."

I feel my cheeks redden, but of course, he has no idea that the thought had actually crossed my mind. He can't possibly know that I can't have children of my own, but it feels like it's written all over my face.

"Now I know that you thought I was her ex, the man they found dead, and that you wanted to protect Frey. But I acted out of instinct, you see."

I get it. The loss of his daughter makes him hyper-sensitive to the fate of other parents. And of children.

"So, how do you stay under the radar?" I ask curiously.

"Fortunately, I know how to work hard and Rogério, a farmer I met here, gave me a piece of land on which I built a cabin. Nothing grand of course. I generate my own electricity, use water from the well, and so on. In exchange, I do some work on the farm for him. Mainly chores, and repairs. Furthermore, I hunt *percebes* when the weather permits."

I debate for a moment whether I should tell him that I am a goose barnacle myself, but decide not to embarrass him too much. He seems so shy, like he's even less used than I am to dealing with people.

"How did you know I was in that hotel?"

"I didn't, but I have a receiver in my van, I was listening to the police radio after I called them. That I got here faster than they did is because I happened to be closer."

"Unfortunately, yes," I say grimly. It's still his fault that Aline was able to escape.

"I'm genuinely sorry. May I ask you something?"

I nod, my mouth full of croissant.

"What I don't understand is why on earth you thought I was that ex-husband of Isa. If you had told me the truth, I could have helped you."

I point to his long sleeves. "You always cover your arms. Why? I thought you wanted to hide a tattoo."

His face turns bright red. I'm happy that I'm not the one with burning cheeks for a change.

"I have psoriasis, a skin disease. It's all over my body. It started when I was on the run. The stress, I guess. The loss of my daughter. It has taken a toll on my body. Besides, I'm not built to live in a sunny country, but in Scandinavia, you just can't disappear as easily as you can here."

Psoriasis. Really? I've put mine and Frey's life in danger because Daniel is ashamed of his skin? It's so absurd that I almost start laughing, but one look at his sad face makes me think again. I hover somewhere between relief and pity.

"Geez. That sucks," I say. My last question is hereby answered, and my stomach is on the verge of exploding. I can't eat another bite.

"Indeed, it does, but I've learned to live with it. I'd love to make it up to you, Michelle."

"Why, you just did, didn't you?"

"Yes, but my actions have put you in an awkward situation, and I'd like to make it right."

"How?"

"Can I relieve you of that spare tire and put a really good one on your car?" he asks sheepishly.

"You may," I smile back.

Chapter 53

After saying goodbye to Daniel and assuring him I was okay now that my car had four decent tires again, I checked out. The manager refused to accept my money and wished me well. In addition, after my generous breakfast, he gave me an extra lunch box and a bottle of wine, which I politely declined. I have to face the fact that I am an addict and that it will be a long time before I have a normal relationship with alcohol again, if ever. At least I know now that I can go for almost three weeks without a drink. That's something.

My pain, your thrill, You're poison, Alice Cooper sings on the radio. Aline is still on the run. The police have sent out a search warrant that has been picked up by all the media. She has been wanted for years in France, where she came from, for arson and involuntary manslaughter. Moreover, she is now wanted for the murders of Remco De Pauw and Trixi Dreher. Nevertheless, I decide to continue my trip. She can't show her face anywhere, so the odds that she'll come after me seem small to me.

It's weird, but since I escaped her, since the moment I thought my last hour had come, I seem to have an extra battery that has only just been connected and which provides me with a dose of unlimited energy.

I wanna taste you but your lips are venomous poison, you're poison, running through my veins, you're poison, I don't want to break these chains, I roar along loudly. The miles of asphalt glide at a fast pace under my car as I drive south. I sing. I shout. I breathe in the warm summer scent. I even make plans, daydream, and occasionally stop by the side of the road to write sheets full of to-do lists. I am on a high. A constant hum echoes in my ears.

There is one more place I want to stop before I reach my final destination. A place I have heard a lot about during my trip. Even Daniel advised me to stop there because it is so beautiful: Bordeira.

He didn't exaggerate. It's already evening when I arrive. I get the lunch I got from the hotel out of the car and climb the dunes next to the large parking lot, which is packed full of surfers returning from the ocean, and families with children playing. As the red fire of the sun extinguishes into the ocean before my eyes, I open the various packages carefully wrapped in aluminum foil. Sandwiches, salted butter, salad, raw vegetables and fruit. The last package feels lumpy. It has a little sticker on it: *Eat today!* I grin and pry open the silver wrapping. It's *percebes*.

"You've got to be kidding me," I say to myself, and look around to see if anyone is secretly filming me with a hidden camera. Which, of course, they aren't.

I chuckle. This is very symbolic. I will devour my old self, Michelle the goose barnacle. It is the best dinner of my life. I enjoy it intensely and eat it all, every morsel of it, down to the last crumb.

Charles Darwin studied the goose barnacle extensively. Moreover, they were invaluable to his life's work The Origin of Species. He used the goose barnacle to test his theory of natural selection, The Survival of the Fittest. Only the strong survive, and all that. Now isn't that interesting? Well, I too developed a theory, also known as Michelle's Law: not the strongest will survive, but those who stay closest to themselves.

The smell of freshly caught fish on the barbecue enters my nostrils. In the parking lot below me, a young father is teaching his son to juggle. An older man in a folding chair watches the scene, a cigarette glued to his lips. I now have enough money to stay at a local B&B, but this is the life I want to live. The outdoor life.

When the last sunrays have disappeared, I stretch myself out in my car and continue reading Eat Pray Love until I fall asleep. My slumber is wonderful and dreamless.

***

When I wake up the sun has not yet risen. It's six in the morning and the energy is still buzzing through my body. I have to get up. The dunes that were almost orange yesterday, now seem black. It's quiet, and I close the door as softly as I can.

Bordeira is a magical place with a mile-long natural beach embraced by beautiful cliffs. There are no houses, no restaurants, absolutely nothing except what you bring yourself. Depending on the tide you sometimes must wade through shallow water before you get to the actual beach, this morning is like that, and I intensely enjoy how my feet touch the cool water.

In the middle, I come to a stop, letting the salty smell of the sea reach my nose. I have never been so awake in my life. It's slowly getting lighter, the sky changes color, and the water ripples.

I wade further and when I reach the other side, I am confronted with a high dune. The wind has drawn beautiful ridges and patterns in its sand, which feels cold to the touch. Foot by foot, I begin my climb. My senses are on edge, I am aware of every grain of sand, every rustle in the dune grass. Like a queen, I now stand on top of the dune. I imagine myself in a desert, as far as I can see, the dunes stretch out. Rolling, smooth, soft. It's almost like I'm alone in the world, and I like that just fine. For now.

The roar of the ocean catches my attention, she seems to be calling me, and I surrender to her demand like I have done every day for the past few weeks. Something about staring at that mass of water feels healing. I walk down the other side of the dune, cross the wide beach, and stand with my feet in the surf.

When, after glancing behind me, I make sure no one is here at this early hour, not even the fishermen, I know I've found my moment. It's time for a tête-à-tête with the ocean. Quickly, I take off my T-shirt and throw it on the sand. I let my shorts drop around my ankles, and then I kick them off. I had put on a bikini under my clothes, but after a brief hesitation, I take it off as well. Now all I have left is the bandage on my belly, it's already coming loose at the corners and I decide to get rid of it with a few painful jerks.

Here I am. I say it out loud, "Here I am."

It sounds crazy when no one is around. The water ripples playfully around my feet, luring me deeper. I can't resist. But why should I? This is why I'm here, isn't it? Why I closed the door behind me and plunged into the unknown. My hands slide protectively to my belly; I wade deeper until I'm up to my knees in the water. Behind me, the sun is rising, and the color of the sky reminds me of the morning I first saw Aline and Trixi. Has it only been a little over a week since I tried to hide from them like a crab between the rock crevices? My desire to belong was so great. They seemed to have their feet in the sand so much more firmly than I did.

How quickly things can change.

Like they did that day, I stretch my arms in the air, moving ever so slowly. The beach is no longer theirs; it is mine now. From out of nowhere, I feel a power surge within me. The buzz in my ears becomes so tangible that my whole body begins to tremble uncontrollably. Whatever is stuck there, it has to come out. And I can only think of one way to do that.

I don't look back; I don't care whether anyone sees me or not. With my arms spread, and my head tilted back, I open my mouth wide and with one long drawn-out cry, I let go. The childhood I missed, the mother who thought only of herself, the babies I was never allowed to hold in my arms, the husband I lost.

When I almost run out of oxygen, I take a deep breath and get up with renewed strength. I start to run as if my life depended on it. I leave the safety of the surf and storm straight into the crashing waves.

"Come on then!" I shout. "I'm not afraid anymore!" I jump up with my arms into the first wave and allow myself to be lifted a little. The salt water burns my belly, but I don't care. I laugh loudly, feeling like a little kid at the fair. A kid without responsibilities, without inhibition. Then the wave gently puts me down again.

"One more time!" I shout. The sensation of the water on my naked skin is beyond description. As I dive through the next wave, I feel little bubbles tickling all over my body. They are having a party on my body. I imagine myself swimming around in a champagne flute, a small white figure with red hair. I come back up and let myself be carried away by the current, floating around on the swell of the ocean. I don't know exactly how long I've been floating like this, but when the sun warms my cheeks, I realize that the buzzing in my ears is gone.

It's time for the last stop of my journey.

Chapter 54

It's over, Belle. They're looking for me. My face is on TV and in all the newspapers. "Have you seen this woman?"

They call me a serial killer, but I never intended to kill. You know that. All my life I hated my mother for what she did to me. She made me an accomplice when I was just a child. But if I had not helped her burn Matthew's corpse, my brothers and sisters would not have had a home. I couldn't let that happen. I know it wasn't my fault. You told me that often enough when I was plagued by nightmares. You said my mother was a psychopath with no conscience. According to you, I was a victim, not a perpetrator.

Now I'm afraid you were mistaken about that, ma belle. The monster that was my mother also resides in me. It was still small when you met me, but your death was like a growth hormone for that dark creature with its long tentacles that ate me from the inside. It first got a voice the night of your death, and since then, its roar has been louder and louder. For the past few days, it has been deafening.

I wanted to kill her, Belle. I didn't want to just possess Michelle, or love her. I didn't want to just lie next to her to feel closer to you. No. I wanted her to be mine, only mine. I wanted to brand her. I wanted to be the last to feel the warmth of her skin before her body became cold and stiff. I wanted to be the last to see the light in her eyes before it would go out forever. I wanted her to be the last, my seventh corpse. But it's all pointless.

This world is ugly and empty without you. I have looked for you everywhere: in the setting of the sun, in the flames of every campfire, in the warmth of my bed, in the taste of red wine. But you are no longer there. I can pretend to talk to you, but I know you will never again answer me.

We were so happy together, so free. Unconstrained. I didn't judge you, you didn't judge me. We could have traveled the world together: harpooning in Polynesia, building houses in Nepal, spotting gorillas in

Uganda. Whereas all that awaits me now is captivity. Four walls, limited daylight. For how long? Too long, is the only thing I know for sure. I won't survive.

I just abandoned the last car I stole in a parking lot. I left all of my things in it, as well as my letters to you, ma belle. These words are my last ode to you. I hope I haven't disappointed you too much. I hope you'll understand the choices I made. It would have all turned out differently if you had still been here.

Here I am, all alone, at the end of the world. Below me the waves are crashing against the rocks, seagulls are flying in and out, shouting at each other. Or at me? Are you trying to tell me something, Belle, ma libelle, my dragonfly? Do you miss me as much as I miss you? Is it you who wakes me up at night, when the dark is too black, and I fall into the deep nothingness that makes me sweat and throw off my sheets? When my heart won't stop pounding? If only I could lie in your arms again, hear your voice. Then you could control the monster. But you can't anymore. I know. I have to take care of it myself. Once and for all.

I take off the blonde wig that hides my short-cut hair. You loved my long hair, remember? I breathe in the sea air, tasting the microscopic water droplets propelled into the air by the waves dozens of feet below me, forming an eternal mist. I imagine the souls of the sailors who perished over the centuries, I feel them waiting for me at the cliffs below. They extend their arms to me up above, while I stand here with my toes over the edge. They are calling me, they know my name. They know I belong there.

I extend my arms beside me and smile. The sun warms my face.

And then I see it, Belle. Your sign. A dragonfly comes flying up just in front of my face and then lingers in the air for a moment. Her transparent wings vibrate and sparkle in the sunlight. Like a jewel made especially for me. I extend my hand to her, to you.

She flies away.

I follow.

I'm coming, Belle. See you soon.

Chapter 55

This is it: The End of the World. I have made it. I have traveled to the end of the world to discover that my world is not ending but has yet to begin. For the first time, I know who and what I am, and most importantly, what I am not.

"Will the real Michelle please stand up!" I say to myself. I chuckle. My road trip has turned out to be an epic therapy session. Even though I know I still have a long way to go, I'm brimming with energy now that I know I have nothing left to lose.

I've looked death in the eye often enough by now to know that my fear of it only impedes my will to live. And is therefore pointless.

Nothing seems impossible. If I've come face to face with a crazy psychopath and survived, then I can also tell my mother that I don't like men. Never did, by the way. That I only realize this now, at thirty-one, may seem strange, but I never learned to think about what I want.

I should never have married William. Was it a stroke of luck that we couldn't have children?

No, I still can't think about it that rationally. I would rather have a baby with William than no baby at all. My desire is too great. But I will have to trust that one day I will be a mother, in some form or another.

Another thing on my list is to look for an apartment that is all my own. Maybe I can even buy a small van, and have my own surfboard, so I can go on trips during school vacations.

And so what if I'm no longer welcome at school? There are other schools out there. I could even go back to college to study psychology, like I always wanted to. Why not?

The world is at my feet. Here, on the very spot where I stand, you can take that literally. I can well imagine how, in the days when people believed the earth was flat, they thought this was the farthest point, and you could fall off it.

I first walked around the courtyard where the lighthouse is, but that was too crowded for me, so I walked back, past the parking lot where dozens of cars and tour buses are parked, past the stands with food ("The last hot dog before America!"), tea towels, knitted sailor sweaters, dried figs, and souvenirs.

I am now walking right next to the cliff edge, on a path. The wind is tugging at my hair. Dozens of feet below me, the waves are pounding furiously against the rocks. They, too, are constantly reinventing themselves; no wave is ever the same. They are unique in all their splendor and power. Sometimes, during heavy storms, the waves reach so high that this place is completely flooded. I've seen it in pictures in the brochure from the tourism office. I feel a kinship with the yellow-red rocks, against which the ocean relentlessly pounds. They can't help but endure the violence, but they're still there, despite everything.

"What a magical planet this is," I whisper in awe. My words blow away in the wind and I let them. This is what I wanted to do, where I wanted to be. And most importantly, how I wanted to feel. I can drive home now with my head held high.

The newspaper articles of the past few days will haunt my mind for a long time, I know. They call Aline The Dragonfly Killer. Is it a coincidence that both Isa and Aline had a connection with dragonflies? Isa because she got the bracelet from Remco, who used to call her Isabelle Libelle, which made her despise dragonflies. Aline, because the real name of the love of her life, a French girl who was raised in a cult and died of cancer, was Lilybelle. She had a dragonfly as her spirit animal.

My opinion? If you look for symbolism, you will find it. For example, Heleen is convinced that her deceased grandmother sends her messages from heaven every time she sees a ladybird. It offers her comfort. Belle and Aline had their dragonflies.

And I do too now. Because, whether I want to or not, I can never look with the same eyes at that insect again. I can never again stand naked in front of a mirror and look at my belly without seeing one. The cuts that Aline scratched into my flesh with her knife that particular night will forever leave me scarred. In the form of… you guessed it.

Aline thought the bracelet was a sign from Lilybelle that they would meet again. When she met me shortly after, with my red hair and pale skin, she was sure Lilybelle had sent me.

Let me tell you this, though, I have seen pictures of that girl. I thought I would look strikingly like her, hence Aline's bizarre behavior, but nothing could have been further from the truth. Yes, we have the same skin and hair color, but that's where the comparison stops like a car crashing into a tree: Lilybelle was a drop-dead-gorgeous beauty with a doll face, cute stub nose, pouty mouth, and delicate freckles. I, on the contrary, am a redheaded beanpole with big ears. Her looks had nothing, absolutely nothing, to do with me.

So, there you go. The resemblance was mostly in Aline's head, along with a host of other insane thoughts.

I walk back, my old Volvo faithfully waiting for me. The gas tank is full, and I have enough provisions with me to get me through the first few days of my trip home. This time, I won't be traveling along the coast, I will drive through the countryside. I will miss the ocean, but at the same time look forward to driving through the mountains. I have finished

Elizabeth Gilbert's book and I am mouthing one of the many quotes I underlined in the text:

It is better to live your own destiny imperfectly than to live an imitation of somebody else's life with perfection.

That sums it up, I think. My life and how I want to live it may not be perfect, but it is always better than trying to squeeze myself into a straitjacket that is two sizes too small. Although I still disagree with Gilbert's views on the existence of God, I admire the journey she has taken, the journey to finding herself.

In my mind, I am planning my next destination. Who knows, maybe it will be India. Why not?

I leave the book on the hood of a van painted with flowers, get into my car, and set the GPS. I leave my cell phone on silent because since the news of my adventure got out, journalists from all over the world are calling to hear my story. My mother also calls me every so often to hear how things are going. She had tried to warn me about William's baby, which is why I had so many missed calls from her. I think she's really worried about me.

I drive away from the lighthouse, away from the end of the world. The streets of Sagres glide by, old fishermen deliver their catch to restaurants, surfers stand barefoot in the sun. Life goes on.

I turn on the radio and sing along loudly to *Summer Of 69*, the sun hot on my roof. I drive past Lagos and Portimão, and in Albufeira, I say goodbye to the southern coast of Portugal and turn onto the highway. My Volvo is just starting to pick up speed when my gaze is drawn to a strange dark cloud. It seems to hover over the road towards me. What makes the phenomenon even more bizarre is that the sky is otherwise bright blue. I glance in my rearview mirror, but I'm driving quasi-alone.

The cloud is getting closer; it looks like a living creature making figures in the air. Is it a swarm of locusts? It must be. Then something smashes against my windshield.

Definitely not a grasshopper.

Then a second thing crashes against the glass, followed by a third and fourth.

I hit the brakes, steering my car to the emergency lane. What the hell? But as quickly as it came, the cloud floats by and the sky is clear blue again. Bewildered, I get out of the Volvo and walk to the front of my car, where one of the things has been left behind.

It is a beautiful dragonfly, the largest I have ever seen. Its wings are spread, its delicate body still trembling slightly. I stare at the strange creature living out her last seconds on this earth and notice how quiet it is. No car drives by, no bird whistles. I, too, am holding my breath.

I don't like dragonflies, Isa said.
Ma belle, Aline whispered, in her husky voice.

Then, the wings of the dragonfly begin to vibrate so fast they seem to play a rhythm on my car window. She straightens up, seems to consider her next move for a moment, and then shoots away, straight up toward the blue sky.

Epilogue
Three Years Later

It is around *apéritif* time. The initial heat is only beginning to subside after an oppressively hot day on the Côte d'Azur, and the swallows are flying low, when the white high-gloss kitchen of a modern sea-view villa will be forever tarnished.

Philippe is the one who finds her body. He will never get over the shock; he was convinced she was happy and will continue to wonder for the rest of his life what he could have done. They have been together for almost three years. The best years of his life.

Clarisse, the housekeeper, will never succeed in removing the stains caused by the arterial blood that has penetrated deep into the pores of the natural stone kitchen worktop. This hurts her almost more than the death of Madame herself. It feels like she has failed. So eventually, a new kitchen worktop will be installed, one of dark gray granite. And Clarisse will also be replaced over time.

And Frey... ah... Never will she understand why her mother decided, for no reason at all, to chop at her wrist with a broken wine glass. During the funeral, she will have to be supported by Philippe, who is holding strong for her.

So why did she do it, why did Isa turn the lives of her loved ones upside down?

In her opinion, she did the opposite. All these years she did everything to protect them, from the voices, from the monster, from herself. But today, it's all over because she won't be able to fight it anymore.

***

Around five o'clock, Isa jerks awake from her afternoon nap. The hammock has made a checkered pattern on her buttocks and her skin itches a little because of the rough rope. A moment ago, she was still lying in the shade of the big palm tree, but now the sun is shining full on her face. Is that why she woke up? Or did she hear something? Is there someone in the garden? She pushes herself up and looks around, but there is no one to be seen.

She tries to remember what she dreamed, but can't focus on the image. It was about Remco, that she knows for sure; most of her dreams are about him. Even now, all these years after his death.

Three years ago, she fled Portugal. Of course, the detectives immediately realized they had made a mistake when they dug up Remco's background and discovered that Isa had kidnapped Frey. She had picked Frey up just in time at Jacco's house in Bordeaux and had then gone into hiding until her face was no longer in the newspapers. It was only since she met Philippe that she was able to relax a bit.

Even though every day she thinks she's being followed.

Even though she can never let Frey out of her sight without feeling sick.

Even though she still can't sleep at night. That's why her eyes fall shut so often during the day, often even without her realizing it.

When will it finally stop? How long can this go on? She's slowly going mad, she feels it. But then again, wasn't she already?

She studies her brown feet with the bright yellow painted nails. Just a little longer and everything will come out, she is sure of it. Only recently, the papers wrote of a couple convicted of a murder they had committed no less than twenty-five years ago. All that time they had been on the run.

But I didn't commit murder, Isa thinks.

You lied, says a voice.

I had no choice, Isa thinks.

That's what Aline said, the voice replies.

Everything started with the birth of Frey. Isa doesn't recall exactly what happened during those first weeks, but she remembers the constant fear she felt from Remco. And the voices. She was sure he wanted to do something to her and Frey; the voices told her. She was so scared; she kept trying to run away with her daughter until he started locking her up and she couldn't leave. Then she started hiding Frey. First in the closet, then in the sauna room, finally in the...

You hurt her.

No, she mustn't think about that now. Remco had her committed. They sent her to a psychiatric hospital and gave her medication and therapy, lots of therapy.

Pregnancy psychosis was the verdict. Very rare.

When things got better, she went home again to Remco. Even though he, of all people, caused everything. At least, that's what she thought then. The only ones who believed her were her parents, but of course, they knew nothing about the voices. She had never told them. As long as she took her medication, the voices stayed away. When, thanks to Dad, she could divorce Remco and live on her own; everything was going well again, and life was smiling at her once more.

But when Dad died, the voices came back.

Isa gets up from the hammock and walks across the mowed lawn, past the pool to the house. Philippe is working in his office and Frey is playing at a friend's house. She walks barefoot through the sliding glass doors into the kitchen and pours herself a glass of white wine, which she drinks sitting at the bar.

You're not allowed to drink.

What difference does it make?

She sees herself reflected in the shiny surface of the kitchen cabinets. Blue circles under her eyes. Skinny. She has dyed her hair red since fleeing Portugal. As red as Michelle's.

About the time after her father's death, her memories are murky. She remembers Remco chasing her and breaking into her apartment. Or so she believed. But the police found no trace. Even the detective she hired couldn't find anything. He said she was imagining it. He had cost her a fortune, just to hear that she was a fantasist. That she had staged everything. That Remco had never set foot in her apartment.

Michelle believed it, as did Jacco.

You lied to them, the voice says.

That's not true. I believed it myself. Then it's not a lie, is it? Besides, what else could I have done?

Not only had Remco applied for and received a restraining order against her — he claimed she was stalking him, which might have been the case — but then it turned out that Social Services had written a scathing report on her and she was going to lose custody of Frey.

She takes a sip of wine. She had gone completely berserk after the news and fled the country. She couldn't tell Michelle that, of course; she would never have helped her. Neither would Jacco. Technically, she kidnapped Frey, although that's a ridiculous word. She's her mother, dammit. Mothers are supposed to be with their children.

Good mothers are, yes. But you are not.

Shut the fuck up.

That a silly bracelet could be the root of all this misery, still seems unbelievable. Why did Remco take it with him while he was looking for her and Frey? He had always been a softie, especially for a police officer.

He was a good father. He loved you and he loved his daughter. It was all in your head. We were in your head.

Oh, cut it out.

Isa blinks away the tears. She had told Michelle that Remco stole the bracelet from her apartment. But when she had left Remco, she hadn't taken anything with her, especially not something she had gotten from him. She preferred never to see that thing again. Why didn't she remember that back then? Why did she believe everything the voices said?

Because you are a drunk.

And then, when she suddenly saw that stupid dragonfly again. When that horrible Aline had that very bracelet on her wrist... Isa sighs and takes another sip of cool white wine. It's a good thing Philippe doesn't know anything about her past.

You can't keep it hidden any longer.

Not now that the voices are back, after all this time. It started a few weeks ago. At first, she didn't understand why she was hearing them again, but since this morning she knows. She puts a hand on her stomach.

You can't keep that hidden any longer, either.

She can't have another child, impossible. It's all happening again. It's a miracle Frey barely remembers anything from back then.

Her father is dead and it's your fault.

I didn't kill him, Aline did, along with Trixi.

And yet, it's your fault. He was innocent, just wanted his daughter back. You, on the other hand, are a bad mother.

Isa clenches her teeth. She can't go through this again.

It's your fault that your daughter no longer has a father.

Nonsense, she has Philippe. Isa gulps back the glass of wine in one go.

You're a murderer.

No, I'm not.

Frey is the daughter of a murderer.

No, she's not!

The police are on to you, just wait and see.

Stop it!

Philippe will hate you.

Shut up, you!

Murderer! Murderer! You murderer! You murderer! Murderer!

Isa pushes her hands against her ears, but it doesn't help. The voices only get louder. She can't tell Philippe about it, he wouldn't understand.

He'll throw you out on the street, without a cent.

He would never do that.

He would if you had his baby taken away. It'll be over for both of you.

You can't, you can't. Frey can't help it. She's innocent.

Like mother, like daughter.

No, Frey is perfectly healthy!

What will they say at school, when they hear that her mother is a madwoman, locked up in a psychiatry ward?

I'll find a way; I know what medication I need. I can still fix it.

Silly woman, you're not allowed to take those pills when you're pregnant. Besides, you're way too far gone. Look at you sitting there, all alone, yet busy talking. You are a terrible mother. Your daughter is better off without you and you know it.

Isa is sobbing, her mascara running out and forming black streaks on her cheeks. She's exhausted. She knows she has to terminate the pregnancy, but Philippe will never understand that. And when she tells him why, everything will come out. Frey will never forgive her.

You know what you have to do. For Frey.

I'll do anything for her, anything.

Then do it. Show her you're a good mother.

Do what?

You know very well what to do. When you're gone, there are no more problems.

But then Frey won't have a mother!

She's better off without you.

Isa clenches the glass in her hand, the muscles in her arm tightening.

Do it.

She sees her face reflected one last time in the high-gloss paint of the kitchen, her mouth set off in a soundless scream.

And then she does it. Because Isa is a good mother.

The Dragonfly – A Totem Animal

Totem animals or spirit animals are creatures that have a personal symbolic meaning. They stem from the traditions of the Native Americans, where each family had its totem. Their characteristics represent character traits and skills that you possess or need to learn in this life.

A totem animal can be a guide for you and protect you, but can also help you learn certain life lessons. According to tradition, this animal will cross your path when you need it. It helps you discover which part of yourself you need to develop and gives you the strength to go through these changes.

***

As a totem animal, the dragonfly represents transformation and the art of being able to adapt to circumstances. When the dragonfly appears in your life, you are about to go through an important change, just as the dragonfly changes color in its life. By daring to look at yourself with fresh eyes and rearrange your life, you can go through a metamorphosis that brings you closer to your true self.

Because the dragonfly can move in all directions, it also represents the endless possibilities in life. The dragonfly spirit animal asks you not to think about limitations and to realize that you mostly impose them yourself.

Finally, the dragonfly also stands for spiritual growth and breaking through illusions. Not everything is as it seems, and so you may wonder whether how you present yourself now, is in line with who you are, or rather with who you want to be, just like Michelle did. Perhaps there are habits you need to break to become yourself. Habits that you have imposed on yourself or that have been created by circumstances. Emotions play a big role, especially if they are emotions you don't allow, or are based on thoughts that don't match reality. The dragonfly offers you a new perspective and the strength to look at your life from a distance. In doing so, the dragonfly encourages you to show your colors and let your light shine.

***

Sources:

www.spiritanimal.info/dragonfly-spirit-animal/

www.dragonfly-site.com/meaning-symbolize.html

Acknowledgments

Traveling around by motor home: my husband is over six feet tall and didn't see the fun of it. Why would he fold himself in two, to fit into an undersized bed for months on end, bump his head on the low ceiling every day, give up his daily hot shower, and gag while cleaning out the chemical toilet, when we had a more than comfortable home?

Why? Because it was my dream.

On September 16, 2017, we left, accompanied by our then ten-year-old daughter. With minimal preparation and only a vague idea of where we wanted to go, we drove down the driveway of our house in Belgium and after an hour we had our first fight. Many more would follow.

We homeschooled our daughter for a school year and visited every museum we came across along the way. My husband and child learned to surf and from then on, the trip became not only the fulfillment of my dream, but of theirs as well.

Dear M. and A.: I could never have done this without you, thank you. You are sweethearts (sometimes). Also, a big hug to son D. who looked after the house and the cat that year, and to the whole family who in turn looked after the son (but that's another story).

***

Many thanks to all the proofreaders (in chronological order): Liselot Overstijns, Tanja Fredriksson, Ilse Mertens, Marieke Scheers, Ink Kroon, Melissa von Wenz, Gisy Van Hove, Joke

Vander Aa, Vicky Maggelet, Danny, Ruth Swallow, Fiona Austin... I don't think you guys realize how valuable it was to receive feedback from you.

Thanks to blogger Sofie Verschueren, I came into contact with Alexandra Seghers and Marijke Segers, women who, like Michelle, were faced with premature pregnancy loss, and with Tine Van de Sompel, the mom of a stillborn baby. Their feedback was of great importance in sending this book out into the world with confidence. They corrected the terminology I used and made sure I described Michelle's experiences as realistically as possible.

A special thank you to César Manuel Prudencio Ferreira, who works for the Portuguese GNR, the military police, who explained to me in great detail the agencies that intervene in cases of murder and kidnapping in Portugal. If there are any errors in this book regarding the actions of the Polícia Judiciária or the GNR, that is entirely down to me and no one else.

Special thanks to Melissa Vandeputte, the Foreign Rights Manager at Hamley Books Publishing, who succeeded in selling the international translation rights of this manuscript. It's a dream come true.

***

Finally, I would like to thank you, dear reader. After the publication of "Alone", my debut novel, I received hundreds of reactions from you. That warm bath of recognition was the reason I wanted to keep writing.

I hope this book has helped you escape reality for a while and that you enjoyed this little holiday in Portugal, even if only in your head.

Barbara.

About the Author

Originally from Antwerp (Belgium), Barbara De Smedt moved to Portugal in 2019 after having fallen in love with the country during a road trip around Europe.

As a lifelong learner, she studied languages and Psychology. For the past 20 years she built her own international health and wellness business, together with her husband.

Today Barbara dedicates her time to writing full time, enjoying her family and taking long dog walks.

Instagram: @barbara_dora_

Subscribe to her newsletter: news.barbaradesmedt.com

www.ingramcontent.com/pod-product-compliance
Lightning Source LLC
Chambersburg PA
CBHW021953010726
47494CB00003B/711